THE SEA GLASS MAP

ISBN: 978-1-83556-073-0 PAPERBACK
ISBN: 978-1-83556-074-7 HARDBACK
ISBN: 978-1-83556-075-4 EBOOK

Book Design by HMDpublishing

PART I

Chapter 1

Sinking down into the warm waters of the Pacific, I giggled as air bubbles bloomed off my fingertips and rose to freedom. I finally settled softly on the sandy ocean floor, twenty-five feet below the surface, my sea glass necklace hovering in front of my face.

There wouldn't be any other kids like me down there, I knew that much, but I did hope to see my pod—the dolphin family that rescued me as a baby.

So far, rocks and seaweed were my only companions. That, and the pelican who'd just dropped me from above. Like a torpedo shot from the sky, she'd knife through the water, slicing the rays of sunshine that beamed down. Neither the powerful seabird nor the reach of the sun could extend deep enough to rescue me though, and I didn't mind. I didn't need rescuing. The ocean was my home.

"Miss Spencer. Akela Spencer?" Mr. King asked again. The classroom laughed as I finally awoke from my flashback daydream.

"There you are, Miss Spencer. Thank you for returning to the eighth grade," Mr. King continued as my classmates chuckled again.

"Yeah, um, sorry, Mr. King," I said as I shook the years-old memory from my head.

The dream felt so real. They always did. I ran my fingers through my hair to see if it was wet. Nope.

"Now, back to the question. If you happened to be walking the Appalachian Trail, where would you find yourself?" Mr. King holstered his hands in his pockets as he nodded to me.

Geography wasn't my favorite subject, but it was one of the easiest, as the answers were always the same. Nothing ever moved on a map unless you wanted to get into the shifting of seismic plates or glaciers migrating or melting from global warming. It was all just memorization, and I was good at that.

I took a deep breath. "The Appalachian Trail is a marked hiking trail in the eastern United States, extending between Springer Mountain in Georgia and Mount Katahdin in Maine," I said somewhat mechanically, but trying not to sound like I was repeating a Wikipedia post, which I was.

"Showoff," Kara sniped from the back of the class. Her comment was followed by muffled laughs.

I turned to see Kara and her gaggle of ghoulish girlfriends sneering at me.

"Settle down," Mr. King said to the rear of the room. "Very impressive, Miss Spencer. Now, did anybody get the extra credit question on where Ponce De Leon's fabled Fountain of Youth was located?"

The class bell rang obnoxiously loud, cutting Mr. King off. He tried to continue, but was overwhelmed by the stampeding students heading out the door.

Kara bumped me, knocking my book off the desk as she exited class with her buddies. "You and your cousin have quite the interesting relationship," Mr. King remarked as he picked my book up off the floor and handed it to me.

"Thanks, I'd choose a different word, but interesting works." I stood up to leave, tucking my necklace into my shirt.

"You know, that necklace you have, the one you're always fidgeting with, has anybody ever told you it's the exact shape of North America?"

Hesitantly, I pulled the blue necklace out of my shirt.

"You see, you wear it horizontally, but vertically, it's a continent." Mr. King pointed at the top corner.

"That's Alaska, Canada, down through the continental US and it even has Mexico. See! Geography is everywhere! It's an amazing piece, Akela. May I ask where you got it?"

I inspected my necklace and shrugged. "It's sea glass, from my parents—my birth parents… I think. I never knew them."

Mr. King's cheery demeanor evaporated. "I'm sorry, Akela. Even more so, you should treasure that necklace, it's quite remarkable."

After school, I walked the long way home, around the park, or the town green, as everybody called it. The green was brown, though, covered with dying grass and nestled up against an even browner, barren hillside which was sparsely peppered with random shrubs. Any other foliage that'd survived the years of drought had been cut away as fire prevention.

Tumbleweeds blew off the foothill, down the street, and raced toward me. Where they were going, I didn't know, but at least they were moving. I kicked at them as they blew by. It hadn't rained here in months, and I hadn't seen the ocean in years.

I plopped down on a faded green bench and reached for my necklace. Mr. King asking about my sea glass got me thinking about things I'd practiced hard at keeping below the surface. But Papa Kaipu always said that feelings, like water, always find their way. I cried a single tear that dried so quickly against the arid wind it was gone before it hit my lips.

Later that night in my bedroom, I took off the necklace for the first time since I'd moved in with Kara and her mom, Matea. With the door closed, I held it in my hand and turned it to see what my teacher saw.

I opened a map of North America on my iPad. The detailed cuts and curves of the glass perfectly matched up to the jigsaw outline of the actual continent. The necklace really was remarkable.

I put my sea glass back around my neck, hanging horizontally as it always did, and pulled my shoulder length brown hair into a ponytail. In the mirror, I saw the piece a little differently now, but it wouldn't change its meaning to me. I was thirteen, far from my true home, and without any family that felt real to me.

Following a long sigh, I flopped down backwards on my bed, splashing down into crystal clear water. Floating weightlessly, I waited for the dolphins to come, and they did. They always came. We started to swim, far away from this house, this school, and this town.

CHAPTER 2

"Bank shot," shouted a boy in a basketball jersey as he shot an empty milk carton off a locker that careened directly toward my head. I detected it and casually deflected it into my bin. My reflexes were surprisingly fast.

"Whoa. Nice block," the boy gasped to his friends. He extended me a fist bump, but I denied that, too.

Every day before lunch, I navigated the crowded halls of my school carrying a blue recycle bin. Convincing the school to buy separate bins for recyclables was easy, but I couldn't force the kids or teachers to use them properly.

A bookish girl from Algebra class stopped to drop in a can.

"Here ya go, Akela."

"Thanks." I started to move away.

"Me and the boys brought our cards today. Care to join us on a journey into the land of spirits and spells during lunch?" Her eyes lit up at the subject.

I thought about saying yes, but I didn't believe in magic. Not like I used to at least, when Papa Kaipu and Nana Alana were alive.

"Nah, I'm cool." I threw her a peace sign and moved on. It's not that I was totally anti-social, it's just that I was doing my best not to get attached to anybody or anything here.

As usual, I could smell what the cooks were preparing from my class way down the hall. Greasy tater tots were easy to pick out over the strong perfume from the girl sitting next to me and the stronger body odor of the boy behind me. At some point in your adolescence, showering everyday isn't just for your own personal hygiene, it's your civic duty. Some kids hadn't gotten the memo yet.

Having a ridiculously strong sense of smell is kinda cool, I guess. Kaipu used to say that I could smell which direction the fish were swimming. He was right, I could. I'm still waiting to discover the real upside of having such a powerful nose though. More than anything else, it's taught me to breathe through my mouth.

The cafeteria had picnic tables inside and outdoors. The weather was hot and there was smoke in the air from a brush fire hundreds of miles away. Even when the Earth seemed to be on fire, more and more these days, I still preferred the view of the open sky.

Grabbing an outside seat, partially shaded by a stretching eucalyptus, I opened my art history book to a drawing of a pelican. The image of the bird in flight carried me back to Hawaii and my previously interrupted daydream.

My Papa Kaipu had left his precious peanut butter and jelly sandwich unprotected on the deck railing of our beach house.

"Hurry, Papa, a hungry bird wants your food," I said.

Kaipu spun around just in time to see the seabird gracefully swooping down to nab his favorite lunch, but not before I grabbed onto the big bird's legs.

"No, no, no, Akela, let go! Akela, let go!" Kaipu hollered.

The startled bird's powerful wings kicked into gear and carried me off our deck, over the beach, past the surfers, and breaking waves.

Kaipu desperately shouted as I flew out, away from our house, and high over a deepening blue sea below.

"Don't let go, Akela!"

Like most kids, I didn't listen of course. Unlike most kids though, the ocean was my second home.

After a few minutes hanging out underwater with no dolphins to talk to, I looked up to see the bottom of surfboards and boats that had rushed to the area to help.

In a flash, I swam the entire distance back underwater, bodysurfing a little swell onto the sandy shore. The same beach Kaipu and Alana found me on as a toddler.

The two of them ran as fast as their eighty-plus-year-old legs could carry them and whisked me away before anybody could ask how a little girl could hold her breath for over five minutes. I waved at my would-be rescuers as we scrambled off the beach.

Kaipu was drying me off when the sandwich-stealing bird circled back and landed on our deck. He watched as the pelican and I stared at each other. Wordlessly, I communicated to the bird that I was fine. She then flew off again.

Telepathically connecting with other species was normal to me, as far back as I could remember. Apparently, this was fresh news to Kaipu though.

"You understand each other, don't you?"

"Yes, Papa. Doesn't everybody?"

Kaipu's expression turned serious. He glanced over at Nana Alana, and then back to me. "Oh, my sweet, little Akela, you know this world is mostly good, and is filled with so much beauty, and even magic, if you know where to look." He squeezed my hand and his eyes glistened with the prelude to a tear. "But there are forces out there that may seek to use your powers against you, or against others. You must keep them a secret. Can you remember that my dear? Can you do that for Papa?"

"Yes, Papa. I can remember."

"Good." The mischievous grin returned to his kind face. "Now, let's call your bird friend back here to make me a new sandwich, why don't we?"

The memory brought a smile to my lips just before a slam on the table snatched my grin away. Kara stood over me with her cafeteria tray and a few of her crew.

"Looks like this is the last open table for people with friends." Kara pronounced the word *friends* slowly and as if it had three syllables. "That means there's not enough room for you and your books."

"Go pull up a blade of grass," one of her lackeys chimed in lamely.

Whatever. It wasn't worth engaging Kara's team over a silly seat. So, I grabbed my stuff and walked away to the shade of an oak.

Comfortably, I rested under the tree until I heard a flock of pigeons land above me. You don't have to communicate with birds to know you shouldn't sit below them.

Looking up, I tried my best to mentally communicate that a move to a nearby tree would be appreciated. Ideally, the one Kara and her friends were sitting under. I wasn't fluent in bird, and it'd been a while since I'd even tried, but I could still get my point across. Poop there, not here. Pretty straightforward.

"Sorry, Kaipu," I whispered to myself, but man, Kara deserved this.

Sure enough, one by one the pigeons relocated directly above Kara's table.

A few moments later, the pigeons did what they do best. I took a satisfying bite of my apple as Kara and her friends screamed and ran for cover.

Ah, the little pleasures life brings.

Unfortunately, living with Kara and her mom was not one of those pleasures.

CHAPTER 3

"Car wash time!" Kara yelled so loudly it echoed throughout the house.

Saturday mornings were Kara's usual swim meet day. It was also the day where the team washed cars to raise money to travel and clothe themselves head to toe in their beloved Bonita Fields Buoy swim gear. Kara had won the team naming contest.

Kara was my age, taller than me, and with long curly hair that went down to her waist. People considered her pretty and I'd agree, as long as she didn't open her mouth. Her voice was shrill, her tone loud, and her words almost always cruel, at least to me. She looked a lot like a younger version of her mom, Matea, before the wear and tear of life had hardened her.

Kara pulled a chair that I was about to sit on out from under me as Matea delivered her an unevenly toasted waffle. Kara drowned it in syrup and tore into it.

I ignored the stolen chair, as did Matea, and circled the table to grab the other seat. I was used to this treatment, but it still bothered me, Kara being a thirteen-year-old and acting like a ten-year-old. And Matea pretending like I didn't exist.

After Kaipu and Alana died, it was either foster homes or moving here, so the courts put me with Matea and Kara. Matea was Kaipu's great niece and only living relative.

The house was small and backed up against a busy freeway. It had three bedrooms, two upstairs for them and one smaller bedroom downstairs for me. Matea was renting the lower room out when I first moved in, so I shared a bedroom with Kara for the first year. That didn't go well.

Space wasn't the only limited resource in the house when I arrived. Whatever happened to Matea before I came into her life, I don't know, but it left her without much love left to give. Kara viewed me as competition for the little that remained, and I learned early on not to fight her for it.

Matea ripped open an envelope and held up a check.

"Your check is here, Akela," Matea said in a fake cheery voice as she tucked the check into her purse.

Kaipu's will paid Matea a monthly stipend for my living expenses and education—a fact that Matea never once failed to remind me of. How thoughtful of her.

The will left only one other stipulation: that I was to go to the beach at least once a week. But that hasn't happened. Ever.

To be fair, Bonita Fields wasn't anywhere near the beach.

"It's not that I don't want to take you, Akela, it's just expensive. I gotta work and gas isn't free, you know. Kaipu didn't exactly leave me a fortune to cover all your expenses," she'd say. It was always about money with Matea.

I constantly fantasized about running away, back to the ocean. But I never did. I was stuck in a quicksand daydream, and I just kept on sinking.

"C'mon, Akela. Get a move on. The Buoys need the money, so hurry up!" Kara barked. Unfortunately, I was focused on a paragraph on how seaweed impacted the Earth's oxygen levels and didn't reply fast enough for her.

"Now, Worm!" Kara yelled in my ear as she started to drip syrup onto my book's page.

I rarely fought back against Kara, but she had a way of getting underneath my skin and she knew not to mess with my books.

Slowly, I glanced up. "The Buoys? Bonita Fields Buoys? Really, Kara?"

Kara was dumbfounded that I was even talking to her.

"Why'd you name a swim team after a stationary object? That'd be like naming the track team the Cones or the Curbs. I mean, I get the alliteration part, but you couldn't think of anything better than the Buoys for your precious, not so fast, usually coming in last, swim team?" Grabbing a roll of paper towels, I wiped the syrup from my book and dropped the paper roll like I was dropping a mic.

Sensing the anger boiling in Kara, I quickly walked to my room and closed my door as I heard her erupt. "Mom!"

Closing my eyes, I drowned out the yelling with the memory of Hawaiian waves. As I breathed slowly, the surf grew bigger and bigger until a giant swell rose and thunderously exploded on the street outside this sandcastle of a house. The saltwater rushed into my room and swept out, taking me with it, where I disappeared back into the deep blue.

Kara turned the hose on me a few times as I washed cars that morning, but I didn't mind. What bothered me more was all the soap and water we washed down the storm drains that wound up in the ocean.

Honestly, I had nothing against the swim team besides their name and the fact that Kara was on it. I should say it was our name, since technically I was on the team, too, but neither of us considered each other teammates. I never swam and had no plans of starting. Chlorine-filled pools bummed me out and just made me miss the ocean more. I was only on the team as a scheduling convenience for Matea.

Today's meet was against four local schools, each with a name and mascot of a fast ocean animal. The Sharks, Barracudas, Sting Rays and of course The Dolphins. Not one of them was named after a floating ball. I didn't go out of my way to point this out to Kara, who was decked out head to toe in Buoy gear.

Sitting high up on the bleachers, I leaned against the back wall.

"I'll be cheering from up here," I yelled sarcastically down at Matea. She waved without looking as she helped Kara get out of her warm-ups.

Coach made me suit up just in case anybody got injured. That never happened, thankfully for me and the other swimmers of course. He'd spent a lot of time encouraging me to swim when I first joined. Now, he just let me be.

Adjusting my nose plugs to protect against the overpowering reek of chemicals, I leaned against the wall with my iPad. I subscribed to a few online news feeds.

My favorite newsletter was called Global Alert. It was published by a group of anonymous scientists and environmental activists. They were always taking on whaling boats, blocking logging operations and fighting against all types of environmental destruction. They sounded like eco-warriors to me. They sounded badass.

The beginning of the newsletter always had an editorial column by somebody with the initials S.S. That was my favorite part. I felt like S.S was writing to me.

S.S's article was titled "Dartivion CEO, Jarvis Dodd, Announces Offshore Rig. Proposes Demolition of Reef."

Dartivion Corp was a global conglomerate with business interests in every country in the world. Its founder and CEO, Jarvis Dodd, was proposing to blow up a portion of the Great Barrier Reef to access cheaper oil. Dartivion Corp was the largest plastic producer on the planet. You can't make plastic without oil.

S.S wrote, "Until our society values a living reef more than a dead reef and a tree worth more than its wood, this economy of destruction will persist."

I agreed with S.S. I usually did.

Something about Dodd and Dartivion Corp smelled fishy to me and if anybody knows what fish smell like, it's me. I remembered Nana Alana's words about the news. She was a journalist, and always said that there was more to the story if you wanted to take the time to dig. I liked to dig.

I got so into my research about Dodd and his companies that I didn't realize that the constant splashing and yelling had stopped. Hours had passed, and the meet was over.

Matea and Kara were already in the parking lot, and it took them a minute to notice I was walking with them.

"Hey, guys," I said extra loud just to make sure they knew I was there.

Matea spun around excitedly. "Akela, could you believe Kara today?"

Unfortunately, I hadn't watched one second of the meet.

"No, I, uh, yeah, I couldn't believe it. Those things she did. Especially that one thing." I kept it as vague as possible.

"I know, I couldn't believe it either." Matea wrapped her arm around Kara. "A first, a third and a fourth. Her best meet ever!"

Wow. Kara had never placed higher than fifth before. Good for her. Whatever made the two of them happy, if it didn't happen at my expense, only made my life easier.

On the car ride home, I sat in the back seat reading silently. The radio was on with a broadcaster listing scores of local sports teams before turning to other news. My ears perked up.

"And in environmental news, Dartivion Corporation CEO, Jarvis Dodd, denies responsibility for a massive fire burning thousands of acres in California. The blaze started near their logging facility—" the broadcaster said before getting cut off by an incoming call for Matea.

Kara took the opportunity to turn around from the front seat. "You know, Akela," she started in a sing-song tone that I knew meant trouble, "maybe if you got into the pool, you could win a couple of these one day."

She dangled her ribbons so that the wind from the open car window had them blowing into my face. I stared at my book and didn't look up. I was doing my best to ignore the red, blue, and yellow fabric tickling my forehead, but Kara wouldn't stop. She stretched a little closer so that her blue first place ribbon was now flapping directly into my eye. I'd had enough.

Without thinking and shockingly fast, I whipped my hand up and snatched the ribbons from her hand and in one motion, tossed them out the window.

We both craned around to see the ribbons fly away. The blue first place sailed over the sidewalk, down the side of a hill, and off into the storm drain. Whoops.

Kara screamed and Matea flinched, taking her eyes off the road just long enough to rear end the brand-new Mercedes in front of us. Fortunately, we weren't going very fast, and nobody was hurt. Unfortunately, we were going just fast enough for the airbags to deploy and give both Kara and Matea a nice smack in the face. Double whoops.

With our car now fully stopped, the Mercedes owner knocking on Matea's side window, and with both Matea and Kara glowering at me, I knew my wish for a peaceful evening was a thing of the past.

When we got home there was a lot of screaming, crying, and finger pointing. I guess I deserved it. I didn't mean to throw away Kara's ribbons, and I especially didn't want to cause an accident.

"The only fair thing to do is to throw some of her stuff away, right, Mom?" Kara circled me like a shark. "Like something really important to her."

Instinctively, I started to reach for my sea glass necklace, but caught myself and scratched my chin instead. Kara eyed me closely.

"Forget about your ribbons, Kara. What about my car? Tell me, who is going to pay for that?" Matea yelled at me.

I promised Matea I'd get a summer job to help pay for the car damage, but she still ranted on. Kara became quiet, though. She only stared and nodded slowly. It freaked me out. If my bedroom had a lock on the door, I would have used it. Living with Matea and Kara was brutal and only getting worse. I had to get out of Bonita Fields.

Chapter 4

I didn't sleep well that night. Still, I forced myself up early and out the door to school before Matea had a chance to yell at me more.

My grades were my way out. Oddly enough, so was my participation on the swim team. My college application didn't have to say whether I swam or not. I was a Buoy and proudly the most stationary of the bunch. That would show me as the well-rounded individual that I was sort of becoming. On paper at least.

Still sleepy, I drifted through my morning classes in a daydream of ditching Bonita Fields. The school classrooms and hallways filled with water and the other students morphed into coral and seaweed as I swam around them, all the way back to Hawaii with a pod of dolphins—my pod.

Floating to my locker in a happy fog of ocean thoughts, I opened it to find my backpack was missing. A note was taped to the back wall. "See Akela read, see books in pool, see Akela in pool?"

My legs took me to the pool faster than I thought I could run. There, snickering at the poolside stood Kara with two of her meanest girl-friends. She was holding my empty backpack. My books were all in the water!

I ran past the girls and dove in with all my clothes on.

Kara laughed. "I told you, the only way to get her into the pool was her books!" The other two girls cackled in unison.

Their laughter pierced my ears as I grabbed and piled my ruined books onto the side of the pool. The water bubbled and frothed around me as my anger boiled over.

"I didn't even know she could swim!" Kara yelled as they walked out of the gym, turning out the lights as they left and leaving me in the dark.

I hated the dark, yet I stayed there, alone in the water. For how long, I don't know. Something was shifting inside me, and it needed time to settle.

Later that afternoon, I lined up poolside with the other swimmers at practice. They eyed me suspiciously, but Coach acted like nothing was different.

Kara laughed under her breath. "Keep the life ring handy, Coach."

More chatter, but I couldn't process the noise. Glaring at the water through a lens of rage, I saw and heard nothing, but the pool and the sound of the coach's voice.

Coach held out his stopwatch and paused with his whistle in his mouth. "Alright, gang, on my whistle. Ready."

I tucked my sea glass into my bathing suit.

At the sound of his breath forcing out the first audible tweet of the whistle, my world became water. The next moment I remembered, I was touching the wall. Coach stared at me. His mouth opened, the whistle falling out as his gaze moved from me to his stopwatch and back to me again. He shook his head a couple of times in disbelief, before looking back up at me.

"So, how'd I do?" I asked.

I hadn't taken notice yet, but the other swimmers were only a few yards away from me, swimming the other direction on their first fifty meters. I had finished one hundred meters. A few swimmers awkwardly sat by the side of the pool for some reason.

Coach walked silently backwards to his tripod where his phone was set up to record every practice. He stumbled over a towel, without taking his eyes off me, and grabbed the phone.

Later, I sat quietly by myself in Coach's office, twirling my sea glass between my fingers and going over how I'd explain what just happened in the pool. The TV on his office wall suddenly turned on and the image of a man came on the screen. The man was tall, skinny, and dressed all in black.

He stood at a podium as if he were addressing a press conference. The emblem on the podium was from the Dartivion Corp website. The camera zoomed in on the man. His skin was pearly white, made more pronounced by his jet-black hair. He had a hawk-like nose and the most piercing blue eyes I'd ever seen. I'd seen his photo before. This was Jarvis Dodd.

He spoke through thin lips. "Dartivion Corporation's actions have been misinterpreted for years now. Yes, we use the Earth's resources, but only to create better ones and a better planet. Let me show you how."

Dodd reached his hand toward the camera. My skin crawled as I felt as though Dodd was reaching out directly to me.

The door opened and I jumped in my chair as Coach walked in.

"Sorry to startle you, Akela," Coach said, and he closed the door behind him.

The monitor was off now. My mind must have been playing tricks on me.

Coach connected his phone to the monitor on the wall. He sat down, let out a big sigh and pressed play.

On the monitor was an image of the swim team lined up at the beginning of practice. Coach blows his whistle and then the video looks like I was fast forwarded, while everybody else moved in slow motion.

In a blur, I swam the full one hundred meters entirely underwater doing a dolphin-like swim movement and without taking a breath. The wake behind me was so big, that two swimmers were launched completely out of the water. The coach rewound and played the video again and again. He looked at me after each play, while I stayed quiet.

Finally, he turned it off.

"Hmm, what you did, Akela… it's beyond amazing. It's closer to impossible, at least what I thought was possible… Have you ever swam like that before?" Coach asked in a concerned and confused manner.

Kaipu's voice came to me, warning me about sharing my secret.

Stalling, I looked around the office at Coach's family photos. One jumped out that I hadn't noticed before. It was Coach holding a surfboard on a tropical island.

"Was that taken in Hawaii?"

Coach eyed me closely. He took a deep breath before he spun his chair around and grabbed the photo. "Yep, on the big island. I wasn't a bad surfer for a mainlander."

He put the photo back, then crossed his arms and waited for me.

"Well?" Coach asked.

"I don't know, Coach. I was always a fast swimmer. It's been so long, though. I guess I kinda forgot how fast? I've never been timed before."

"Timed? Timed! You swam one hundred meters in twelve seconds, without a breath or even using your arms!" Coach stood up and gestured wildly. "If you'd swam that distance in thirty, forty, I'd be astonished. You'd be on the evening news, the Guinness Book of World Records, maybe even in a tank at SeaWorld!"

My stomach jumped at the SeaWorld comment. The idea of animals in containment for human entertainment appalled me. Now, I was being compared to one. Kaipu was right! I could wind up in a tank or a science lab, while doctors ran tests on me. I shook off the horrible thought.

Coach read my agitation and took a deep breath. "But twelve… twelve seconds, it's not right… it's not human." He stared past me and out the window.

Maybe Coach was onto something, and I wasn't completely human? Having never known my real parents, it might be true.

"I'm going to have to call your mom about this, Akela."

"Go ahead." I put my hand up on my necklace. "And she's not my mom."

Whatever fear I'd had of Matea and Kara was gone, and soon I would be, too.

That evening I sat there as Matea and Kara took turns yelling at me for being awesome.

"You're so grounded! You're so off the swim team! You're… you're… I don't know what else, but you're in big trouble, right, Mom?" Kara screamed through sobs of tears.

Apparently, Coach's iPhone wasn't the only recording device at the practice. One of my teammates had her phone set up as well and up-loaded our practice session to YouTube. The video showed me break-ing all US, Olympic, and known universe records for the one hundred meter freestyle. Instead of being given awards, interviewed by inter-national sports outlets, and put on the front a cereal box, I was being flogged by my not-so-understanding sort of family.

"This video, Akela, I don't understand it. What were you thinking?" Matea asked.

"Thinking? I wasn't thinking anything. I was just trying to swim fast, I guess." I shrugged. "Looks like I did."

Comments like those weren't going to help me.

"See, Mom! Now Akela's bragging and trying to make me feel worse." Kara grabbed Matea's phone. "This video… wait. It's gone?"

Matea swiped her phone back from Kara. "Me and some other par-ents called the school and made them take the video down. They don't have permission to put you kids online."

That was good, but the video had already had a few hundred thou-sand views. The reality started to set in that my secret might now be exposed. I began to get paranoid.

How many people saw what I did? If the audience was limited to lo-cal school kids and their parents, I guess I'd be considered a freak and ostracized, which probably wouldn't change my usual day to day. But what if someone else saw it? Someone who, like Kaipu warned me, might have bad intentions. I didn't want to wind up in a science lab.

Lost in my own thoughts again, I finally returned to Kara's angry voice raining down on me.

"Enough, Kara!" Matea said firmly.

Kara stopped crying instantly, almost too fast, and ran upstairs.

Matea stood up to follow her but stopped. "You know, Akela, every day this gets harder for us. All of us. I can't lose Kara, too," she said to herself as she bowed her head and walked away.

I couldn't think of anything to say. I knew about loss.

That night I lay in my bed, holding my necklace against my chest. I was tired. Tired from the swimming, the endorphin rush, and from the fallout afterwards. That video must have shocked people and that worried me.

Opening my journal, I wrote down, *"run away/escape/swim(?) to Hawaii. I need to get out of here!"*. Those words stared back at me until my eyes grew heavy.

A noise startled me from my sleep. Sitting upright in my bed, I glanced to where my clock was supposed to be, but it wasn't there. I leaned over to grab my journal from my nightstand, but the nightstand was gone, too. I was in my room, but everything was slightly off. Then I saw him.

How he had gotten into my room, I'm not sure, but he was there. He stood against the far wall looking just like he did in the video appearance. He was very tall with oil black, slicked back hair and topaz blue eyes that I found I couldn't pull away from. I knew instantly that this was Jarvis Dodd.

"Akela Spencer. We finally meet." Dodd spoke calmly, but his words somehow carried a physical force. "Are you ready to join me, Akela? It is time. The battle has begun."

The room began to spin, slowly at first, then faster and faster into a whirlpool. My mouth opened to scream, but nothing came out. My arms and legs were frozen. Help!

"Join me, Akela!" Dodd laughed, a high pitched, hyena-like laugh. "Whether you want to or not!"

I woke up in a sweat. My room was empty. My clock read three a.m., my journal and nightstand had returned. I'd passed out on top of my sheets. Overwhelmed with relief that I was only dreaming, I crawled underneath the covers and hugged my pillow. Sleep returned fast and heavy.

CHAPTER 5

Sunlight had snuck in through the opening of my fraying shades. I'd overslept and was the last one up, as I heard voices echoing from the kitchen. Happy ones, too, which could only mean something was going on.

Kara had to be pissed off still. I suppose I'd be too, if the person who I despised the most, out of nowhere, without practice or any warning, annihilated my best performance in the one thing I took the most pride in. That would be a slap to anybody's ego.

Oh well, nothing I could do about that now. Awesome is as awesome does. And I did awesome. Unfortunately, it wasn't going to make my life any easier.

My crazy, realistic nightmare about Jarvis Dodd still lingered over me as I sat up in bed. Something was wrong. My heart stopped as I felt for my necklace and it was gone! Without being noticed, I swept into the kitchen to find Kara and Matea hovering over the computer.

"Five thousand dollars!" Kara squealed. "That'll pay for a private swim coach!"

"And to fix my car," Matea said.

When she moved her head, I got a glimpse of the screen. They'd placed my necklace on an auction site for sale.

"You can't sell what isn't yours!" They both jumped at the sound of my voice.

"The necklace is my property… my only property." My hands balled into fists. "Where is it?" I demanded with a seriousness that snapped both Matea and Kara out of their greed-infused trance.

"Gone, Akela. We sold it. Figured it was the least you could do for us, considering all we've done for you." Kara's eyes glimmered with malice.

"I don't know about that, Kara, but it'll help pay for the accident you caused, Akela." Matea pointed at me. "If I'd known it was worth so much, we'd have sold it sooner. You know we need the money," she said without any emotion.

"It can't be gone. I mean, you couldn't have sold it and shipped it already?" I hoped beyond hope that this was just another cruel Kara joke.

"Nope, we put it up last night and immediately found a buyer. Some rich chick. Said she'd come pick it up this morning. Sorry, Akela, you snooze, you lose, loser." Kara snickered again.

"Shut it, Kara." Matea snapped her fingers. "Sorry, Akela. We all have to make sacrifices." Matea looked back down at the computer screen.

My necklace… my only connection to my birth parents. How could they be so monstrously mean to take that away from me? And why would anybody want to buy it?

Rushing into my bedroom, I reached under the mattress and grabbed an envelope I'd stashed. It held a little bit of money, a family photo, and a drawing. I carefully unfolded the pencil sketch Kaipu had made of my first memory. The reason why he told me to keep to myself.

What would people think if I told them the truth? That my first memory was of being underwater. Not swimming, not bathing in a tub, but sinking slowly into the dark, deep blue water of the open ocean. I can remember the fading light as I continued to sink. I wasn't cold and I wasn't scared. Even weirder, I wasn't struggling for air.

It was a peaceful memory, which was odd, considering I was a toddler alone in the middle of the Pacific. Alone, until I saw them—two dolphins, their eyes directly in front of mine. They were a couple, somehow, I just knew that. I can still feel the texture of the skin on the female dolphin's nose as she gently pushed me toward the surface, the male directly by her side.

Kaipu had drawn me smiling and holding hands with the dolphin couple, my sea glass necklace floating in front of me. In the background was the rest of the pod that helped deliver me safely to Hawaii.

I was lucky to be found by Kaipu and Alana on the beach that morning. Luckier still, they'd adopted me.

Staring at the family photo of the three of us, I started to cry. The smiling kid in the drawing and the family in the photo were both gone. I don't remember being that person. I tried to stop the tears, but I couldn't. Water always finds its way.

I sobbed uncontrollably until my face and hands were wet. I'd never felt so alone, but as the tears streamed down my cheeks, I could sense a strength returning to me.

There was no way I was going down without a fight. I'd wait until this rich, sea glass craving lady showed up. Matea would have to bring my necklace out in the open. At that point, I'd make my move.

Then, I heard a helicopter. It was louder than the usual traffic copters and was getting closer, so close that the house started to shake and rumble.

I pulled back the shades and threw the window open high enough to poke my head out to see a Coast Guard style helicopter hovering directly over our house. This was one huge copter, and somehow different than any other I'd ever seen. What the heck was it doing in this neighborhood?

It paused over our house before landing in a vacant lot across the street. The blades began to slow as the pilot cut the engine.

Then it hit me. My swim video! Somebody in the government or military saw my supernatural swimming and they wanted me.

I'd seen the movie and Kaipu had warned me about what would happen next. Government goons would use some secret ray gun technology to stun me and whisk me away to a science lab where they kept aliens and other oddities in giant fluid filled tanks. I wasn't going to be part of their freak collection. I might have been a freak, but I was nobody's collectible.

It was time to run for it. The window in my room wasn't big enough for me to get out. Our backyard shared a wall with the highway, which left the only way out through the front door. Grabbing my envelope of memories, I sprinted into the living room where Matea and Kara had crawled underneath a table.

"Earthquake, Akela!" yelled Matea. "Get under something!"

For a heartbeat, I paused to look at the two of them cowering together on the floor, and then continued running to the front door and opened it wide.

There, to my surprise, stood a woman. She had raven black hair, dark skin speckled with freckles, and darker eyes. The woman wore a pilot's jumpsuit and looked like could have walked off the cover of an aviation fashion magazine. A metal briefcase was in her hand.

I stared, awestruck, before snapping out of it. This chick was my enemy, I needed to do something. Just before I mustered up the nerve, I was abruptly pushed out of the way by Kara.

"Well, hello! You must be our buyer?" Kara asked while looking around the mysterious lady at the helicopter across the street. "Nice chopper, lady."

The woman stared at Kara without saying a word. Kara shuffled uncomfortably back and forth on her feet as Matea filled in behind her. None of us could keep our eyes off this woman. Kara's hands were noticeably shaking as she tucked them under her armpits.

Matea puffed up her chest and stepped closer to the stranger. "Wow. If you can afford that chopper, you can afford 10 Gs. We can call it my commission," Matea forced out with feigned confidence.

As if Matea was invisible, the woman walked right past her and into the house. "Well, come on in," Matea said sarcastically as we followed her inside.

The woman scanned the room, seemingly unimpressed. She held my stare for a moment before turning to Matea.

"Can we sit?" the mystery lady asked in a tone that was more of an order than a question.

Matea, Kara, and the helicopter fashion model lady all took seats at the kitchen table while I stood with my arms crossed, leaning against the fridge.

This woman was here for my necklace. Why was it so valuable to her? It was only sea glass, a keepsake from my dead parents. It wasn't worth anything. Or was it? Whatever her reasons for wanting my necklace, I wasn't about to give it up without a fight.

"My name is Mikanna. I put a bid in for the necklace you posted. May I see it?" Mikanna spoke clearly and with the confidence of a courtroom lawyer.

"Yeah, yeah, of course. But first, let's—" Matea started to say, but was stopped short as Mikanna cut in.

"Now, Matea," she said forcefully while slamming her briefcase on the table so loud that both Kara and Matea flinched.

Matea motioned to Kara, who hopped up. She pulled the drawstring up from inside her sweatpants. My necklace was tied to it. Kara quickly untied the knot holding the two together and handed it to her mom, who reluctantly put it in Mikanna's hand. She eyed my necklace as if examining a jewel.

I wanted to grab it from her, but still I waited.

Mikanna opened her briefcase and placed a large stack of bound hundred-dollar bills on the table. Kara's eyes widened and reached for the money, but Mikanna placed her hand down over it hard and fast.

"Ouch!" Kara pulled her hand away.

"Not so fast." Mikanna turned to me. "Akela, sit down and join us."

How'd she know my name? My eyes narrowed at Mikanna. Just like Alana and Kaipu, I could see something kind in her gaze. I sat down.

"That's my necklace and I didn't agree to sell it. They stole it from me," I said and glared hard at both Matea and Kara.

Mikanna motioned to me with her hand to pause as she reached into her briefcase to pull out a stack of papers.

"What's this all about?" Matea asked. "We don't need a contract or nothing fancy. Just give us the money, we give you the necklace."

"I'm proposing a package deal here. I want the necklace, but I'm also here to take a big burden off your hands, Matea."

"Are you going to pay off my mortgage?" Matea asked.

"Not quite, but there is a payoff. I'm here to adopt Akela."

"Excuse me?" Matea and I said in unison.

I literally shook my head to make sure I was hearing correctly as the word 'adopt' bounced around my brain. Leaving Kara and Matea and returning to the ocean was my plan. Not joining yet another family. I didn't need anybody anymore. And who was this woman, anyhow?

"You heard me right. I have the legal paperwork all prepared. I've gotten pre-approval from the relevant authorities and only requires your signature to move the adoption forward." Mikanna paused. "And you'll still get the monthly stipend."

Mikanna's eyes were telling me not to worry, but I was worried. Who was she, and where did she want to take me?

"Excuse us for a moment," Mikanna said, motioning for Kara and Matea to leave the table. Kara reached again for the money, but Mikanna, with lightning-fast quickness, slapped her hand. Harder this time. Kara yelped in pain.

"I need two minutes with Akela. After that, I'll be on my way and the money is yours." Mikanna flicked her wrist. "Now, move into the other room."

Mikanna had a presence that demanded respect. Matea got up and took Kara into the living room.

"Wait," Mikanna said. "Take this and read it." She handed the paperwork on the table to Matea. Matea's eyes briefly caught mine before she looked away.

"So, Miss Akela Spencer, I have to say, it's a pleasure to see you." Mikanna unveiled a glowing smile at me.

In an instant, the hard demeanor she portrayed to Kara and Matea was gone. Her body language and the light in her eyes were both soft and welcoming.

"Here, put this back on please." She picked my sea glass necklace up off the table and stood up. "May I?" She reached to place the necklace on my neck.

I nodded hesitantly as she lifted my hair up to allow the necklace to rest against my skin.

She sat back down in front of me. "Thank you, Mikanna," I said.

"It's yours, Akela, and call me Mik. I don't think you have any idea how special that necklace is. Or how special you are for that matter."

"I am a little bit different, I guess." I wasn't sure why I was confessing this to Mik, but I had an odd sense of safety in her presence. "Are you really here to adopt me? Who are you?"

"I work for an organization, Akela. A secret one. My boss sent me for you." She paused as if debating whether to say something. "That's not all."

Mik slid a photo across the desk of a young couple holding an infant. A younger Mik stood next to them, smiling.

I looked at the photo and then back to Mik. "Who is this?" I asked.

"That's you, Akela," Mik said softly.

"That's me? And are those my parents?"

"Yes, honey. I knew your parents." She reached out and grabbed my hand. I pulled my hand back at first, but then gave it to her. I didn't know what to say, but I knew how I felt. Tears streamed down my cheeks.

"You know why you feel better after you cry?" She wiped away a tear from my cheek. "Saltwater, there's saltwater in our tears."

"I miss the ocean so much."

"That's why I'm here, Akela. To take you back." Mik got to her feet and reached her hand to me.

"I want to come with you." My eyes swept the room. The refrigerator was covered with photos of Kara, none of me. I lived here, but this wasn't my home. It never was. I took Mik's hand and stood up. "There's nothing for me here."

Chapter 6

Mik settled affairs with Matea in the kitchen while I packed. Listening through the two closed doors, I didn't hear any protest from Matea as she signed off on allowing me to go. It was probably the best for all of us.

I grabbed my backpack, some clothes, a few favorite books, and my envelope.

As I walked back into the kitchen, Mik closed her briefcase and stood up. Matea and Kara sat at the table staring down at the stack of signed paperwork.

"Ready?" Mik asked me.

Nodding, I followed Mik to the door. She stopped though and gestured back to Matea and Kara. I raised an eyebrow and Mik only nodded to me. I knew what she wanted me to do.

Locking eyes with Matea and then Kara, I quietly said, "thank you."

Kara eyed me with a combination of surprise and relief. Matea closed her eyes.

"Be good to each other," I said, following Mik out the front door.

A crowd had gathered around the helicopter, Mik pulled a remote starter from her flight suit and the blades started turning before we hit the sidewalk. The roar of the engine and turn of the rotors sent the onlookers scrambling back.

We were in the middle of the street when I noticed the black car speeding toward us. Usually, I would've heard the car coming, but my ears were overwhelmed with the sounds of the helicopter engine. Before I had time to react, Mik pushed me out of the way of the sedan. I landed hard on the opposing sidewalk, slightly scraping my knee and elbow. The car unsuccessfully tried to hit Mik, who'd somersaulted out of the way. The car skidded to a halt as the doors flew open. Two men in black suits and sunglasses jumped out. Mik stood between me and the men as they converged on us.

"Run to the chopper, now!" Mik commanded me.

"What about you, Mikanna?"

"Run kid. I got this and I said to call me Mik." She winked at me with outrageous confidence.

What have I gotten into? I said to myself as I sprinted to the helicopter. As I ran, a rush of hot air blew by me. I had a strange sensation that somebody was there, but when I looked to see, there wasn't anybody. Putting my head down, I focused on getting to the safety of the mechanical bird.

"Little late to the party, aren't we boys?" Mik said as she calmly waited for the men to come within striking distance. The first goon threw a punch which she deftly dodged before throwing a lightning fast, spinning round kick that knocked the glasses off the man and sent him to the ground.

"We don't want you, we just want the girl," said the man who was still standing.

"And her necklace," said the other, getting back up off the ground.

Mik just smiled at the men. "The girl and I package are a deal. And so are my fists."

The second goon attempted a leg kick which she easily blocked with her shin, then launched herself into a front flip, ending with a perfectly placed elbow to the man's nose.

"Whoops, did I forget to mention, my elbow is part of the package too?" Mik said as another elbow followed the first.

I climbed into the chopper and watched from the co-pilot seat as Mik dismantled the two men with ninja-like karate moves. It wasn't long before both men were taking sidewalk naps.

My hand rested on my necklace as I breathed a sigh of relief.

Briefcase in hand, Mik walked briskly to the chopper. How was her hair still perfect? Suddenly, the door to my side of the helicopter flew open. I felt that same hot rush of air that happened moments before, but this time standing there was another man in a dark suit. It was Jarvis Dodd.

"You don't know whose side you are on yet, do you, Akela Spencer?" Dodd's voice cut through the noise of the helicopter engine. Once again, I found myself frozen and unable to scream.

The pilot's door opened and Mik hopped in.

"Close your door, kiddo, it's time for liftoff," she said and pointed at the open door.

It took me a moment to realize that I could move and speak again. Turning back to the door, I expected to see Dodd, but he was gone.

"Did you see him, Mik? Did you see Dodd?" I yelled, wide eyed and scared.

Mik's expression changed to pure seriousness.

"Close the door now Akela."

Within seconds we were aloft. I pulled a headset over my ears and scanned all directions for signs of Jarvis Dodd. As we lifted higher above, the men in black slowly moved back into the car, but just two of them, nobody else. Police cars were visible and approaching from all directions.

I lost my view of them as Mik flew the massive chopper higher and higher into the sky. Cars turned to ants, buildings to Lego pieces and before long they altogether disappeared as we ascended above the cloud line, climbing until the mountain peaks disappeared as well. We were soon sailing above a sea of cotton candy.

"Where are we going?" I asked.

Mik just turned to me and smiled. "You'll see."

"Good things the cops probably arrested those goons, right?" I asked, hoping for a yes.

"I'm not going to lie to you, Akela. Those cops didn't do a thing, not to Dodd's men." She smiled. "Don't worry. You're safe now, kid."

"What about Dodd? He was there, too. Just like in my dream."

Mik paused before replying. "We don't know the extent of his powers, but I'm not surprised. We'll be home soon. It's safe. Trust me."

Mik focused her attention on the console where she simultaneously used her left hand to engage a switch on the flight controls, while her right hand punched a code into the main interface. A voice came from the speaker system. "Verbal password to engage vehicle transition."

"Big Blue Whale," Mik answered back as she grinned again. "Hold on, kiddo."

I felt and heard mechanical activity all around me. Looking out the window I could see panels quickly extending from my side of the helicopter, at least I thought it was a helicopter. When the panel was fully deployed, each section locked into a wing shape. The exact same process took place on Mik's side. Mik flipped another switch which transformed the military bench seating into two luxury recliner chairs. A flat screen TV lowered from the ceiling.

I looked over at her and mouthed the word, "Wow."

"Here's the part where you trust me, okay?" Mik said.

I just nodded as she said, "Final transition to Big Blue Whale. Now."

The helicopter rotors engine cut off, and for a moment, my heart felt like it stopped, too. Before any panic could set in, the noise of the chopper engine was replaced by the hum of jet engines. I was pushed back into my chair as we rapidly accelerated forward.

"We've got a long way to go. You should get some rest."

Mik put the copter jet into cruise control and let go of the handles with a dramatic release, but I didn't flinch. She mocked a fake frown. I followed her into the main cabin where luxury chairs reclined into full lay down beds. She handed me a blanket and blackout eyeshades.

A thought occurred to me. "This may be a silly question, but I'm not supposed to call you Mom, am I?" I asked.

Mik laughed and wrapped an arm around my shoulder. "You can call me whatever you want, sweetie, but I prefer Mik."

She sat me down on the bed.

"What'd my parents call me?"

"Jane," Mik said with a smile.

I thought for a moment. "Akela Jane. I kinda like that."

"Me, too." Mik stood up. "I know this is a lot to take in. Get some rest and I'll fill you in more later." She walked back into the cockpit. "Oh, by the way, this turns into a boat, too, so don't be surprised when you wake up."

I didn't think much else could have surprised me at that point. My mind was a jumble of questions and excitement, it was hard to rest. I stared out the window at the expanse of the Pacific Ocean. The largest ocean in the world. For the first time in a very long time, I felt movement in my life. I wasn't stuck or sinking anymore; I was flying.

CHAPTER 7

It'd been hours since I woke up, and the JetCopterBoat—or JCB, as Mik called it—was now a boat motoring full tilt toward the horizon. We both had our eyes fixed forward. She looked down at the center console and flipped a switch.

A holographic image materialized out of a cone-shaped device embedded in the center console. The face of a smiling, bald, black man crystallized in front of us.

"It doesn't appear you've been followed, Mik," said the man in the image. "Launching escort craft."

"Thanks, Des," Mik said as the holograph disappeared.

She quickly redirected her gaze to the ocean ahead and smiled as a helicopter seemed to materialize out of thin air in front of us.

"Where'd that come from?!" I shouted. "Is that another hologram?"

The helicopter buzzed overhead. I could see the pilot. The man wore an LA Lakers hat and sunglasses. Mik waved, and instinctively, so did I. The helicopter continued above us and then vanished out of sight surprisingly fast.

"Where'd they go?!" I yelled over the roar of the engine.

"Any second now!" Mik shouted back, ignoring my question.

Suddenly, a massive vessel materialized out of thin air. It was less than a hundred yards in front of us, and it was so gigantic that I couldn't see around it. There was nowhere to turn.

"Ship!" I screamed.

We were so close I couldn't take in the size of it. A small city floating atop the water had appeared in front of us. It could've been Atlantis risen for all I could tell, but really all I cared about was that we were flying at breakneck speed right at it.

"Mikanna! Do something!" I screamed again.

Mik just turned to me and smiled. "Call me, Mik!" she yelled with a laugh. Great, I was adopted by a murderous psychopath. Just my luck.

I reached toward the steering wheel, but I couldn't move against the centrifugal force pushing me back.

The boat was right in front of us. Closing my eyes, I waited for the impact, but nothing happened.

Was I dead? If I opened my eyes, would I see angels, devils or maybe my parents? I didn't feel dead, whatever that meant. I felt the same. Kinda like a thirteen-year-old girl, but also kinda weird. Basically, I felt like myself.

I slowly opened my eyes to see that a forty-foot high and two-hundred-foot-wide panel on the side of the massive ship had slid open and allowed our boat to pass into an under-boat garage that appeared large enough to house a football stadium.

The JCB guided itself into a slip next to an identical looking JCB craft. There were three of the hybrid crafts in all. Besides that, I counted boats of all sizes, jet skis, submersible units, and some vehicles that I didn't know how to classify.

All these vessels floated comfortably in what I thought must be the world's biggest floating garage. If this was heaven, God really liked her toys. I don't blame her either, as this stuff looked super cool.

Mik unbuckled her belt and mine as I too was preoccupied taking in my surroundings.

"Welcome to *Spirit of the Sea*, Akela."

Chapter 8

We walked off the gangplank into the interior of the vessel and stopped in a small, nondescript room. A voice sounded from a wall monitor.

"Welcome back, Mik. Who do you have with you?"

Mik motioned for me to come forward to the screen. "This is Akela. Akela, open your eyes wide."

"Retina scan engaging," the voice said.

The two walls next to the monitor slid open to reveal a glass pod-like chamber. The room was about the size of a train car with space to seat close to thirty people.

"To the dining area, please, but slowly." Mik grinned at me. "I want Akela to see the view."

The doors closed behind us, and we started moving through a tunnel of white walls, floor, and ceiling.

A voice came through the speakers. "First stop, Rainforest Climate."

Suddenly, the glass chamber was flooded with light, sound, and color.

The roof of the white tunnel was replaced by a jungle canopy of trees. Hundreds of green, yellow, and brown leaves sparkled like jewels under the spotlight of a sun, somehow shining indoors. Beads of moisture appeared on the train windows as we rode into a dense jungle. A movement to my right caught my eye, and I turned to see a monkey cradling it's baby and using her tail and other hand to swing from branch to branch. To the left, we passed a panther napping peacefully fifteen feet off the ground in a tree.

The sounds, colors, and sights were so vivid that I wondered if I was delirious from my recent ridiculous voyage.

I gently slapped my face. "I'm not dreaming,"

Mik gave me a raised eyebrow, which I returned with a thumbs up.

The train passed through an opening in the tree coverage and once again was filled with light and blue-sky. Looking upward, I saw a flock of multi-colored toucans pass overhead.

I craned my neck all the way to take in the floor to ceiling sun-filled view. Was this a biodome? Where was all the light coming from?

"Retractable roof," Mik said. "And when outside weather isn't conducive for the environment, we have the ability to create our own atmospheres inside."

Slowly turning around, I tried to take it all in. The green reminded me of home, my real home of Hawaii, but the animals were more than I could have imagined.

"Can we stop and get out?" I asked excitedly as I saw the end of the biodome nearing. Mik shook her head.

I quickly jogged to the back of the glass train, not wanting to leave the greenery. Soon we were back in a tunnel, but only for a moment before being blinded by the glare of white and sun. Mik handed me a pair of sunglasses.

"Second stop, Polar Climate," the overhead voice chimed in again.

The Polar Dome was a winter wonderland of white and bright. As I looked out through the glass windows, I realized how many different shades of white existed. I giggled out loud as a polar bear jumped from a snow-covered perch into an icy pool of water.

Higher up in the dome, an eagle circled before diving bombing to pick a salmon out of the water. The eagle landed in a tree, the salmon still writhing in its claws. Nature at work.

"How big is this ship?"

"Big. Very big. Powered by sun and water, too." Mik pointed at the polar bear before it passed out of sight. "Endangered." She then nodded toward a speckled owl resting in a tree. "Endangered as well."

"And that panther, right? I read about it being hunted close to extinction. Deforestation in the Amazon rainforest has almost eliminated their natural habitat." I found myself almost yelling.

Mik nodded at me with an expression that asked me to continue my thought and hand gesture to lower my voice.

"Sorry, so this is a sanctuary for endangered species, right?"

"Yes and no, but mostly yes. The *Spirit of the Sea*, or SOS as we call it, is a biodome capable of accommodating, with a few exceptions, almost every different type of species on Earth."

"Amazing."

"It is amazing, and you've only seen a small portion of it."

I paced excitedly back and forth the length of the glass train. My mind raced while trying to process everything. How many more animals were on this boat? How big was the SOS, and how in the world could anybody afford to build it?

My excitement turned to anxiety when I saw a man and woman in lab coats drawing blood from what had to be a tranquilized snow leopard. I imagined my body replacing that of the sedated big cat and quickly snapped out of it. Reality hit me fast, along with Kaipu's warning. I didn't know where I was or who I was really with.

I reminded myself that I trusted Mik enough to leave Bonita Fields, but not so much to leave my guard down completely. The train passed into the next chamber. "What's next? Desert climate? Mountain region? Or a laboratory possibly?" I asked.

Mik ignored my question as the train moved into another section. Excitedly, I ran to the front to see where we were next. I was surprised when we emerged into what I could only describe as an outdoor city promenade. There was a single lane street that our train was passing down. A pizzeria, coffee shop, karate studio, gym, bookstore, and restaurant named *Chez Shipman* all lined the sidewalk. A small park area was adjacent to the storefront. The park had a large grass lawn, a towering oak tree, two eucalyptus trees and a few palm trees that were scattered around the perimeter, along with park benches. Sparrows, doves, and crows could be seen passing from tree to tree.

Also, there were people. Quite a few of them. They all appeared to be going about their everyday lives. I even noticed a boy who looked to be around my own age.

The train stopped. The voice overhead said, "Stop Three, Montana Avenue."

"This is our stop. Hungry kiddo?"

"Yes!" My stomach grumbled so loud that I almost forgot I had just ridden a glass train through the rainforest and Antarctic.

Mik and I stepped out of the train, across the street, and onto the sidewalk. The same kid I'd seen earlier was now practicing handstands in the park. He noticed us and started hand-walking our direction before suddenly flipping himself back onto his feet in one swift movement. Mik waved and we caught eyes for a moment. The boy had dime-sized dimples that were possibly visible from space. He smiled and I did a double take as I watched him run off. His jog accelerated into a sprint, which turned into a blur before he disappeared.

Before I could ask who the boy was, Mik's watch beeped loudly. She spoke into it. "Mik here, you need me on this one?"

A man's voice came through her watch, "No. Get Akela situated. We can handle this."

Mik nodded and closed her watch as the lights of the *Chez Shipman* restaurant turned off. The OPEN sign switched to CLOSED.

"Looks like it's pizza today, kiddo." She slapped me on the back. "You'll have to wait a little longer to meet our benefactor."

A large pineapple pizza and a pitcher of strawberry flavored sparkling water were delivered to our table and I dug in.

I didn't completely understand what was going on, where I was, or who I was with, but I felt something in my belly that I hadn't felt in a long time. It was more than just delicious food. The constant knot that I'd gotten so used to being there had loosened ever so slightly. I was out of Bonita Fields, finally.

CHAPTER 9

After dinner, Mik took me to my room. We followed the path the fast kid had taken through the park. It took us through an internal corridor that eventually led into a huge central atrium that opened to the sky.

"Another retractable roof?

"Yup, on the SOS, we do our best to harness Mother Nature, but she's an impulsive mother. Climate change is only making things worse." Mik talked and walked briskly toward the stairs.

We stopped on the fifth level in front of a long hallway of numbered doors.

"How many people live on the SOS?"

"Including you, a little under a thousand. That includes the maintenance team, scientists, crew, and all other roles. Most play more than one. Oh, and the operations team. That's your team kid, once you are ready." Mik smiled.

"I'm part of a team?" The nerves in my gut started to tighten again. The only team I'd ever felt part of in my life was with Kaipu and Alana. I guess I was on the Bakersfield Buoy swim team, too, but I didn't want to count that.

Mik nodded. "Yes, that's the plan. In time."

"What does an operations team do?"

Mik paused, her eyes raising skyward before returning to meet mine. "We protect the environment."

"So, kinda like the Environmental Protection Agency?" I asked.

"Sort of, but our job is a little more hands-on, you might say." Mik patted me hard on the back. "You'll see soon enough, kiddo."

"Is it dangerous? Do I need to train? And how will I know when I'm ready?" I asked in rapid fire, stopping in the hallway.

"Yes, what we do can be dangerous and yes, you'll need to train." Mik stopped and walked back to me. She put a hand on each of my shoulders. "You're brave, Akela. Brave to live so long away from the ocean, brave to stand up to me when I came for your sea glass, and even braver to come with me." Mik looked at me intensely. "You have a deep reservoir of courage, kid. As deep as the ocean. You'll be fine. I have no doubt about that."

"Thank you," I said. I didn't know what else to say, but I instantly felt better. For now.

We kept walking until Mik stopped in front of a room. She grandly opened the door. "Your suite, Miss Akela."

"Wow. Brave and sweet? I'm starting to grow on myself."

Mik laughed and followed me into my new digs.

Spirit of the Sea was so incredibly immense that I'd forgotten that I was on a boat surrounded by the Pacific Ocean. Walking in, I could see the ocean through the balcony doors. I got so excited, I charged toward the deck, sprinting past a small desk and a bed with clothes laid out on top of it. My eagerness to taste the salty air overwhelmed the reality that I should be smelling it much more clearly. I leaned forward toward the deck like a runner about to break through the tape at the finish line.

"Door!" Mik yelled just as I smacked face-first into a clear glass sliding door that led to the balcony.

Bouncing backwards, I fell onto my butt as the door finally opened automatically. I checked my nose for blood. Nothing. Mik came walking up beside me and knelt to examine my face.

The automatic door was now opening and closing as it bumped against my legs sprawled out in the door opening..

"Major props to your cleaning crew," I said through my laughter. "That is one clean door."

Mik helped me up. "I think your excitement and speed was a little too much for the sensors."

"Apparently." I tried rubbing my nose back into its normal shape. "But you know, what if somebody needed to get outside quickly, like for a fire or an emergency or something?"

"I'll talk to the techs." Mik nodded.

We walked out onto the deck and soaked in the view of the Pacific Ocean, the largest ocean in the world.

"Around fifty percent of the entire Oceanic water of the Earth is represented in this ocean. The Pacific," Mik said quietly and with great reverence.

The spray of the ocean air danced lightly on my skin as my senses came to life. Slowly, I closed and opened my eyes and blinked hard.

For a long while, Mik stood silently beside me as we drank in the sight, sound, and smells of the Pacific. After being gone for so long, it was hard to be this close to the ocean and not be in it.

"When do I get to swim?"

"Tomorrow, kiddo." Mik walked back into the room and I followed. "There's clothes on the bed. Take a shower and get some sleep. When you wake up give me a buzz on this. Don't worry about the time. I'll take you to your physical." She handed me a brand-new phone. "I'm in your favorites."

Thumbing through the shirts, I tried to hide my unease about having a physical, but the image of the sedated mountain lion wouldn't lay down in my head. "Will-do. Oh, and I just had a physical at school, I'm all set.

"Everybody on SOS gets one. Sam's rules.," Mik said.

"Who is Sam anyhow, and when do I meet him?" I changed the subject and tried to stifle a yawn.

"Soon enough. He'll fill you in on everything."

"My parents, too?" I asked and this time really yawned.

"Yes, honey. He will."

Slowly, I lowered myself down onto the bed. The few hours of sleep over the past two days had finally caught up to me. I'd deal with ditching my doctor's appointment after some sleep.

Mik turned and walked toward the door.

"There's a saltwater option in the shower by the way," she said as she closed the door to my room.

The moment the saltwater hit my skin my senses kicked into overdrive. Every pore on my body tingled with energy.

The pajamas fit perfectly as I sat at the desk and combed my hair back. Looking in the mirror, I pulled my hair up. Maybe I'd cut it even shorter now that I was going to be part of an operations team, whatever that really was.

The saltwater had done its job. Feeling relaxed, I smiled at myself in the mirror. Strangely, I couldn't remember ever doing that before. My eyes moved up with my rising cheeks as I wriggled my nose. It wasn't a very big nose, but it had an ever so slight bend to the left that made it look like it was planning on turning a corner before the rest of my body. That made me smile even more. If anybody walked in right then, they'd have thought I was nuts.

Laying down on my bed, I held my necklace close against my chest and moved my fingers along the jagged outline of North America. I was out there, somewhere left of the west coast. Finally. My last thought before passing out was that I should smile more.

CHAPTER 10

I dreamt that I was swimming in the open ocean alongside a pod of dolphins. We were all gliding in and out of a gigantic boat wake, surfing up and down the never-ending waves pushing off the hull. The dream was so realistic that I'd even felt the wetness of the ocean water on my face.

Lifting my head, I saw the giant puddle of drool that I'd created on my pillow. What a sleep, and what an even better dream.

In a daze, I walked over to the door leading to the balcony, but slowly this time. Opening it, I laughed as I noticed the outline of my nose. My small deck had two chairs, a table, and a reclining chair.

As soon as I walked outside, I heard a sound that I hadn't heard in forever. It was from my earliest memory. Scanning the horizon, I saw nothing but open ocean.

Gradually, I moved my line of sight closer and closer. Was I experiencing some sort of auditory hallucination, an echo from my recent dream? Or maybe I was still dreaming? That was it! The dream. I walked to the balcony railing and peered over the edge.

There, fifty or so feet down below, I saw them—a pod of dolphins. There must have been close to thirty, swimming and launching themselves in and out of the wake of the boat. Just like in my dream. I smiled and hollered a 'hello!' to them.

The pod concentrated their jumping, flipping, and wake surfing right below my stateroom. As I watched their actions and listened to their sounds, I suddenly felt that they were calling to me!

Leaning over the balcony, I saw that it was a good five-story drop into the ocean below. I'd jumped from higher cliffs and even from a pelican's leg in Hawaii, I could do this.

Maybe I'd get in trouble, and I'd definitely miss my physical, but I didn't want any doctors inspecting me anyhow.

My nerves were on overdrive, but I knew that I had to make this jump.

Scaling up the rail of the boat, I braced myself against the sidewall of my deck. I smiled at the thought of Kaipu and Alana looking down at me as I jumped.

While I might have been the world's greatest swimmer, my arsenal of dives consisted of a cannonball and a belly flop. Midair, I quickly decided that feet first would be the best approach. As I rapidly neared the ocean surface, I realized I might hit one of the dolphins. At an average of six hundred pounds of pure muscle versus me—little old me—a collision wouldn't end well. Fortunately, the dolphins thought of this as well and created a circle of clear water for my body to enter the Pacific.

My feet pierced the seal of the sea and my entire body followed in a flash. Instinctively, I exhaled water out of my nose as I opened my eyes to see the blur of bubbles and blue surrounding me as I passed five feet, ten feet, twenty feet, thirty feet, forty feet below the surface. Wow, I was going deep.

My momentum slowed and I was able to more clearly see and hear the world of life around me. Dolphin life. The pod gracefully circled me, but not in a menacing way. Their bodies were sleek and muscular, perfectly designed for swimming and ramming, but they were only monitoring, protecting, and welcoming me.

Absorbed in the moment, it took a second for me to realize that the dolphins were all communicating to me and that I could understand them.

"Swim, swim, swim!" they called to me.

For a heartbeat, I panicked when I saw the hull of the boat moving away from us. Could I still swim with and keep up with the pod?

With a kick of my legs and a pull of my arms, I started moving. The pod instantly broke formation and swam with me.

My speed increased until I was swimming as fast as the boat. Locking my legs together, I pushed my arms ahead of me in a diving position and breached the surface for a quick breath. It took a few moments to get my rhythm down, but once it kicked in, I could feel the water pulling faster and faster against my body. I was really moving now and felt strong as I broke the surface again. This time I completely breached and was joined in the air by the dolphin pod.

When I landed, I found myself perfectly positioned right in the curl of the boat wake, and started surfing back and forth over the face of the wave. It was all happening just like in my dream. A dream that was starting to feel more like a premonition.

The pod and I continued racing, playing, surfing, and jumping until I noticed that the boat was slowing, and dolphins were beginning to slow with it.

We took a more relaxing pace and began to swim around each other, slowly and deliberately. Each mammal had a unique face and distinct tone to their voice. The shape and light of their eyes were all slightly different. Some had a serious expression, while others came across as carefree. The size of their bodies, shapes of their fins, their way of swimming and tone of voice. All very much individualistic, just like any human.

Since jumping in, I hadn't tried communicating back to the pod other than using facial and hand gestures. It'd be so many years since I'd seen a dolphin, and my recollection of how I understood and spoke with them was a distant memory. I knew it happened, but trying to hold onto the details was like grasping at the ocean mist.

I said 'hello friends' in my best attempt at dolphin language that my waterlogged brain could handle. I wasn't sure they could hear me over the hum of the *Spirit of the Sea*'s engine, but then I remembered I was speaking telepathically.

"Hello, ocean friends."

The two closest dolphins regarded me for a moment before swimming around and closely by, barely caressing my back with their fins as they passed. My heart backflipped as they allowed my hand to run along the length of their torso. The second one, the largest male in the pod, came back around and swam next to me.

"Hello again," he said. *"My name is Jon."*

"My name is Akela." I paused. *"Wait, you said hello again?"*

He silently gazed into my eyes as I glanced back and forth between the two mammals. A long-lost image slowly materialized in my head, as if moving from a great distance into focus, until at once, it hit me like a tsunami. I recognized them! These were the dolphins that saved me. This was the pod that had delivered me to Hawaii—to Kaipu and Alana.

The second dolphin, a female, swam up next to Jon. I could tell right away that they were a couple, the two Kaipu had sketched from my memory *"I'm Ana. We've always known you, Akela. We were worried you might have forgotten about us."*

"Forgotten? You guys are all I've thought about for years." My mind flashed back to the years I spent landlocked and living with Kara and Matea. I started to cry, my tears reuniting with the salt of the ocean water.

Of all the dolphins in the ocean, the odds of being reunited with Jon and Ana were astronomical. This had to be more than a coincidence.

I touched the sea glass necklace around my neck and the two dolphins wiggled happily in front of me. The pod had formed a larger circle around the three of us and, like a welcoming line at a wedding, each dolphin introduced themselves.

"Hi, Akela. I'm Rhino," said a smaller adolescent male with some scar tissue on his head that gave him a horned look.

"He belongs to us," said Jon.

Then came a tough looking female. *"My name is Laila."*

"Hi, Akela," called another adolescent, *"I'm Bingo."*

And the introductions continued as all thirty dolphins said hello.

Last to come forward was an older dolphin, covered in scars from nose to tail. He'd clearly won many battles to have survived this long, but the fight appeared to have taken its toll. He moved slowly and deliberately. The joy that was evident in the other dolphins was not here with this one. The pod viewed him with respect and fear.

"Everybody calls me Grandpa, Akela. You might as well, too."

I bowed my head respectfully, as Grandpa grunted dismissively and swam away.

The bottom of a small boat appeared above us.

"I think your friends above might want to spend a little time with you," Jon said.

"But… I… we just reunited. I'm not ready to leave you guys."

Jon and Ana wiggled gently. *"You are of the sea and the land, Akela. Go up. We will have plenty of time together."*

"When? How? Are you guys leaving?"

"No, no. We are with the Spirit of the Sea and the Spirit of the Sea is with us." The dolphin couple both nudged me with their noses upwards, just like they'd done when I was a baby. *"Go up and see for yourself."*

Slowly, I swam away from Dolphin Ana and Dolphin Jon. It felt odd leaving them so quickly after reuniting, but they'd said they were a part of the *Spirit of the Sea*. I trusted I would see them again.

My head popped up next to the boat to see Mik at the helm and two men standing on deck with their arms crossed. The first was a young blond man wearing diving gear. The other was the bald man I had seen in the holograph. He was gigantic.

Mik smiled at me while shaking her head and wearing a 'what the heck were you thinking' look on her face.

"Why don't you come aboard, Ariel," Mik said. That was probably not the first *Little Mermaid* reference I was going to hear.

I breaststroked to the swim ladder and started to pull myself up, before suddenly remembering that I was swimming in my pajamas. I also realized how tired I was. My hands gripped the ladder, but my arms refused to pull me up more than halfway. They were dead. I was running on adrenaline. I wasn't in any type of shape to swim like that for an extended period. The enormous man grabbed a towel, leaned over the ladder, and effortlessly picked me up. He gently placed me on the deck as I wrapped myself in the towel.

He was the biggest man I had ever seen. I had to tilt my head backward to take him all in. I guessed he was more than six and half feet tall and made of stone. A salt and pepper beard covered his sharply chiseled jawline. If it weren't for a smile that could melt an iceberg, I would've found him very intimidating.

"Thank you," I said.

As he leaned forward to shake my hand, I noticed the sea glass necklace hanging around his neck. It was unmistakably shaped like the continent of Africa. I instinctively reached for my necklace, and as I did, I felt it rise off my chest and move toward the giant man in front of me. As he bent lower, our necklaces hovered near each other without touching, as if they were magnetically drawn together. I stood mouth agape at the sight of our sea glass pieces meeting each other. The smaller man's eyes also transfixed on the two glass pieces.

"Hello," I said shyly. "Our necklaces appear to be introducing themselves as well?"

"It's my pleasure. My name is Desmond, and yes, our necklaces are once again connected," he said casually as if it was a totally normal occurrence. Desmond spoke in a thick accent. "And this is Johan." He gestured toward the diver.

"Hello, Akela," Johan said, but his eyes were still locked on our necklaces. He had very blue eyes.

Johan came up to Desmond's shoulders and was probably almost six feet tall himself. He reminded me of the guys you'd see in an action sports advertisement with his shoulder length hair, pirate style mustache and beard, and steel blue eyes. He was older than me, probably around college age, and German based upon his accent.

I felt myself blushing. Mik picked up on it and jumped in, "We weren't sure how your little diving act was going to go, so we scrambled our best divers in case you needed a little assistance. Next time you plan on going for a swim, do me a favor and let me know, okay, kiddo?" Mik said in a serious tone.

I nodded.

"If she knew what was really down there, she wouldn't have jumped at all," Johan said and was immediately stared down by Mik.

I figured Johan was referring to sharks, but I was confident that the dolphin pod had my back if any showed up. Still, seeing their smiling and somewhat concerned faces, I realized that what I'd done was very inconsiderate.

"I'm sorry, I didn't really think about what I was doing. I just did it."

"Downright reckless is what it was," Desmond boomed. I felt awful, but before I could apologize, Desmond shouted out, laughing, "But my goodness, young lady, can you swim!"

My blushing went from pink to bright red.

"How'd it feel?" Johan added. "I mean, as a diver, I've only dreamt of swimming like that."

Mik guided the boat back into the underwater garage as I did my best to explain everything from my dream to swimming with the pod.

"Amazing, Akela," said Mik as Johan and Desmond tied off the boat. The two of us stepped off as Desmond and Johan cleaned the boat and put away their gear. We all walked back together to the main station.

"You know, while you were down there, Akela, we could hear all of the dolphin chatter," Mik said, matter of fact.

"Yeah, and it sounded different than normal," Johan said. "You can understand them, can't you?"

"Yes." I took a deep breath and a leap of faith. "And they can understand me. I don't know how, but I've always been able to speak Dolphin. That and some other animals as well. Maybe not speak to them, but somehow communicate with them. Telepathically. It's hard to explain."

I must have looked a little nervous as I spoke. Mik put her around me and I turned to Desmond, who had caught up with us.

"You have a gift, my dear," Desmond said. "We will help you unwrap it."

A dolphin breached the water just as I looked up. It was Rhino. We made eye contact as he waved his tail before he returned to the water.

For a moment, I thought to tell them that this pod, Dolphin Jon and Dolphin Ana's family, was the same pod that saved me while I was baby. But I didn't. It was too much, too soon.

"See you in the mess hall, Little Mermaid," Johan joked as he hosed down the boat. I smiled, but couldn't think of anything to say.

I was better at communicating with dolphins than I was with boys.

CHAPTER 12

That night Mik met me at my room. We strolled down a glass encased hallway and onto the longest escalator I'd ever seen. The escalator passed by and through the biodomes as we descended. My eyes followed the path of the monarch penguins sliding down a small glacier into the water. In another dome, a family of gorillas groomed each other while resting easily along a small, winding river. On the other side of the escalator, I saw a flash of movement and turned to see a pack of wolves blazing across a valley flush with wildflowers. Funny, I almost thought I saw a human sprinting with them, but before I could focus my eyes the pack disappeared around a large rock formation next to a rolling river.

"The ship can desalinate ocean water faster than any other water processing facility to date," Mik said as we passed the river. "Sam is working to bring the technology to the local level. Access to clean drinking water can be the difference between life and death."

"Righteous," I said. "Sam's the boss man, right?"

"Yes, he is."

"Can't wait to meet him and thank him," I said, but I wasn't totally sure what I was thanking him for yet. It was great to be out of Bonita Fields, but I had an uncomfortable feeling that I was getting involved in something that I wasn't ready for.

We continued down the escalator for a few awkward moments until I broke the silence. "So, what's the deal with Desmond and my necklace? I mean, you had to have seen them move toward each other on the boat, right?"

"They are pieces of a map, Akela. A sea glass map." She continued facing straight down the path of the escalator, until finally turning to me. Her eyes sparkled. "It's why we brought you here. One of the reasons at least."

"A sea glass map to what? Wait, is that what Jarvis Dodd was after—"

Mik jumped in before I could finish.

"Those are questions for Sam, Akela. We'll meet with him when he returns. For the moment, you must be careful not to discuss the sea glass map with anybody, but me. I promise that you're safe here."

I didn't understand how I was 'safe', but also needed to be careful about talking about my necklace. I started to ask, but Mik gave me a hand signal to hold off. A gesture that by most would come across as rude, but from her, it was graceful.

I pulled my necklace out of my shirt and looked at its shape. My whole life I'd been unknowingly wearing a map piece, something part of a larger puzzle that Sam, Mik and the SOS team wanted to solve. Jarvis Dodd, too, apparently. If Dodd was trying to finish the same puzzle, my necklace might as well be a lure. I tucked it back into my shirt.

The steepness of the escalator slowly leveled off and I recognized the entrance to the promenade area. I'd assumed we were going there to eat, but we passed by and continued until the moving sidewalk came to an end. I could hear music, laughter, and the friendly chatter of a large group of people coming from down the hallway.

I sniffed the air. "Nice, I love eggplant."

Mik stopped and eyed me.

"What? I told you I have a very strong sense of smell," I said and immediately remembered the physical I ditched. Thankfully, Mik didn't bring it up.

We turned a corner and walked into a large open room filled with people, food, and music.

Surveying the room, it was the size of ten basketball courts, but felt way bigger due to a glass ceiling that soared at least two hundred feet above the floor. The night sky above gave the sensation that we were outside. Projected into the open area above was a three-dimensional moving image of our solar system. It rotated high above us, our Earth three stones away from the sun, with the moon slowly orbiting it. I stood there staring upwards, watching the planets swim around each other.

"Helpful reminder of where we are, isn't it?" Mik elbowed me to keep moving.

"Now that you bring it up, where are we exactly?"

"The dining hall of course." Mik laughed and walked off ahead of me. I didn't find it funny being kept in the dark, but I was quickly distracted by the scene around me.

The furthermost wall from the entrance had a little indention, allowing room for a stage. A bluegrass band was happily picking out a playful tune for the diners. An older couple danced at the front of the room as people clapped in between bites of food and sips of drinks. I noticed many younger kids around my age leaning against the wall watching the band. So, there were other kids on the SOS besides me and the fast kid in the park. I surveyed the room for him, but he wasn't there.

The seating was bench-style and spread out across oversized picnic tables. Food was available at a buffet through a long open window that ran almost the entirety of the room.

The energy in the room was so vibrant and positive. Everybody seemed happy. It felt odd to me.

"Is it always like this?" I grabbed trays for our plates and stepped into the food line.

"Well, there's always music. There's a lot of talented people aboard the SOS, and these Sunday night dinners are a great opportunity to share those talents with the rest of the crew."

"Do you play an instrument?" I selected a piece of oven fresh sourdough for my plate.

Mik coughed out a laugh as she eyed me scooping heaps of salad. "Me? No, no. Sam likes for everybody to get up once a year and contribute something artistic—a song, poetry, humor, a play, paintings, whatever. Last year I told a few jokes."

"How'd that go over?"

She stared back at me, quiet and expressionless for a few long seconds. "That was my impersonation of the crowd's response."

"Hey, that's good! You should add that to your routine."

Mik ignored my comeback as we took our food trays and sat down across from Desmond, Johan and two women I hadn't yet met.

Mik introduced me. "Akela, you know Des and Johan already. This is Ericka and Ahimsa."

I tried not to stare, but there was something about the women that I couldn't take my eyes off of. Ericka was a blue-eyed blonde with long wavy hair and very sharp, attractive facial features. Ahimsa had black hair, dark skin, and beautiful brown eyes. I would've guessed she was of Egyptian descent.

"How do you like it here so far, Akela?" Ahimsa, asked.

"Uh, good. So far so good, I guess," I said somewhat haltingly when it finally hit me. Ahimsa had the same exact facial features as Ericka. Identical. "You and Ericka, you're sisters, right?"

Ericka and Ahimsa both laughed at the exact same time. Ericka spoke first. "Yup. We are what some people call biracial identical. Our mother is Swedish and—"

"Our father was Moroccan," Ahimsa said, seamlessly finishing Ericka's sentence.

"Wow. I mean, sorry to stare, but you're both so beautiful. So different and yet the same," I said awkwardly.

"Aren't we all?" Desmond said. I nodded, a little embarrassed at my candid comments. Desmond picked up on that immediately.

"You like my painting?" Desmond gestured to the nearby wall, which was covered with many different paintings of all shapes and sizes.

"The whale?" I asked, pointing at an acrylic painting of a giant blue whale that was so realistic that I thought it might just come to life.

"Desmond is a man of many talents," Mik said.

"It's amazing. I like to draw, but you could be a professional," I said.

"Thank you. I'd love to see your drawings, Akela."

"Me, too," Ahimsa and Erika chimed in unison.

I found myself smiling. Why'd I feel so comfortable with these people I'd just met? And why was my comfort level now making me feel uneasy? I tried to stop thinking so much. It wasn't working.

"Ahimsa and Ericka are both scientists, Akela." Mik opened her arms wide. "Their work allows us to be able to stay at sea year-round."

"And for our biodomes to operate," Johan added. "They're both beyond brilliant." His gaze held Ahimsa's for what I felt was a little longer than an appropriate amount of time. Just as inappropriately, I took that opportunity to stare at Johan. The dude was handsome.

I averted my eyes. I felt like I needed to say something. Conversation wasn't something I was used to, and I reminded myself of Mik's assertion that I was in a safe and welcoming environment.

"How'd you guys get here?" I asked. "I mean, this type of job isn't something you'd find on a job board. Mik here had to practically kidnap me, right?"

Everyone turned toward Mik. I'd figured by now that she was a leader, but this was confirmation.

"One person… Sam Shipman," Mik said.

The others nodded in agreement. I waited for anybody to volunteer more information, but nothing came.

"Did Jarvis Dodd attempt to get to any of you guys first, like he did with me?"

I saw Ahimsa's eyes jump at the name of Dodd.

"Whoa. I didn't know that, Ak—"

"Why talk Dodd when we can dance!" Johan grabbed Ahimsa's hand and pulled her toward the stage.

The band had just kicked into a rousing rendition of Peter Rowan's famous *Midnight Moonlight*. Kaipu had loved bluegrass.

Mik crossed her arms and was giving me a stern look.

"Be patient, Akela." She started to walk away before stopping. "Oh, and speaking of patience, your physical has been rescheduled for tomorrow."

Dang it. I didn't need any examination to confirm I was a freak, but Mik was gone before I could think of another excuse.

Dodging my physical was just another concern added onto finding out more about my parents, my necklace, and why I was there. The information was coming in bits and pieces, but I wanted it faster. I was happy to be out of Bonita Fields, back in the ocean, and reunited with my pod. It wasn't enough, though, just to be along for the ride. I needed to talk to Sam.

I was about to ask another question when Desmond stood up. Towering over the table, he sweetly bent down and extended his hand out to me.

"May I have the pleasure, young lady?"

I spent the rest of the evening dancing the night away while my questions simmered on the back burner of my mind.

CHAPTER 13

To say I slept well that night would have been a massive understatement. My body felt sore, but strong. I knew I had to get stronger to keep pace with the pod and I couldn't wait to swim with them again.

While my body was tired, my mind was overwhelmed. Thoughts, questions, and ideas raced through my brain, careening off each other like bumper cars.

For years I had dreamt of returning to the ocean, but never in my wildest daydreams did I think this would happen. I wasn't sure about anything yet other than that if the SOS team worked to protect the ocean, then I was with them. Regardless, there was no going back to Bonita Fields.

Lazily, I rolled over and checked the clock sitting on the bedside table. I had nowhere to be, so I just laid there staring at the lifelike mural of a coral reef on my ceiling when a loud knock came at my door.

"Who is it?" I shouted.

"Leo."

"And Warren," chimed in another male voice.

I sat up in my bed. "Okay. Hold on a sec." Who were these guys, and why were they making me get up?

Begrudgingly, I pulled myself out of bed. I'd been sleeping in pajama pants and a Keep Tahoe Blue t-shirt.

There stood the two boys. I instantly sized them up. I'd seen Warren in the park before, walking on his hands and running like a gazelle. He was a little taller than me and built like a sprinter. I'd guess he was around my age, and he had an amazing shock of thick brown hair that matched his amber eyes. This boy was definitely way cuter up close. On top of it all, he spoke with a strong accent that I couldn't put my finger on, but I figured was from somewhere in Eastern Europe. And those huge dimples, which instantly brought the warmth out in my cheeks.

The other boy appeared a bit older. He was tall, with dark hair and sharp eyes behind glasses that seemed to be calculating everything they saw. In addition to intelligence, kindness projected from those eyes as well.

Both boys had backpacks on. Backpacks. Right. Slowly and reluctantly, I put two and two together.

The older boy introduced himself. "I'm Leo."

"That must make me Warren," Warren said as he saw me eyeing his backpack. "Yeah, I thought the same thing, too, when I first got here."

"School," I said. "Right. I guess my head was thinking more about saving the planet than it was about school. "Where you guys from?"

"It's easy to do. I mean, not saving the planet, that's hard, really hard actually. What I'm trying to say is that it's easy to forget about school," Warren added. "Oh, and I'm from Poland."

Leo shook his head and sighed loudly. "And I'm from Japan. We'll wait here while you get ready. The school labs are hard to find the first time around. Look in the desk, you'll find everything you need for class."

In my desk I found a fully packed backpack and a laptop. I quickly dressed, only stopping to look at my family photo, Kaipu's drawing, and the photo Mik had given me of my birth parents that I'd pinned up above my desk. I was dying to meet Sam and learn more about my family.

We moved quickly through a maze of corridors with Warren leading the way. He walked exceptionally fast, as if he were gliding instead of walking. He kept pulling further ahead us, only to slow down again.

We passed several laboratories scattered throughout the ship, mostly adjacent to the various biodomes. At one point we stopped at another bio chamber. I couldn't tell what climate this dome was replicating. There weren't any animals in view, just a cold desert environment and a robotic vehicle driving around through the red sand.

"Mars climate," Leo said in a quiet voice.

"Mars?"

They both nodded. "Sam Shipman doesn't miss anything. He says if we can figure out if and how life existed on Mars, we could apply some of those learnings here on Earth," Leo answered.

"Also, a getaway plan if Dodd makes things really bad here," Warren said.

"Are you guys worried about Dodd?" I asked, trying not to sound like I was worried.

"Sometimes, yeah—" Warren started to answer before Leo jumped in.

"Have you met with Sam yet?"

"Nope," I said, "and it's really starting to irritate me."

"Warren, you know that technically Sam is the only one on the ship allowed to debrief newcomers on Dodd," Leo said.

"Right. Sorry, Akela." Warren nodded in agreement.

"What's the deal with this Sam guy, anyhow? Seems a bit on the controlling side, no?" I asked.

"He's the boss, so he gets to make the rules on the SOS," Leo said as we exited the Mars biodome area and walked through a door into a large open-air section of the ship. "He also made the most amazing ship on Earth our home, so I'm good with a couple of rules here and there."

I tilted my head back to take in the cloudless blue sky. The ceiling above was another retractable roof design that allowed fresh air and sunlight into the space. It felt like we were outdoors. We walked along a path bordered by a grassy lawn with benches, a fountain and a wide variety of trees that led to the entrance of the ship's school. Warren kicked his flip flops off and masterfully caught one in each hand as he moved from the walkway to the grass.

"There aren't many things as good as fresh grass on your feet," Warren said.

Following suit, I kicked off my flip flops, with one hitting me in the face and other bouncing off Leo's shoulder.

"Sorry, Leo!" I said as Warren scrambled over to grab one sandal and I picked up the other.

Leo stayed on the sidewalk. The grass did feel great.

"You don't know what you're missing," I said to Leo and gave Warren a fist bump as we walked toward the school building.

It stood three stories high and had a red brick facade. 'The Spirit of the Sea University' was carved in stone above the hallway. The whole scene reminded me of many of the college campus brochures I'd researched online. I loved it.

I stopped and did a full turn to take in my surroundings. For the first time, I was starting to comprehend the full scope of the *Spirit of the Sea*, the size of the staff and how many other kids there were on board.

Leo touched my shoulder. "Akela, I'm sure you've realized that this is one massive invisible floating city by now, correct?"

"Yeah, of course I did," I said, not too convincingly. "Mik told me, but I guess I didn't really think about it."

"Well," Warren said with a big inhale, "as much as this boat has in automation, there is still a huge crew that includes engineers, scientists, doctors, cooks, janitors, accountants, lawyers, us of course, and let's not forget, dentists, pilots, teachers—"

Leo abruptly shouted, "Warren! I think she gets it. The *Spirit of the Sea* takes an army of people to operate, and guess what?"

"They have kids who go to school?" I said through a choked back laugh.

"Yes! That's what I was going to get to eventually." Warren started to walk away. "I can't be late again. See ya after class," he called over his shoulder.

"What do your parents do onboard?"

"Well, my parents both passed away, but my Uncle Gadgis is a scientist on the ship." Leo paused. "You should know, Warren's parents are gone, too."

My stomach sank and my heart followed it down, as the tide of sadness swept over me. I couldn't believe all three of us lost our parents. "Crap, I'm sorry. You know, mine are gone as well. Birth and adopted parents," I said.

"Geez, Akela, that's totally awful." Leo brushed my arm again. We both stared at the grass as an emotional rip current pulled us into the past.

"Get a load of us, three orphans of the ocean," I tried to joke, forcing a smile.

"Well, I don't feel like an orphan here. Hopefully you won't either." Leo smiled back kindly, then checked his watch. "C'mon, we're gonna be late."

As I followed him into the *Spirit of the Sea* University, I imagined Kaipu and Alana standing on the grass, holding hands, and waving to me. My eyes started to water and I let them. Water finds its way, and so will I.

CHAPTER 14

Weeks came and went in the blink of an eye, and I still hadn't had a physical. It always appeared on my daily schedule, and I always conveniently missed it. I was good with that.

Otherwise, my schedule was nonstop. Math, marine biology, sustainable development. I ate that stuff up, so all the studying didn't bother me. Plus, I liked hanging with Warren and Leo. We had class and ate lunch everyday together. Everything was going well enough, I guess.

Lies didn't surround me on the SOS, but neither did honesty. Nobody was totally forthcoming as to what we were doing on a giant floating invisible fortress. I'd get surface level answers from the boys, but the minute I dug deeper, I was told 'Sam will tell you that.' The same Sam I hadn't even met yet. Mik told me that he was frequently off the boat on 'missions', but that the three of us were going to have dinner when he returned, supposedly.

Life on the SOS was a thousand times better than Bonita Fields, but I wondered if Mik gave me such a busy schedule to keep me from digging more. Before and after class, she had me constantly training. I was getting pretty good at martial arts under Mik's instruction, but it was being back in the ocean that I craved the most.

Johan was the ship's lead dive instructor, and I met him at five a.m. every morning in the Aqua Hold. The ship surrounded the Aqua Hold on all sides, except the bottom, which led the way to the ocean floor. Glass-walled classrooms bordered the water, giving the students and researchers front-row, underwater viewing access to the pod and any other aquatic life in the space.

The first time I followed Johan's flowing blond hair through the entrance to the Aqua Hold, I understood what Dolphin Jon and Dolphin Ana had meant when they said they were part of the SOS team. The pod was there waiting to join us for our morning swims.

It was there every day that I swam with the pod. It was there I got my saltwater groove back.

And Johan, well, he had more questions about me than I had about the boat.

"That necklace looks good on you, Akela."

I smiled and said, "Thanks", in my head, but no words came out.

"Do you know where you got it?"

"Nope."

"Nothing?" Johan's chiseled face appeared genuinely and handsomely confused.

I shrugged. "It's always just been there. As far back as I can remember. I'm not really supposed to talk about it?"

Johan ignored my question. "What about Sam? He tell you anything about it or our mission yet?"

"Nada. Haven't even met him."

"Huh. Well, he obviously told you about your birth parents?" Johan eyed me closely.

"No, I still know nothing about my real parents, either. Do you know anything?" I asked, smiling and hoping that maybe I'd finally learn something.

Johan grunted and returned to fiddling with his gear.

I liked Johan taking an interest in me, but this conversation was annoying. It was frustrating enough not meeting Sam yet or learning about my parents. I didn't need a reminder.

Johan pulled his mask down and fiddled with his golden locks. He'd put it up into one of those man buns.

"How's it look?"

"Your mask? It looks straight." Standing at the water's edge, I couldn't wait much longer to dive in.

"No, my hair. Is the bun centered? Ahimsa's teaching in the glass class this morning. You know, in case she sees me."

I drew on my years of eye roll restraint training with Kara and maintained a straight face.

"Yes, Johan. Your hair is centered." I dove into the water.

Johan couldn't keep up with me, of course, but he was always there. A constant presence. Anytime I tried to swim further off with the pod, he'd eventually corral me back.

"I'm only following Mik's orders, Akela. Don't get mad at me."

What I wasn't being told by my human contacts, maybe I could find out from my underwater friends. And, while I didn't think that Johan, or anybody else on board, could understand dolphin, I needed to be sure. For my own and the pod's safety, I had to do it alone.

Late that night, I made my way down to the Aqua Hold. Some people were still up and about, but nobody said anything other than 'hi' or 'good evening'. Just like friendly people passing each other on a normal street. Did they know who I was?

Walking into the Aqua Hold, it was so quiet I could hear the water lapping up against the stairs. The only light came from the entrance stairwell and the floor lights outlining the dock. Otherwise, the water was the deep blue of a night just before the stars came out. A peaceful setting if I weren't still afraid of the dark.

"Be brave," I said out loud as I dove into the water, reminding myself that I was safe on the SOS. At least, I hoped so. Every few strokes I swam deeper, I couldn't stop myself from nervously looking around. The borderlines of the ship's Aqua Hold were barely visible, but they were there. Still, I worried what else was in the water with me—until I heard them.

First Ana, then Jon, Laila, Rhino, and Bingo. One by one they appeared and started playfully circling me, faster and faster. I stretched my arms out wide as they graced my fingertips with each pass. The control they had over their bodies mesmerized me. Grandpa appeared last and watched from a distance. We were all laughing, save Grandpa, who didn't crack any hint of a smile.

Not wanting Johan to spoil my plan, I began to ask questions.

"It's a little bit of everything," Ana said while we swam figure eights around each other. *"What we know is limited to what happens in the ocean, but our sense is that the SOS leads the global effort against evil forces."*

"To protect the ocean?" I communicated back.

"More than the ocean, Akela. Everything is interconnected."

Jon swam up and playfully bumped me toward the oncoming Laila. I locked eyes with Laila and smiled as we instinctively swerved in opposite directions.

"We've seen the SOS engaged in plastic removal, oil spill clean ups, as well as interference with whaling vessels," Jon added.

"And with dolphin hunts. Humans." Grandpa shook his head somberly before swimming away.

"Grandpa lost a lot of friends and family over the years. He's slow to trust humans," Jon said, watching his father swim away.

"I don't blame him, so am I. Some of us—no, many of us—are here to help. That's why I'm here, I think."

Jon and Ana dove deeper. *"Grandpa and the pod have been swimming with the SOS for years now. He remembers you, Akela, but that was when you were a baby. Babies don't know any better other than to love. To harm is mostly learned,"* said Ana.

I put my hand on my necklace and held it up to them. *"Do you know anything about this?"*

"Only that it's the same sea trash you were wearing when we first found you," Jon answered.

Sea trash. I laughed so hard that bubbles came out my nose. At least I knew for certain that the sea glass map wasn't something the pod was aware of.

A light shot through the darkness, landing on us. It was coming from one of the submerged research classrooms, along with strange squeaking sounds from a speaker near the glass. Grandpa shook his head and swam away into the dark

"You'll have to earn Grandpa's trust again, Akela," Ana said before facing the classroom window. *"And can you please ask them to keep whatever that is down a bit?"*

I laughed. *"Ana, I think those 'strange sounds' are them trying to communicate to you."*

Johan's voice came through the speaker next. "Akela, get out of the water please. You're going to get both of us in trouble with Mik."

Johan and Ahimsa pressed their faces against the bubble-shaped window of the classroom. They both had earphones on and were watching us closely. Johan was filming us with his phone.

Ana swam so close to me that our heads were touching. *"I don't know what he's saying, but I do know why you're so important, Akela. You can bridge the gap between our worlds like nobody else before."*

Great. As if I wasn't stressed out enough, already.

CHAPTER 15

I was stirred from my sleep by a noise coming from the deck. It wasn't unusual for a sea bird to land outside, but it was odd for it to happen in the middle of the night.

As I sat up, the outline of a man's body shifted in one of my deck chairs.

"Hello?" I called, slowly creeping outside. No response came from the silhouette. There was a man there, sitting with his back to me, looking out over the dark ocean and night combining into one.

"Hello, Miss Spencer." Dodd's voice slithered through the salt air. His words wrapped around me.

"What do you want with me, Dodd?"

Dodd put both hands on the chair's armrests, slowly stood, and faced me. His ice blue eyes glowed against the dark.

"You are fighting on the wrong side, Akela. I'm the one you want to fight for, not Sam. You don't even know who Sam is, do you?" Dodd reached his hand out as his words tightened around me, constricting my breathing. "Join me," he said.

My feet slid across the damp deck until I bumped into the table. I was being pulled toward him and couldn't stop. I tried to shout for help, but the words drowned in my mouth. My right hand moved on its own and reached up to meet Dodd's. He smiled, and I awoke.

The nightmare of Dodd stayed with me as I moved through my day. After school, I found myself kicking and punching faster and harder than ever during my daily martial arts training.

Mik had pads on each hand and shin that she kept moving, and I kept following with strike after strike. As usual, I was blowing my hair back out of my face after each attack.

"I told you I'm pretty good with the scissors if you want a haircut," Mik said as she blocked a spinning round kick. Her hair looked perfect as always.

"No offense, Mik, but the only appointment I want is with Sam. I can't wait any longer." I was frustrated and scared. Last night's dream had me fed up. "You know, I trusted you. I'm here, I'm training, and I'm doing everything you asked of me."

"You haven't had a physical yet," Mik fired back. She was right, but that was the last thing I wanted to hear right now.

"Well, besides that! I want to know about my parents. I want to know what I'm training for and why Dodd keeps showing up in my dreams!" I yelled and threw a flurry of punches and kicks as fast as I could.

Mik blocked all my attacks before sweeping my front leg out from under me. Next thing I knew I was staring straight up at the studio ceiling. Mik stood over me. "Nice combinations, kid. We're having dinner with Sam tonight," she said as she offered a hand and picked me back up.

"Why didn't you tell me that earlier?" I grabbed a towel and tossed another one to Mik.

"I did, Akela, but you're too in your own head. Like just now, you were in fight mode. You were here, but not mentally." She put her hand on my shoulder. "There'll be many times, in life and in operations, where things don't go your way. The sooner you learn how to channel your energy and your power without losing control, without losing focus, the sooner you'll be able to help us fight Dodd."

Back in my room, I quickly showered off. In the mirror, I couldn't resist flexing muscles that weren't there before. Living in the saltwater and training every day was bringing me back to life.

I tossed on comfortable sweatpants, a "Save The Whales" t-shirt, and a pair of flip flops, then headed out the door. My anger from earlier was gone, and had been replaced with the excitement of meeting Sam.

"Hmm," I said out loud as I realized that Mik hadn't told me where to meet this mysterious Sam Shipman.

The phone in my pocket had Mik's number, but I decided it might be a good time to explore my new surroundings on my own. I had relied on Mik, Leo, and Warren to lead me through the massive maze that the SOS seemed to be at times. If I ever wanted to figure this place out, I had to stop relying on my friends as a GPS system. It was time to explore.

I walked around the hallway that made a ring of fifth-floor rooms and went up a flight of stairs to the next level. This floor resembled mine. More crew housing. Every now and then I stopped to look at the varied works of art, murals, and plant life on display. I pictured my drawings hanging along these walls. Catching myself in another daydream, I snapped back and continued up to the next level.

At the top of the stairwell landing, it was clear that this floor was different. Glass walls wrapped the entirety of the level. It was dizzying looking around and seeing straight through to the blue Pacific in a 360-degree rotation. Something about the perspective seemed a little off, but I couldn't put my finger on it.

Peering through each windowpane, I waited for one to be an electronic door and allow me entrance to the room. Nothing happened. I tried saying open, 'abracadabra,' in Spanish, French and even in dolphin language, but no words opened the door. I completed two full circles until realizing that I wasn't going to get in. As I finally turned away, I heard the sliding of a door open behind me.

When I entered the room, it dawned on me that the ocean I was seeing from the outside, through the glass were monitors projecting images of the ocean. At least for most of the room. TV screens covered ninety percent of the walls, with small openings leading to observation decks every twenty yards or so. The monitors mirrored the actual light of day outside, so the connection from real to virtual was seamless.

As the doors closed behind me, the images immediately all switched over to what appeared to be live shots. Over three hundred separate screens showed whales swimming, fishing boats, oil rigs, coal stacks, protests, forest fires, plastic bottles, government meetings, on and on and on it went. I felt like I walked into a sports bar dedicated to environmental activism.

One bank of monitors was dedicated to the ship's internal biodomes: Rainforest, Arctic, Desert, Mountains, Mars, Ocean. I looked closer at the screen labeled 'SOS Ocean' and saw what appeared to be an enormous open water pool within the ship. It was the Aqua Hold.

I wondered how many times Sam had watched me interact with the dolphins on these screens. The idea of being secretly observed pissed me off.

Eight large chairs were assembled on a circular platform toward the middle of the room. I'd watched a few documentaries on NASA, and while this didn't look like mission control at Cape Canaveral, it did look like a command center of sorts.

I maneuvered my way past the chairs, directly in front of the large image of whales. They appeared to be in a completely different part of the ocean than the sea life in the SOS. How was this being filmed?

"Cameras, attached—humanely, of course—to the whales," a man's voice said from behind me.

I spun quickly to see a man sitting in one of the eight control chairs. He wore a Hawaiian button-down shirt, board shorts, and flip flops that looked like they were made from rubber. This was the man I had seen flying the helicopter that escorted Mik and I into the SOS. This was Sam Shipman. Finally.

I eyed his shoes.

"I got these in Mali, Africa. A man there can make them from recycled car tires. He can make you a pair and get them within a millimeter of your correct size, just by looking at your feet."

Sam hit a button on the armrest of his chair. All the screens turned off, except for one showing an African Elephant grazing peacefully with her two adolescent children.

"Johanna and her family. The land is a protected sanctuary now. The local tribesmen are the wardens." He zoomed in on the elephants and smiled. "They are safe again, for now."

"One of what Mik called operations?" I asked.

"Yes, Akela." He smiled, offering me his hand. "Sam Shipman. You have no idea how happy I am to see you."

"Akela," I said and shook his hand. I had planned on giving him an ear-full about making me wait so long, but instead I said, "I'm happy to be here, too."

Sam pointed at the seat next to him and I sat. "Tell me, Akela. What do you think we're doing here on the SOS?"

"Well, I know from the biodomes that you are rescuing endangered species."

"Yes, that's one thing we do. Go on."

"And from what you just told me about the Mali *operation*—" I put my fingers up in air quotes for the word operation, "—I'd say you're fighting for animal rights?" I was going to add what the dolphins had told me about the SOS's activities, but I wanted to hear it from Sam.

"Yes, that, too. Not just animals, though." Sam flicked all the monitors back on and had the images rotate left to right across the screen directly in front us. Images of landfills, oil spills, factory pollution, vaccine researchers, and senate hearings moved past our eyes. One screen had an image of the Dartivion Corporation headquarters.

"You fight for the environment, for Mother Earth. You also fight against Dartivion and Jarvis Dodd," I said softly.

Sam nodded. "Yes. Now, follow me."

I followed him back through the control center, past the sliding door, and into the open-air hallway. The oval-shaped walkways that ringed this portion of the ship were broken up by stairwells and an elevator at each end. Sam stopped at a little outcropping of an observation area that allowed us to step out over the atrium floor, seventy feet below us.

From way up high, I could see that the floor of the circular atrium was decorated with a large painting of our planet. Every continent, ocean and body of water was meticulously recreated in a swirl of blues and greens.

Sam pointed down at the image of our Earth. "Our most obvious impact on our planet has been on the land. Rainforests once covered thirteen percent of the Earth's land surface. Now they only cover six percent. Wait a moment and watch."

Within seconds, I watched as the image below shifted. More of the green disappeared in Brazil and other areas where I knew rainforests existed.

"The Earth is four-point-six billion years old. In human proportions, let's call it forty-six years, which means humans have only been on Earth for four hours, our industrial revolution began one minute ago." Sam sighed.

"And we've already destroyed fifty percent of the world's rainforests!" I said angrily, taking another look at the image. "Humans. We're like locusts."

Sam gave me a sad, knowing smile. "You look like your mom when you get angry." His eyes drifted to the sea glass necklace hanging from my neck.

"Did she give this necklace to me?" I pulled my sea glass out from my shirt.

Sam's eyes lit up at the sight of my sea glass. "C'mon, let's eat, and I'll tell you everything I know." The Earth image on the floor reverted to its original state as we walked down the stairs. My pain and anger faded along with it.

CHAPTER 16

We entered *Chez Shipman* and were directed to an open French-style courtyard. Mik was already seated at the table, and Sam pulled my chair out for me.

"Hi, boss," a waiter said congenially before addressing me. "I've heard all about you, Akela. Welcome aboard. What'll you have to drink?"

He took our orders and whisked himself back to the kitchen. Mik was getting used to my variety of facial expressions and was starting to know my questions before I asked them.

"He's an engineer on the ship. One of the best and brightest." She paused as the waiter delivered our drinks and walked away. "Everybody on the SOS wears multiple hats. You will, too." She winked at me.

"He said he's heard all about me, how much does he know?" I asked with some concern.

Sam straightened up in this chair. "Akela, the *Spirit of the Sea* is a vessel with a mission. Everybody on it is part of the team. Whether they have, let's call them *unique*, abilities like yourself, or are just talented and passionate about saving our planet, you have nothing to worry about here." He held my gaze until I smiled. I still felt worried.

"Got it. Just might take a little while to get used to." The waiter returned with our food. I thanked him and quickly took a big bite. "So, you said everybody on the ship has multiple jobs. What are yours?" I asked Mik.

Mik looked toward Sam.

"Mik, she's my jack of all trades," Sam said while sipping sparkling water. "She has her PhD in Marine Biology, a black belt in three different martial arts, and, as you already know, the ability to fly or drive anything with an engine."

"You really know how to flatter a girl." Mik laughed.

Sam continued, "And like me, Mik has studied more than just the top layers of our planet's environmental issues. She has peeled back the onion, so to speak, to seek deeper into the root cause of our challenges. She and your parents were all doing so together." Sam paused and looked at me for a reaction. I waited for him to continue.

Mik jumped in instead. "Your father, Tom, was a geologist. Your mom, Lisa, was an anthropologist as well as a doctor. She was one smart cookie, just like you. They were both brilliant, caring, and dedicated friends and parents. Two of my favorite people, and our earliest colleagues," she said with a big smile, placing her hand on top of mine.

"So, both of my parents were human?" I said slowly, not realizing how weird that would sound once I said it out loud.

Sam and Mik both let out a loud laugh. Sam shook his head and smiled widely. "Uh, yes! You've seen the photo, right?

"I know, it's in my room. Mik gave it to me. It's just that, you know, I'm very different."

Sam smiled gently. "Your parents were both as human as you, me and all of the other non-biodome creatures on this ship. You may have some aquatic attributes that make you unique, but you're as human as any of us."

I had no idea that my subconscious brain still harbored doubts or would be so relieved to know that I had a pair of two-legged parents. I mean, nothing against my dolphin brethren, I guessed, but I didn't know. Maybe every thirteen-year-old kid needed some reaffirmation that they're human sometimes.

A quick daydream washed over me. My parents worked together in a lush, tropical environment with me crawling happily between the two of them. We had on matching khaki explorer outfits, mine with a diaper bulging out of the back. All of us cheerfully went about our family business together until they disappeared from my vision. I snapped out of it with a wave of sadness.

"What happened to my parents?" I asked in a voice that didn't sound like my own.

Sam looked at me, as if waiting to decide if he wanted to continue.

"Tell me what happened to my parents,"

Mik nodded at Sam.

"We lost them," Sam said with a deep sigh.

"Lost them at sea?" I asked.

Sam again paused, staring deep in my eyes and then redirected his stare at Mik.

"Yes, lost at sea. After you came along, of course," Sam added with a sad smile.

"They were out on a mission to interrupt a whaling operation. We aren't sure if a whaling vessel hit them or a rogue wave. Their bodies were never recovered," Mik said somberly. "Yours either, or so we thought."

"They took me on a whaling mission?"

Sam adjusted his silverware on the table. "They took you everywhere. Your parents lived on that boat when they weren't with me at our initial institute in Monterey. That boat was your family's home."

Sam looked up from his utensils and directly into my eyes. "Akela, you experienced and survived many dangerous adventures on land and sea. For every one of them, until now, you were always with your parents."

After all this time, I'd finally heard the whole story. There wasn't much to it after all. My parents died doing what they loved, protecting the planet. Now, I was following in their footsteps. Hopefully, without the dying part.

Chapter 17

Throughout dinner, Sam and Mik took turns telling stories about my parents. Funny stories, sad stories, friendship stories, adventure stories and love stories. My mom and dad started to transform from ghost-like images I'd conjured in my head to fully formed, flawed, interesting, adventurous, and caring people. My parents.

So much time, so much loneliness, so many unanswered questions. I felt it all wash away as the life and times of my parents materialized in front of me.

The strongest sensation welled up in me, that my other parents, Kaipu and Alana, knew my birth parents. Intellectually, I didn't believe that to be true, yet still I sensed a larger connection between all of us and while none of them were physically here now, I could feel all of them.

"How'd you meet my parents?"

"Well, we met your parents deep in the mountains of South America. We were independently working on the same, umm, let's call it a history mystery of sorts," Sam said with a twinkle in his eyes.

"A history mystery. Cool. I like history, mysteries, and rhymes."

Sam straightened up. "Well, Mark Twain once told me, I mean, he once said that history doesn't tend to repeat itself, but it often rhymes. At least in my experience, I find that to be true."

"Twain also said that if you have to eat two frogs for breakfast, eat the bigger one first," I added.

"Yes, he did," Sam said with a faraway look in his eyes.

"Back to your question about your parents. You see, Akela, a few years prior to meeting them, my team had been conducting an archaeological dig in the region. We uncovered two stone slabs with a lengthy inscription on them."

"What'd they say?"

"It wasn't totally clear at first. We believed the slabs to be of Mayan origin and published our findings. We didn't disclose the location of where we'd found them, though. We needed help with the translations, as some of the words were unfamiliar to our linguistic team. Our researchers interpreted the slabs as clues to a Mayan prophecy about the Earth and what was causing us to destroy it."

"Did you believe that?" I asked.

"I didn't until your parents contacted me and said they had found a completely different source with a strikingly similar story. It was from a different culture, Incan, but communicated the same tale of an ancient prophecy. Two peoples, two civilizations, who had no known interaction with each other, both with the same story."

Sam's eyes lit up. "As an anthropologist, this double confirmation was a clear indication of something real!" Sam said with a pounding of his fist on the table.

"Isn't a real myth kinda contradictory? An oxymoron?" I asked.

"Some things are only impossible until they aren't," Sam said cryptically.

Mik leaned in closer to me. "Within both sources were clues as to where another artifact could be found, Akela. That's how our journeys intersected with your parents."

Sam reached over to his wrist and hit the screen on his watch. A panel appeared in the center of our table and a holographic image presented itself three dimensionally in front of us.

An image of Mayan ruins appeared. It was so realistic, I reached out my hand to touch and went through the light display with no change.

Sam gestured to the hologram. "These two separate cultures of indigenous people told a story about a pair of powerful spirits, Htmalo and Chixtal. Htmalo was the spirit of earth, sky and all things living. Htmalo was a good spirit, the provider of life. Chixtal, though, was a trickster. These people used Chixtal to explain anything that was wrong or evil in the world. Htmalo and Chixtal were always at odds with each other. As Htmalo would provide the people land, food, and the bounties of life, Chixtal would bring famine and the subsequent fighting over scarce resources.

"As the story was transcribed by both the Incas and Mayans, Htmalo and Chixtal made a wager. Each spirit allowed that men would have free will to do exactly what they pleased. If they chose to protect the Earth and its resources, Htmalo would win. If they built recklessly and wasted the Earth's bounty, Chixtal, the spirit of destruction, would win."

"So, in this bet, we're the good guys on the side of Htmalo. Did I say that right? Htmalo."

Mik nodded.

"And Dodd is the bad guy, along with Chixtal?" I said as a vision of Dodd and those ghostly blue eyes flashed in my mind. I shook it off.

"Exactly," Sam said.

Sam's hologram shifted to ruins. "This prophecy foretold the end of both civilizations," Sam said. "And if Dodd and Chixtal get their way, possibly ours as well."

I always prided myself on being a realist, and I was having a hard time taking the story at face value.

"Or you could blame it on disease and destruction brought to them by the Spaniards," I tried to say respectfully, but my voice didn't cooperate. "Assuming you're among those who don't necessarily believe in prophecies, right? I mean, c'mon, do you guys also believe in the Bermuda Triangle, The Fountain of Youth, and the Loch Ness Monster?"

I asked with a smile, but maybe a little too carelessly from the looks on Sam and Mik's faces.

I backtracked. "Okay, okay, sorry. So, what does that have to do with us, me, and my parents? Do you really believe that the prophecy is real?"

Mik put her hand on mine. "It is real, and there's more. That artifact we found with your parents, it read that as part of the wager, the two spirits had hidden clues and tools across the globe which, if discovered, would aid in helping their side win."

Sam again pointed his watch at the hologram. The paused image continued. "Htmalo, according to legend, drank from a glass chalice. A chalice which gave him the power to control the forces of nature. Afraid that Chixtal would try to steal the cup and use it against him, Htmalo smashed the chalice into seven pieces. One piece for each continent."

Sam pointed at my necklace. His eyes fixated on my sea glass in a way that left me feeling like he didn't see me anymore. It made me sit up straight and clutch my sea glass.

"I know. It's part of a sea glass map. Mik told me that much," I said. "But what does that really mean, a map of what or to what?"

I stared at my perfectly designed sea glass of North America.

"I have North America, and I saw that Desmond has Africa, so maybe we could start trying to figure out what they form… wait, wouldn't they just form a map of the world?"

Sam's smile returned and his eyes moved back up to meet mine. "Well, yes, good observation, but the prophecy says that once assembled—" Sam turned his attention to the hologram and hit play. "—the pieces will allow access to an island. The Isle of Green. A sanctuary, a place where the world has experienced no scars, and where healing can begin. A rebirth, if you will."

"Wait, like this boat?"

"Yes, smarty pants," Mik said. "The *Spirit of the Sea* is Sam's vision of this island sanctuary. We believe your necklace is another piece of the puzzle toward us finding the real thing."

The hologram transformed and now displayed a three-dimensional animated mockup of the Isle of Green. The camera angle, as if being flown by a helicopter, swooped down over a lush green mountainous landscape. In the distance, a family of whales playfully breached and rested under a waterfall. I could see polar bears in the distance jogging across a giant slab of frozen earth. Animals roamed wild and free as far as I could see. As the camera backed away and climbed high in the sky above the island, I saw the rich rainforest with no trees destroyed. The images were breathtaking.

"If Dodd had my sea glass, he could stop your plans," I said.

"Our plans," Mik corrected me.

The prophecy made some sense, I guessed. I was sure that whoever had invented plastic didn't do so with the intent or forethought that it would someday put our oceans on the brink of disaster. Humans had outsmarted ourselves, and maybe now, many years later, we were finally realizing the predicament that put us in.

The part that I didn't buy was that something other than humans and our egos forced us into this downward spiral of climate change. That Chixtal had somehow motivated and continued to influence his minions, Dodd especially, to destroy our Mother Earth.

"Okay, it doesn't take a PhD, no offense Mik, to know that humans are responsible for ruining the environment. But the whole notion that this evil spirit Chixtal was pulling the strings behind the scenes, sea glass maps, wagers, you know it all seems a little farfetched to me." I was being honest.

"So says the dolphin girl," Sam said and winked at me. "May I see your necklace, Akela?" He put his hand out as I took the necklace off from my neck and laid it gently in his hand.

"This is hundreds of generations old?" I asked.

"More, and so is this," Sam said as he reached into his shirt and pulled out a necklace, on the end of which was a brilliant-colored green piece of glass. He held the necklace away from his chest, so it dangled, glistening in the light.

I stared at the green carving intently until I could see the shape.

"South America!" I exclaimed. Just as I did, my blue sea glass necklace leapt off his hand as if it were swept up by an invisible wind and attached itself on top of the green piece of glass.

We all jumped in surprise as the two pieces of the map connected.

"Aha!" shouted Sam as he stared delightedly at the two map pieces.

"Well, that definitely helps my skepticism!"

Sam barked out a laugh. He continued to hold the necklace up as the two sea glass pieces danced in the light together. "You said that you noticed Desmond's necklace when you two met?" Sam asked.

"I did, but our necklaces only moved toward each other, they didn't meet like ours are doing." Sam smirked, but didn't reply.

"Oh! Duh. South America and North America touch each other, Africa doesn't. I can't believe I didn't figure that out sooner." I slapped my hand against my forehead in embarrassment.

"You figured it out faster than I did, kid," Mik said in a hushed voice.

"So how did my parents find my piece, Desmond his, and you yours? Where are the others and are they all equally powerful?" I asked.

Sam laughed. "Slow down, Akela. Last question first. No, they are not all equally powerful." Sam paused.

"And?" I asked.

"We don't know, exactly. Some think the sea glass finds the owner more so than the other way around, if that makes sense," Sam said slowly, as if he was choosing his words very carefully. "Much of what we know about them and Dodd still remains a mystery."

"Well, at least it's pretty clear to me now why Dodd wants me to join him?"

"What did you just say?" Sam asked.

"Dodd, he keeps showing up. I mean, in my dreams, Dodd keeps telling me I'm on the wrong side," I said.

Mik and Sam exchanged concerned looks. Before I could ask a follow up question, a siren went off.

Sam and Mik jumped to their feet and looked at their digital watches. A hologram appeared out of Sam's watch that was visible for all of us to see. It was Desmond.

"Oil tanker, Sam. Three hundred miles west of here, slowly spilling its cargo," Desmond said.

"What caused it?" asked Mik.

"Unclear. All I know is that the tanker is losing hundreds of gallons a minute. Could be an internal issue, but it seems suspicious," Desmond replied.

"At the present, the 'why' doesn't matter," Sam said sharply. "That location is directly in the migratory path of the blue whales, not to mention thousands of other forms of wildlife that would be impacted, including us."

"Desmond, prepare the proper craft and see if you can contact the pod. We'll meet upstairs in five." Sam clicked off the hologram.

I felt like I was watching an episode of some cool action show unfolding in front of me. So much was happening so fast, it was tough to follow at times. I mean, how would Desmond contact the pod? Maybe the pod was the name of one of the operation's boats?

"Are we entertaining you?" Mik asked.

The comment snapped me out of my stupor. "Yes! I mean, no, but kinda, I guess," I said.

"Well, are you ready to walk the walk, Ms. Save the Whales t-shirt?" Mik asked me while she walked briskly toward the door.

I looked down, forgetting that I was wearing the 'Save the Whales' shirt they'd left for me in my room.

Launching to my feet, I yelled, "I was born ready!" and proceeded to spill my drink all over my new shirt.

I took my seat at the command center. Desmond stood in front of us, pointing at the main monitor, which showed an overhead view of the oil tanker. The ship wasn't moving beyond a slight push from the ocean currents. Black oil pooled off its port side, creating a contrast of blue, green, and black along the water's surface. The juxtaposition of colors struck me as beautiful and deadly all at once.

The monitor view pulled further and further out until the pod of whales became visible.

"How far away are they?" Mik asked.

Desmond walked up to the screen, putting one finger on the boat and the other on the pod of whales. A line appeared on the monitor that showed the exact distance between the points.

"About three miles," Desmond said.

"Get lower, Leo," Sam said as a chair in front of me spun around to show my buddy Leo operating what appeared to be the controls of a drone.

"Sure thing, boss," Leo said.

I couldn't believe that Leo was part of the operations team and he hadn't told me. Our eyes met. Leo shrugged and smiled. I gave him nothing in return. Just stone.

Mik put her hand on my shoulder. "We don't advertise our membership for security reasons."

"Jarvis Dodd would love to get his hands on any one of us. He's tried many times to infiltrate the SOS already," Sam said.

"Sorry, Akela," Leo said.

Leo, with his Greenpeace hat turned backwards on his head, maneuvered the drone lower. The drone camera zoomed in on the tanker. An English flag flew from the ship. Oddly, nobody appeared on deck.

"Where did the crew go?" I asked.

"Good observation," Mik replied. "We'll drop Warren down there to investigate."

"Wait, Warren's part of the ops team too?!" I shouted. "I knew that kid was up to something. Why am I the last to learn everything!"

Leo turned around in his chair. "Oh, so you suspected Warren of being special enough to be part of the ops team, but not me?"

I shrugged. "Sorry bud, you, you're not so special." I was irritated and couldn't resist the easy jab.

"Where's Warren?" shouted Johan as he came sprinting into the room.

"Forget Warren, what took you so long Johan?" Mik said.

"I was getting the chopper ready." Johan put his hands up in defense before running them through his hair. The man was always primping.

Warren came flying in with a blur of movement. "Sorry, boss, I got the alert deep in the mountain dome. I was with the pack."

Warren saw me and sheepishly waved.

I nodded back.

Desmond shook his head. "Enough. All of you." He switched the next closest monitor to the underwater image of the whales. The sounds of the whales communicating with each other came through the speaker. "They are heading directly toward the spill. Get me in there. Fast."

Mik's watch beeped. "The plane's ready and the chopper's spinning. Let's do this."

Sam and Mik locked eyes. Sam nodded.

Mik turned to me. "You ready, Akela?"

All I could muster was another nod.

CHAPTER 18

I followed Mik and Desmond to a corner in the ops room. Desmond tapped a panel and the wall quickly retracted to reveal a long slide lit by flashing lights with rails descending steeply into darkness. He barely slowed down before jumping in and shooting out of sight. Mik stopped at the top and waved for me to go.

I hesitated.

"Akela, it's the quickest way to our plane. Go." Mik stared me down hard.

The slide looked fast, slick, and vanished into nothingness, as far as I could tell. Just as I was about to muster up the courage to go, I felt a kick to the back of my knees. My legs flew up and just before I was about to land on my back, Mik cushioned me just enough to land perfectly on the slide.

"Sorry, kid, I couldn't wait any longer!" She yelled as I rocketed down the chute, winding around tight corners, and through a quick tunnel before exiting onto a soft cushion. I quickly got up and got out of the way as Mik came flying out headfirst in a tight somersault forward roll. She got up onto her feet and sprinted past me.

"Showoff," I muttered.

The hangar space was filled with all types of aircraft. Mik pointed to a midsize jet fighter-looking plane, and I followed Desmond up the retractable stairs and got in.

The plane had a small cabin with a pilot and co-pilot seat. Behind that were four more seats, configured back-to-back.

"Where's the runway?" I asked as I put my headset on.

"Up top, but we don't need one with this," Desmond said.

Desmond and I buckled into the two seats behind Mik as she engaged the aircraft.

Desmond tapped me on the shoulder and gestured for me to look at the wings. The engines, which were facing horizontally to the ground, slowly redirected themselves to point vertically. In a burst, we lifted straight up in the air, like a helicopter.

Mik piloted the jet above the giant *Spirit of the Sea*. It wasn't until we were more than a few hundred yards above it that I could see the surrounding ocean. The SOS was beyond massive. As we moved higher up, the SOS's cloaking technologies kicked in, and in an instant, our giant floating city of a home disappeared completely from sight.

I was about to ask Desmond where the other team members were when Mik engaged the engines into their horizontal positions and I slammed backwards into my seat.

Out of the corner of my eye, I saw us fly past a helicopter.

"Warren and Johan?" I asked.

Desmond nodded. He wasn't his normal, jovial self. He wore an expression of grave concern.

Mik's voice came over the headset. "Des, at full speed we'll be over the scene in less than ten minutes."

Desmond set his watch and then closed his eyes. He rested his hands on either leg, with his palms facing up in the air. His breathing became very deep and rhythmic.

I watched closely as his chest and stomach swelled with air and then he exhaled. In a matter of moments, that stern and concerned expression on his face had transformed. He looked peaceful now. I assumed he was meditating.

My nerves were taking over, and I couldn't sit still. There were so many questions I wanted to ask, but I couldn't bug Des while he looked so focused and relaxed. I tried to meditate, myself, but I kept opening my eyes every few seconds to see what was going on. When I closed them, my mind raced with thoughts of failing and getting in the way of the operations team. I'd no idea what I was supposed to do, or if I was ready to do it, whatever 'it' was. I was freaking out.

Finally, Desmond's watch beeped, and his eyes slowly opened. From the look on Desmond's face, despite my best efforts, he could tell I was panicking.

"I can teach you how to meditate, Akela, if you'd like that," he said calmly. His smile had returned.

I nodded. I was afraid that if I tried to talk I might throw up.

Mik's voice reappeared in our headsets. "Prep Akela on protocol."

Desmond stood slightly hunched over as the bubble cockpit was barely taller than his head. He slipped on a neoprene vest wetsuit, but it wasn't a normal wetsuit. The vest had an underwater communication module networked into the seams that connected with an earpiece. The lower half had a belt which contained a knife, taser and a few other gadgets I couldn't identify.

Desmond gave me a similar vest to put on. It zippered in the front and fit as though it was made for me.

I slipped off my headset and put in the earpiece.

"You'll be able to communicate with everyone above and underwater with that, AK" Desmond said.

I nodded nervously.

Sam's voice came over the channel. "We're right behind you guys. Des, I need you and AK to get with the pod. We're going to the boat with the Sea Swarm bots."

"AK? I mean me? Sea Swarm bots?" I said out loud, forgetting that I was also on the communication channel. Did I just get a nickname?

"Akela is one too many syllables for an operation," Sam said. "You're AK until we get back to the SOS."

Mik filled me in on the plans. She spoke quickly as she piloted the jet closer to our destination.

"Our mission is to intercept the pod and move them in the direction of clean, safe water," she said without taking her eyes off the controls. "Sam's team is bringing in the Sea Swarm to address the oil spill."

"What's a Sea Swarm?"

"Sea Swarm is a fleet of oil-absorbing robots used to clean up spills," Desmond said while stretching his arms out wide.

"Leo and his Uncle Gadgis developed them," Mik added.

All I could say was, "Cool."

"How's the vest fit?" Mik's voice came into my ear.

"Perfect," I said nervously.

Desmond briefed me that the two of us were going to drop in next to the whale pod and try to divert them away from the direction of the spill. It should be a simple and safe operation. All I had to do was follow his lead.

I listened intently, but all the while was wondering how the heck Desmond was planning on swimming with a pod of whales, as well as keeping up with me. Before I had a chance to ask, Mik's voice returned to my ear.

"Guys, the pod is directly below us. I'm going to get you a few hundred yards in front of them. At that point, out you go."

Desmond grabbed my hand. "Don't worry, Akela," he said gently. "Remember, we are of the sea. Down there, we will be in our element."

"What'd you say?" I asked, even though I heard Desmond loud and clear.

Desmond grabbed both my hands. "We are both of the sea, Akela. We are family reunited."

"Alright guys, prepare for drop." Mik slowed the jet down until we were hovering above the water.

A small circular opening appeared toward the back of the cabin. It had a second glass door that allowed us to see that we were about thirty feet above the ocean surface. The door then slid away and the sound of the plane, ocean, and wind all came flooding in.

"Pencil dive," Desmond said as he let go of my hands and stepped through the hole like he was casually hopping into a swimming pool.

I peered through the opening and saw the splash as he penetrated the sea. A quick second later, he reappeared and gave me a thumbs up.

"All good, now you, AK," Desmond said.

I turned to look at the cockpit. "Go get 'em, kiddo," Mik said with a reassuring look before I stepped off into thin air.

The time it took me to fall from the jet down to the water couldn't have been more than a second, but in that moment, time stood still. My mind swept back all the way to swimming with dolphins as a baby.

I then saw the kind, beautiful brown eyes of Kaipu, and Alana kissing me goodnight. I even saw myself sitting at the kitchen table at Matea's reading a book while Matea braided Kara's hair. All those chapters of my life. Every moment and every step had led me to where I was right now—jumping from a modified military jet as part of a team of environmental warriors fighting to save Mother Earth from the forces of destruction.

Badass. You're a Badass Akela Spencer, I told myself as my toes hit the water.

I penetrated the surface and then extended my legs into a scissor position to quickly stop my descent. With two powerful kicks, I shot back toward the surface. I was amped and wound up launching myself completely out of the water into a front flip. In midair, I waved up to Mik in the Harrier cockpit.

"I made it!"

"I can see that kid," Mik said as I landed back in the water and swam next to Desmond.

Mik spoke quickly now. "The whales dove deep, guys. I got too low with the jet and spooked them. Unfortunately, they're still on the course with the spill. They could surface right in the middle of the oil."

"We're on it. Preparing to dive," Desmond said, grabbing my hand again.

"You're like me, aren't you?" I asked.

Desmond dove and I followed.

"We are all like each other in one way or another, child. If you look for similarities, you find them. If you look for differences, you find them. We find what we are looking for. Follow me."

Desmond swam gracefully and without moving his arms. He looked back to make sure I was with him. I gave him a thumbs up and we continued deeper down.

"We have another hundred meters to go. I can hear them.".

I could hear them as well. Taking a leap of intuition, I asked, "You know what they're saying, don't you, Des?"

Desmond turned again as he continued his long, powerful full body swim. He closed his eyes and nodded to me.

My heart swelled. I felt something I'd never experienced before in my life. I wasn't the only one. I wasn't alone.

I quickened my pace and stayed within a few feet of Desmond. I felt strong, but I also knew that I couldn't continue this indefinitely. I was in far better shape than when I'd first arrived at the SOS, but I wasn't in operational shape yet. Endorphins carried me along as we finally saw the pod.

The pod swam spread out, but together, mothers, calves, and fathers. They were immensely beautiful. It struck me how peaceful they looked, as they moved completely unaware of the human-caused danger ahead.

"Fifty meters from contact," Desmond said.

"Good." Sam spoke quickly. "Redirect them south, southwest, and do it fast."

"Roger that," Desmond responded.

"We're at the boat dropping the Sea Swarm now. Warren is heading on board to get a closer look. Get the whales to safety now."

Desmond and I swam swiftly and silently toward our target.

I wondered if Leo and Warren were also of the sea as Desmond and I positioned ourselves to contact the whales. There was something about the way Warren moved that I couldn't put my finger on, something animal-like. If he wasn't of the sea, he was different.

Lost in thought, I swam directly into Desmond. He gave me a disapproving look as we both stopped and focused our attention on the pod. The lead whale noticed us and slowed.

There we held our position. Two hundred meters below the sea, floating in the open ocean in front of twenty whales, each of which was bigger and weighed more than a school bus.

The lead whale was now in front of us, curiously taking us in. Desmond opened his mouth wide, and out came a whale-like song. The lead whale's eyes flashed as he looked intently at Desmond. The depth of intelligence and compassion in the whale's face gave me chills. He instantly sang back to Desmond. Desmond responded and moved himself within a few feet of the massive creature. Slowly extending his hand, the whale moved to allow Desmond's hand to run across its face.

I couldn't believe what I was hearing. I communicated telepathically, but Desmond actually spoke their language.

I listened to them speaking. Other whales were now chiming in and circling around us.

With a jolt, I realized I could understand what they were singing to each other. I could speak whale! Without thinking, I projected a whale song to the pod.

Desmond smiled at me. "Akela, were you trying to tell the whales, 'That we come in peace'?"

"You heard my telecommunication?"

"I did."

More chills swept through my body. Desmond could hear me. "Yeah, I didn't realize I was fluent in whale until about thirty seconds ago, figured I'd give it a try. I couldn't think of anything better to say. Did I insult them?"

"No, not at all. But you said, 'We come in Pizza'."

Sam's voice returned. "AK, Des, I'm picking up one of the whales heading to the surface. Right into the middle of the spill!"

A young calf had separated from the pod and was quickly swimming away from us. Des and the calf's mother both noticed the stray youngster at the same time and took off together after him.

"Akela, I need you to lead the rest of the pod clear of the oil," Desmond said as he swam away.

Desmond moved through the water like a torpedo with the mother whale by his side. I swam closer to the pod.

I mentally sang *'follow me, friends, to safety'*. I didn't have Desmond to confirm whether I'd said what I'd intended to say, but I knew it was right. The language had clicked with me. I waited and stared at the closest whale, as he stared back at me.

Finally, the lead whale spoke. *"We will follow you."*

I swam away with the whale pod closely behind me as we moved quickly toward safer waters.

Suddenly, Des yelled. "I've got a whaling boat directly above us! Where did that come from?"

"Are they firing?" Leo responded.

"Yes, but not harpoons. I've dodged two nets already! I'm trying to lead the boat away from the whales and whales away from the spill."

"Get yourself and the whales deep, Des. I'm coming in hot for that whaling boat. Missile's ready!" Mik barked.

"AK, what's your status?" Sam asked quickly.

"I've got the pod moving, no boats here," I said as I scanned above me. "How far do we need to go?" Now that I was swimming hard again, I realized I needed air. I'd never been underwater this long before.

Leo jumped in. "I've got you exiting the oil spill danger radius in approximately forty-five seconds."

Darn it. I needed to come up for air sooner than that.

"You get that, AK?" Sam asked.

I just grunted back as I didn't want to waste any more air. I was getting lightheaded. If I hadn't committed to saving the whales, I would have surfaced immediately, but I couldn't do that to the pod. Especially not with oil and a whaling boat somewhere above us.

If I swam faster, we'd be clear of danger sooner, but I was already way beyond what I thought was possible for myself. I kicked harder and drove my body to swim.

"Des, check in," Sam said calmly.

"We are out of range from the whaling boat," Des said through heavy breaths. "What direction is it heading, Mik?"

"It's gone. The boats gone. Vanished into thin air?" Mik replied.

"Cloaking device, maybe?" Leo asked.

"Maybe, maybe not," Sam replied slowly.

All this information wasn't helping my ability to remain calm and keep the pod safe. I was struggling to stay below the surface.

"Out of danger radius in twenty-five seconds, AK," Leo said. "But if you angle yourself five degrees to the west, you'll cut that in half."

He knows I'm running on fumes. I checked the compass on my watch and angled west. I counted the seconds as I swam full speed ahead.

"Clear!" Leo finally said.

I bolted straight for the light of the surface and burst through. Gasping for air, I swallowed a few big gulps.

"You did it, AK," Sam said. "The whales are safe now."

I needed more air before I could talk. The entire pod had followed me up and circled around me in a protective circle. The largest of the males stopped right beneath me, allowing me to rest on his back.

I pumped my fist. *Dolphin girl to the rescue,* I congratulated myself.

"What's the status of the stray?" I said through big breaths.

'Stray retrieved before reaching the spill. Stay there. I'm coming with Mama Whale right to you," Desmond said.

"I'm circling the area looking for that boat. Nothing on radar either. It's gone like a ghost," Mik said.

Dodd's ghostly image flashed before me, but only for a moment. What just happened started to sink in, and a smile formed on my lips. Here I was, swimming in the largest ocean in the world, leading the biggest mammals in the world out of harm's way. Protecting the one thing that meant more to me than anything else—the ocean. I didn't truly understand why that was, until today, when Desmond said, 'we are family united'. This was my purpose; I had returned home.

Dipping my head back underneath the water to look for Des, I noticed an odd sparkle of light about fifty meters below. It was a dolphin, and it appeared to be tangled up in a fishing line and hooks. The poor thing thrashed awkwardly trying to release itself.

"AK, you see what I'm seeing?" Johan asked.

Johan's chopper passed overhead. "Roger, that," I said and dove deep.

I called out to the injured dolphin as I swam in its direction. As I got closer, I kept calling out, but the dolphin didn't respond.

"AK, I see you moving away from us,?" Sam asked. "What's going on?"

"There's a tangled-up dolphin here. I'm going in to help," I replied.

I got within a few meters of the dolphin when suddenly my vision of the dolphin shifted completely. Instead of a dolphin tangled in a fishing line, now in front of me was an octopus-like creature with tentacles over ten feet long and that had razor sharp teeth.

I stopped immediately. "What the?!" I yelled without taking my eyes off the giant octopus.

"You alright, Akela?" I heard Desmond's voice, but before I could reply, one of the tentacles of the creature reached out and grabbed my arm. Another latched onto my leg. A third tentacle darted out and deftly switched off my communications module.

The octopus beast looked directly into the eyes. *"I didn't think it'd be so easy to trick you. I mean, after all I've heard about you."* The beast spoke a language that I had never heard before, yet I understood its words as clearly as I understood English. Its voice was deep, hollow, and made my skin crawl. The mouth that it originated from had long, knife-like teeth leading into what looked like an abyss of darkness.

"Let me go," I responded in a harsh mental tongue I had never used before.

The beast laughed. *"Right, now that we finally have you in our clutches. You and your..."* Another tentacle reached up toward my neck. *"And your necklace."*

The tentacle awkwardly tried to pull out the necklace chain, but it couldn't do it. I could sense the octopus's frustration as it continued to try to reach my sea glass, but it was tucked under my tight wetsuit.

"You're not taking my necklace," I said, but I couldn't break free.

The creature squeezed me tighter, pushing more air out of my lungs. I wasn't going to be able to stay underwater for too much longer struggling like this.

The octopus pulled me deeper and deeper below the surface. I felt helpless. The light was getting darker. I racked my brain, thinking of how I could alert the team, but as my oxygen level receded, so did my ability to problem solve. I'd been submerged for a long time. Hopefully, Sam and the rest of the ops team knew something was up and would come help soon.

I focused my thoughts on projecting a message. *"Help me."*

Repeatedly, I sent it out over and over as the octopus pulled me down. My eyesight was slowly fading away. I was losing consciousness.

I heard the sea monster hiss, *"Home!"* and I saw what looked like the outline of a giant vessel moving toward us from a distance. As he pulled me closer, I could now see that it was an enormous submarine. Next to it swam a monstrous, multi-colored creature that looked as though it had come straight out of ancient myth. I must have been hallucinating from lack of oxygen.

I focused my thoughts one last time. *"Please, help me!"*

Out of the blue, I felt a surge of water followed by streaks of darkness. I was spun around, surrounded by a flurry of movement and bubbles. In an instant, I was floating free again. The pod of whales had returned! They had the creature surrounded and were chasing it away into deeper water by ramming its body with their heads and striking it with their tails.

I tried to process everything that was going on, but I was in desperate need of air. I kicked for the surface as hard as I could. The gigantic shadow of the submarine descended out of sight as I moved upward. I wasn't surfacing fast enough.

Desmond appeared at my side and pulled my auto-inflate cord. In a burst, my vest filled with air and I propelled to the surface. I swallowed for air as I penetrated the surface. Desmond was soon by my side.

"In through your nose, out through your mouth, Akela. Breathe," he said calmly.

I couldn't slow my breathing. In my mind, I was still in the octopus's arms, and I couldn't break free. I began to hyperventilate.

"You are here now, Akela. Breathe with me." Des slowly inhaled and even more slowly exhaled. He did it again and again, and soon my breathing began to even out with his.

"Extending your exhale will help steady your breathing," he said as he breathed with me. I started to sob.

"I've got her, Sam," Desmond said. "Come get us."

CHAPTER 20

Back on the SOS, I was taken to the medical wing to make sure that I didn't have internal injuries from my fight with the octopus or from my auto-inflate vest. The bruises on my arms and ribs were deep purple. They were sensitive to the probes of the nurses, but otherwise I felt okay. Still, my hands were shaking.

Why did Sam send me on that mission? Earlier in the day he had said the words, 'When I'm ready.' Maybe it was the urgency of the whale's plight. Maybe he just wanted to see me in action. I was surprising myself. I wondered if Sam was surprised as well, or if he knew more about me than I knew about myself. That thought made me uncomfortable.

My medical gown hung loosely over my limbs as I waited in a room with a west-facing window. The sun had just set, and the sky was painted in pastels. The physical that I'd successfully dodged to date was about to happen. I could make a run for it, but in the end, I knew I'd eventually wind up getting evaluated. It suddenly occurred to me that maybe I had nothing to be worried about. If Sam had wanted me in a tank or to be a medical experiment, I'd already be one by now. Desmond would be, too. I also already found out that both my parents were human. That thought made me laugh out loud.

A team of doctors came in, drew blood, ran tests, and asked me questions. My labs and vitals gave no hint to my aquatic talents or extra sensory powers whatsoever. Turns out, I'm normal, by medical standards at least. My childhood fears of becoming a lab experiment slowly melted away as they treated me with care and kindness. A vision of Kaipu came to me. I knew he only wanted to protect me. Papa didn't know at the time that there were others like me.

After a quick shower, I made my way upstairs, where the team was regrouping in the operations room. The ambush had me shaken up a bit, but the high from saving the whales overrode whatever nerves I'd felt.

I could smell the melted cheese well before I entered the room and bee-lined to a beautiful Gorgonzola and spinach pizza. Show time, my stomach told my brain.

My hands had finally stopped shaking and I happily ate while Sam went over a report with Mik.

She looked over at me and gave me a thumbs up and a questioning look.

I returned her thumbs up. "All good," I said.

Desmond joined me at my table.

"Thank you," I said quietly.

Desmond nodded graciously then smiled. "How many languages can you communicate in, Akela?"

"Not sure. I didn't realize I knew anything other than Dolphin, English, a tiny bit of bird, and some Spanish before yesterday." I shrugged. "How about you?"

"Only with the whales, but my skills are limited. Enough to get my point across, but not much more. You are already fluent. A native speaker. You are a bit of a miracle, aren't you?" Des said.

I wanted to tell Des that Kaipu used to call me his 'little miracle', but I chose to take a huge bite of pizza instead.

"Okay," Sam finally said as he put the report aside. "Let's start with what we don't know." "Akela, what happened down there?"

The still-melting cheese dangled between my mouth and the slice in my hand as all eyes turned on me. Desmond, Mik, Warren, Ahimsa, Erika, Johan, Leo and of course Sam, rotated their chairs and waited as I failed miserably to not get cheese all over my shirt. Warren giggled at my efforts.

The details were a little fuzzy, but I did my best to explain to the team my experience with the octopus-like creature. I didn't tell them about the larger beast I saw, though, because I wasn't even sure I saw it.

When I told them that I understood and could communicate with the octopus, Mik and Sam made extended eye contact with each other.

When I finished, Sam stood up.

"So, you were able to summon the whales without knowing if they were nearby or even able to see them?"

"I'm not sure summon is the right word. I mean it was more of me just putting out a message than being able to control their actions. I asked for help. They could have ignored me if they'd wanted to."

Sam nodded.

"But they didn't," Desmond said. "Neither did I. The whales knew that you were like them."

"Yeah, so, speaking of that… Anybody else here got any special powers I should be aware of?" I asked, turning my gaze toward Warren, but he looked away.

"*Special* is a subjective word, Akela. Be careful of how you label yourself and others." Sam walked over to me. "We weren't planning on having you in the operation today, but it seemed so routine at the time. I shouldn't have put you in such danger. I'm sorry. I should've seen it coming."

"Seen the octopus?" I asked.

"And the whaling boat?" Des asked.

Mik walked up next to Sam and grabbed a controller.

"You were lucky today, Akela, Desmond. We all were. Those weren't the only threats in the water."

Images of the oil tanker from Leo's drone appeared on the screen. The footage of the drone covered the entirety of the ship from end to end and above as well as the sides. The aerial footage paused momentarily before suddenly falling from the sky, penetrating the ocean's surface, and then showing us images of the vessel from below.

I gave Leo a nod of respect. I was still annoyed that both he and Warren had kept secret their part in the SOS operations team, but Leo carried on like everything was good between us.

"Yeah, pretty cool huh?" Leo said. "I modified my drone to be submersible as well."

"Obviously." I smiled.

It was official, our spat was over.

The image from under the ship showed a large opening in the hull.

"Are those teeth marks?" Ahimsa asked as she sat down next to me and grabbed a slice of pizza. "May I?"

"Of course."

My fantasy of eating an entire pizza would fall to one slice short, but whatever. Sharing is caring. The waiter from *Chez Shipman* came walking in carrying three more boxes of pizza. Holy moly. Maybe my telepathic powers worked when I was hungry, too.

"Definitely bite marks," Mik said as she paused and zoomed in on the image. Long teeth-shaped incisions were clearly visible along with spiked holes that ran lengthwise and vertically near the opening.

The air went out of the room at the sight of the damaged ship and the idea that something capable of biting its way through steel was swimming in the ocean with us. My appetite immediately left me.

"What could've made incisions like that, boss?" Johan asked.

Sam walked in front of the monitor. "A kraken. Dodd's kraken."

"A kraken? Like from mythology?" Warren asked.

"Yes, Warren, from mythology," Sam said while he looked directly at me.

Leo cleared his throat. "The kraken is a legendary creature that resembled a giant squid and was known for destroying ships. In the

Greek myths, Perseus faced the Cetus, a sea serpent. The kraken came from the myths or sagas of the Norse, more than a thousand years after the Greeks," he said enthusiastically.

"Well done, Leo." Sam circled us as he talked. "But all mythology is based upon some kernel of truth."

"Are you sure it was a kraken?" Leo asked as he brought up an image of the beast on one of the monitors.

"Some scientists, myself included—" Ahimsa raised her hand, "—believe the mysterious kraken *did* actually exist. Researchers have found digested bones of large animals that must have been eaten by an even larger, unidentified animal."

I took a deep breath. "It was a kraken. I saw it." Everyone else drew silent and turned to me. "The kraken was with Dodd's submarine. The octopus was trying to bring me there. Do you think the octopus that grabbed me was a baby kraken?" I asked.

"I'd say no. Look at the image. The creature that attacked the tanker would've been over two hundred feet long, which would make its babies the size of a school bus," Ahimsa replied.

Sam stood up. "The creature that grabbed you was Octavius. He works for Dodd."

Sam hit a button, and the image of a handsome young man in his late teens or early twenties appeared on the screen.

"That cute guy is the octopus that grabbed me?"

Warren sat upright at my 'cute' comment.

Sam nodded before turning the monitor off. "Yup. We don't know much about Octavius, other than he's a bit like you and Desmond here."

"Yes, but he also takes the form of a sea creature apparently. I don't look like a dolphin when I'm underwater." I paused. "Wait a minute, do I? I mean, I've never seen myself in a mirror underwater."

Warren spit out his water and laughed. Mik just shook her head.

"Regardless, you were very lucky to get away, Akela," Desmond said.

"Very. And only because of you and your whale friends," I replied. It hadn't really sunk in until now, how close I had been to being captured or killed by Dodd.

"*Our* friends, Akela, our friends." Sam smiled. "Yes, you were lucky, and I was careless putting both of you out there. This was more than an act of environmental terrorism; it was an ambush. We're still trying to figure out how the kraken and the whaling boat avoided being detected on our surveillance monitors. Leo, pull up the tanker's manifest."

On another monitor, a document appeared on the screen. Mik read it aloud. "The tanker is registered in the United Kingdom."

Leo quickly searched deeper into the ship's paper trail. "Fake company, another fake company, ah, here we go. Dartivion Corp is the real owner."

"Dartivion and Jarvis Dodd again. Figures. You guys must read Global Alert, right? They've covered Dartivion's crimes for a long time." I looked around the room.

"Did you like my writing?" Sam said, smirking.

I sat, staring at Sam and then slapped my palm against my forehead. "S.S, Sam Shipman, you're S.S. Duh!"

I gotta stop hitting myself.

"And the SOS is Global Alert. Oh man."

The fact I didn't put two and two together bothered me, but I tried not to let it show.

Sam continued, "Usually, in some one way or another, we can trace most of our operations as a direct response to Dodd."

"Why would he attack his own boat? And, more importantly, who the heck has a pet kraken hanging around to do their bidding?" I asked.

"Jarvis Dodd's actions always have a methodology to them. It was clear he knew you were aboard the SOS. Desmond as well. He wanted both of you in the water to capture you and your sea glass." Sam looked down for a moment before raising his eyes back up to the team. "And Dodd almost got what he wanted. Rest assured, it's only a matter of time before he and his monster surface again."

Mik walked over and stood next to Sam. "Team, there's more,"

The image on the monitor shifted to show a large, football-shaped missile.

"I hope that's not what I think it is," Leo said.

Mik sighed. "Unfortunately, it is, Leo. Our intel is reporting that Dodd is acquiring materials to develop a virus for a bio-attack. It's critical we find him and stop him."

"He really is mad, isn't he?" I quickly caught eyes with Leo and then Warren. Worry was clear on their faces. I know I felt the same. We all wanted this meeting to be over.

Sam lifted the Lakers hat off his head and ran his fingers through his hair. "The stakes have never been higher, and we all must stay alert," Sam said, putting his hat back on and slowly nodded. "Dodd clearly knew where to find us."

I fidgeted in my chair as the memory of Octavius's voice came into my head.

"How'd Dodd know that? The SOS is invisible," Warren asked what we were all thinking.

Sam's face grew grim, and he slowly scanned the room. "Because there's a mole on the SOS, Warren." The air went out of the room.

Sam went on, "The ambush was too convenient. Dodd not only knew where we were, but how we'd respond. Our mission appears to be compromised and will remain so until we find the reason why."

Sam moved toward the door and stopped just before exiting. He took a deep breath and let it out with an audible sigh.

"This meeting is over. Rest up. You're gonna need it."

CHAPTER 21

The post-operation meeting had left me overwhelmed with questions. Restless with worry, I couldn't sleep without getting some answers. Specifically, from my two friends and surprise operations teammates, Leo and Warren.

I hadn't known the boys for long, but I couldn't see them as traitors. Still, they'd kept a secret from me.

I got out of bed, threw on some sweats, a hat, and headed out my door.

By now, I'd figured out that Leo's role on the operations team was somewhat of a jack of all trade's technologist. His work with the amphibious drone had been instrumental in figuring out that the kraken was responsible for the Sea Swarm attack. His quick calculations also helped guide me and the pod to safety.

While I spent time training in and out of the water, Leo was tinkering in Professor Gadgis's lab. Gadgis was Leo's uncle and legal guardian. They both could build the coolest gadgets and tools from the most random objects.

Leo was supremely smart, yet I was still surprised to find out he was a team member. I didn't know much else about him, and I knew less about Warren besides the obvious facts that he was fast, funny and I couldn't help blushing when he smiled.

I heard Leo's voice through a door, so I knocked on that one.

"C'mon in." Warren opened the door into a suite much larger than mine. He was wearing sweatpants and a t-shirt. His hair was a delightful mess that seemed to go in every direction all at once.

Leo poked his head out from a small kitchen.

"Hey, AK. Couldn't sleep either, huh?" Leo said.

I nodded and surveyed the room.

The boys shared a large, two-bedroom suite with a common area that had a small couch and table situated in front of their glass deck sliders. A photo of Leo and his Uncle Gadgis rested on an end table. Another of him as a baby with a young couple sat next to it. There were no photos of Warren in the room.

Leo made three cups of tea and carried them out on a tray, which he placed on the coffee table. He plopped down on the floor. I looked at the couch, then followed Warren's lead down to the ground. We sipped quietly, as a small, circular, robotic, device circled us while emitting a low humming sound. Suddenly, it attached itself to Warren's shirt and started to eat it.

"Hey! Make it stop!" Warren howled.

Leo tossed a small Doritos bag at the device. It let go of Warren's now half-shredded shirt and ate up the bag instead.

"Dude, your little monster here is a menace to society." Warren inspected his tattered shirt.

"Sorry, it's a prototype. A variation of the Sea Swarm bots. This one sucks in and shreds up. I'm working on an amphibious unit, too."

"To clean our oceans of trash. Very cool." I bowed my head slightly in respect. Leo grinned in reply.

Did you always want to build things?" I asked.

"No. Back in Japan, beekeeping was the family business," Leo said.

Warren rolled his eyes. "Bee facts 101, here we go."

Leo held up a hand. "One-third of the food grown on Earth relies on pollination, mainly by bees. That's nothing to roll your eyes over."

"Sorry dude," Warren said, rolling his eyes again with a smile in my direction

"My uncle and I still maintain a large beekeeper operation on the SOS, you know." Leo paused for a long while before slowly speaking again. "My mom and my Aunt Gadgis died in an accident with the bees one day during a freak storm. My Uncle Gadgis was off delivering honey and was stranded for days before being able to return home. I was only a toddler at the time. Nobody knows for sure what happened, but somehow I survived the storm."

Whoa. Leo, like me, was just a baby when his parents died.

He put his hand inside his shirt and pulled out a necklace. It was sea glass.

"Asia," I said in awe of the glowing red glass hanging from his neck.

"I have no memory of how I got this," he said, while staring down at the glass. "My uncle says it wasn't there the morning he left."

"I don't know how I got mine either." I pulled my sea glass out from beneath my shirt. "Do you have any powers? Can you fly?" I asked, thinking maybe he had bee-like abilities.

"Nope."

"You ever tried?" I asked.

"I mean, I've sort of tried a few times. Jumping out over the water, but I always wound-up swimming." Leo had a determined look in his eye. "It's only just a matter of time though, until I build something that will allow me to fly."

We sat there quietly for a few moments sipping our tea. I couldn't believe I'd spent all that time talking about sea glass with Sam and Mik, and neither of them bothered to mention that there were other sea glass bearers on the ship. I'd never asked, so technically they didn't lie to me, but still.

Security precautions or not, I was mad at myself for not asking and annoyed at everybody else for keeping me in the dark. I tried not to be upset, but I couldn't help it.

"Sam is just trying to protect us," Leo said.

I gave him an eyebrow raise.

"You'd be a horrible poker player, Akela," Leo said as his real smile returned.

"So, what's your story?" I turned to Warren. I mean, Desmond is of the sea like me, and Leo's here is, well he's a genius."

Leo nodded in not so humble acceptance.

"And Sam Shipman, well, I'm not sure what his power is beyond being the creator of our SOS universe, so I'd say he's pretty powerful."

Leo and Warren nodded silently in agreement.

"So that's all the sea glass holders on the SOS." Warren couldn't hold my stare. "All of them, unless of course if you too have a sea glass Warren? C'mon. Let's cut the bull. I've seen you run."

I sat and waited for a response.

Warren finally stood up, took a deep breath, closed his eyes, leaned his head back and opened his mouth and started howling! A wolf-like primal cry that all at once made me scared and excited.

"Shut up, dude! People are trying to sleep." Leo covered his ears.

Warren finished his howl and stood with his hands on his hips. "So?"

"Tell me everything!" I grabbed Warren's hand and he sat back down on the floor next to Leo."

"Everything?"

"Yup."

Warren nodded. "Well, I was born just outside of Bialowieza Forest in Poland. My parents were forest rangers, big nature lovers, apparently. Kinda like you guys. Well, the nature-loving part, not the forest or Poland part."

"Oh man, this is going to be a long night," Leo said, followed by a loud sigh.

"Bialowieza, Forest. I've read about it. Hundreds of mammals and birds live there. Bison, elk, lynx, eagles and more," I said.

"Yes, AK. And wolves." Warren smiled.

Wolves. I knew it.

"And it's not a long story Leo, you know that." Warren shrugged and ran his hand through his bushy hair. "I don't remember much. Some of what I know is from what Mik told me, other parts are just pieces of my memory." Warren paused.

"My parents were killed in a logging accident. A logging truck flipped while carrying its load and flattened the pickup my parents and I were in."

Warren lost his parents in an accident, too. I shook my head.

"Somehow I survived. I was only five years old at the time. I don't remember much other than the smell of gasoline and fire. Then the face of a wolf poking its head into the truck. He gnawed my seatbelt off and pulled me into the woods."

"Were you afraid?"

"No. I knew the wolf was there to help me."

"How'd you know that?"

"I could communicate with him. Just like you, Akela. Mentally. My parents were gone, so the pack became my family. It's hard to say how long I lived with them, but long enough where it felt natural."

"Can you still communicate with wolves?" I asked, hoping the answer was yes and wondering now if I could mentally connect with Warren.

Warren looked down at the floor and brushed the rug lightly with his fingertips. "No. Somewhere along the line I lost it. I mean, we understand each other a bit, but nothing like when I lived with the pack. I keep trying though."

Warren swiped at the rug this time. His inability to reconnect with the wolves clearly bothered him. I changed the subject.

"Did you hunt with them?" I asked, somewhat morbidly interested.

Warren's face lit up and he opened his eyes wide. "Yes, I would bring down deer with my teeth and drink their blood!" He laughed a fake maniacal laugh and smiled wide showing his very normal looking teeth. "Do you think these could do much good in the wild?"

"I guess not," I said, laughing. "I do crave fish, but I've never caught one with my teeth. Tell me more."

"That's it, really. I lived with the wolves. I ran with them day and night. Shared their food, shelter, and everything. They took me in. It was the only thing I knew and was the only life I knew until the SOS found me."

"How?"

"A camper caught me on video running with the pack on a full moon night. The video was up on YouTube for only a few hours before it got pulled. A day later, Mik arrived."

"That's crazy, Warren. Our stories are so similar," I said.

Warren reached into his shirt and pulled a brilliant orange piece of sea glass. It was Europe.

"I had the sea glass necklace around my neck for as long as I can remember. Where it came from or how I got it, I don't know. I'd no idea it was the shape of Europe until Mik told me," Warren said with a thoughtful, but far off look in his eyes.

"Of course, you have sea glass, too," I said.

We all took our sea glass and held them in our hands. The pieces moved toward each other, hovering off our hands, but they did not touch. We sat there for maybe a minute, watching our pieces float in the air.

"I wonder if our losses, along with our unusual nature experiences, are what brought us the sea glass?" Leo said thoughtfully, breaking the silence.

"Maybe. I guess I understand now why Mik and Sam didn't want us advertising our sea glass. You know, with Dodd having a mole on board and all," I said and put my necklace back inside my shirt. The boys did the same.

I then told them my story from the beginning. When I finished, it was three a.m. and we all decided to call it a night.

Deep in thought, I took my time walking back to my room. The boys were more like me than I could've ever imagined. Still, I felt lost. With every step further into this journey, with every question answered, I found myself with ten new questions that I had to find the answer to. I needed to know more about Dodd, Sam and about the sea glass.

The connection of loss between the team members and the sea glass couldn't be a coincidence.

Chapter 22

Back in my room, I'd psyched myself out of falling asleep. I reached into my bedside table and took out my journal for the first time since I'd come aboard the *Spirit of the Sea.*

Leafing through drawings and entries I'd written over the past few years, I stopped and stared at my last journal entry. It was from the night I decided I was going to run away. Of course, I never had to run. Mik came and rescued me.

The words I wrote jumped off the page. 'run away/escape/swim(?) to Hawaii. I need to get out of here!' I still remembered the feelings of fear and doubt as I put those words onto paper. I looked at my hands as I held the journal. They were the same hands, but I felt like a different person who wrote that entry.

My life had friends in it now, and the first real sense of family since Kaipu and Alana had passed. The anxiety and loneliness that had become my constant companions in Bonita Fields were now in the background. Still, I could always sense their presence somewhere out on the horizon. Like guests thrown out of a party who were forced to watch the event from across the street. They were still there, though, almost as if they were waiting for an invitation. No, *expecting* to be invited back in at some point.

Jarvis Dodd suddenly came to mind. Why'd I think of him in that exact instant when I was analyzing my fears? A chill trickled down my spine. Those cold blue eyes stared right through me as he stood just inches away when we were leaving Bonita Fields. Why didn't Mik see him? Why'd I keep dreaming about him?

I picked up my iPad and Googled Jarvis Dodd and Dartivion Corporation. I'd done this before back in Bonita Fields and skipped the links at the top that would tell me what I already knew.

Dodd was a mystery. Not just to me, but to the world. It wasn't until Dartivion Corporation was founded in the early 1970s that Jarvis Dodd showed up on the radar.

Dartivion Corporation had started in oil, but quickly diversified into plastic manufacturing, coal mining, logging, whaling, net fishing, and a ton of other business units. The common thread throughout all Dartivion was that every activity was tied into reaping profits from Mother Nature's natural resources. The company was under continuous assault by environmental activists, but still the stock price soared, and Dodd had become one of the richest men in the world.

Clicking through the new links, I found the same dead ends. That is, until a few pages deep on the Google search, when I found an article titled, 'Does Dodd Exist?'. It had appeared in an issue of *National Wildlife* over three years ago. The reporter had found an old interview where Dodd claimed he was born in Tofino, Canada in 1950.

The reporter had traveled to Tofino in search of anybody who knew Dodd or anything about Dodd's family. In every instance, she only found people who claimed not to remember the family or those who refused to cooperate with her questions.

While some had concluded that the remoteness of Tofino would've made it easy for a family to live in isolation, this article claimed the exact opposite. That in towns on the frontier, with few inhabitants, the norm was that everybody knew everybody. Not only because of the small population, but because of the necessity of having to rely on each other for survival.

The fact that Dodd claimed his father was a fisherman and his mother a nurse made the idea of their family not interacting with others even harder to believe.

The article's conclusion was that either Dodd materialized out of thin air, or, more likely, his account of his childhood was fabricated. He had used his immense wealth, power, and influence to cover his actual story.

When I went to find the reporters contact information, I came across a news article detailing her death in a freak construction accident. A building crane fell on her during a windstorm. It didn't take me long to connect the dots. The crane company was a far-removed subsidiary of Dartivion Corporation, and the woman who was killed was a harsh critic of Dodd.

Nobody took the time or energy to make that connection. And if they had, they'd have disappeared. How convenient.

CHAPTER 23

A short three hours later, I woke up with my iPad on my lap and the boys knocking on my door. It was going to be a long day.

My tiredness and anxiety over Dodd seemed to disappear the moment I reunited with Warren and Leo.

Warren handed me a large coffee. "Hurry up, we can't be late for Track Wild's class."

"That's sweet of you," I said.

He paused and smiled. We held each other's gaze for an extended moment.

"Oh brother!" Leo wrapped an arm around both of us and herded us down the hall.

"Here it is," Warren said as he maneuvered ahead of us and opened what looked like a service doorway. I followed Warren and Leo up a long stairwell that seemed to go up higher than I thought the ship was tall. "It's faster than waiting in line for the elevator."

Finally, we reached the top of the stairs and walked into a large room with tables arranged along the outer walls. On top of the tables were birds. Dead, stuffed birds. My feathered flying friends in every conceivable size and shape were all there on display. If somebody told me I'd walk into a room of dead birds and I wouldn't be horrified, I'd have called them a liar, but this was different. These birds were there for a reason.

Tiny hummingbirds to six-foot-tall ostriches were everywhere, and all of them appeared to be staring right at me. Warren tugged at my sleeve.

"Quick, these are the seats we want." He pointed to the chairs situated along the north wall.

Leo was huffing and puffing after the long walk up the stairs and slouched into the seat next to me. The other kids leisurely strolled out of the elevator and grabbed the remaining chairs on the opposite side. The center of the room had one chair with a glass ceiling above it.

"Why these chairs?"

"Trust me," Warren whispered.

Leo looked at his watch. "And now," he said as the hidden door opened from the wall and a short man with disheveled dark hair and a beard entered the room. He was wearing a lab coat and multi-colored hat with ear flaps, even though the temperature had to be seventy degrees in the room. The concealed door was directly behind the last seats taken by the straggling students.

Leo whispered to me. "Professor Wild has identified over eight hundred species of birds throughout his career. He's probably helped save thousands more as an investigator into avian-related crimes."

"How does he do that from the ship?" I asked before getting shushed by Professor Wild.

Wild held up a honeysuckle flower in his right hand and made a whistle call with his fingers from his left. Three hummingbirds appeared, coming from the door of his office. They buzzed around the heads of the kids sitting in front of the door, making one boy fall out of his seat.

Their wings beat so fast that they were a blur and made an audible hum as they circled the room before moving in to partake in the honeysuckle sweets Wild offered them.

"The hummingbirds are marvels of aviation, aren't they?" Wild asked. "Yet they are so small and delicate in comparison to humans, that to think that we could take advantage of these beautiful yet tiny creatures seems savage.

"Certain cultures use the hummingbirds and other exotic birds as charms or spiritual tokens," said Leo as he edged forward in his seat "The dead and decorated birds then become a part of an illegal and international trade."

Wild shook his head at Leo. "Yes, the rude young man who didn't raise his hand to be called upon is correct." Leo sank back in his seat.

Wild looked lovingly at the tiny birds in front of him. "Understanding how humans can view, in their minds, lesser creatures, is a critical part in being able to combat crimes against innocent animals."

Wild hit a button and the birds darted back through his office door as the kids dove out of the way of the tiny missiles.

Warren leaned into my shoulder. "Rumor has it that Wild has a collection of live birds in his office that are among the rarest in the world."

"Really?" I asked as Warren's eyes widened and averted from mine quickly. I knew that look. The teacher was coming. Great.

I mouthed, "Thanks dude," to Warren before looking up.

Wild turned to me. "You, young lady. Just the volunteer I was looking for."

"Me?"

"Yes. Please come forward."

Professor Wild spoke as I walked to the center of the room. "Crows are incredibly clever birds, capable of using tools, recognizing faces and even more astounding acts that demonstrate an obvious high level of intelligence."

Wild reached into his briefcase and took out a carefully wrapped package. Slowly unfolding the cloth wrapping, he unveiled a dead crow. The colors of its wings were beautiful upon close examination. Not just black, but shades of auburn, blue and red all blended together. He placed the crow on the chair in the center of the room, directly next to where I was standing.

I looked from Wild to the boys, waiting for some sign as to what my role in this could be.

Wild continued, "Researchers have even found that crows mourn their dead and hold funerals."

He pressed a button on his watch and the glass ceiling above us opened wide. I stared upward for a minute, seeing nothing but blue sky and passing clouds until we heard a single caw. A crow appeared, perched upon the opening to our class. Soon, another appeared, followed by many more.

"The SOS has a large population of crows. When we left port, they were part of our crew, and their numbers have multiplied over the years."

Wild spoke loudly over the birds' calls. "Upon spotting one of its dead, the flock attends to the fallen bird with their loud calls." He held his head solemnly as if he were a preacher starting a sermon. "We are all attending a crow funeral."

I estimated there to be at least sixty crows now sitting around the opening, all cawing in unison. It seemed like some sort of pagan ritual to me. The body of the dead crow had invoked the presence of those still living.

Wild turned and looked at me. "Now here is where the girl who likes to speak in class comes into play."

I smirked, finally having some idea of my role.

"Rumor has it you can communicate with fish," Wild said, a little too condescendingly to my ears.

"Dolphins. Not fish, at least not yet," I corrected him with probably a little too much attitude for my first day in class.

Wild's head ticked up as I spoke, as if taunting me to say more than I probably should. I kept my mouth shut as I could see Warren and Leo in the background both shaking their heads.

"Yes, dolphins are clever creatures and maybe you've taught them to sit and roll over," Wild said, goading me, but I didn't take the bait.

"But revenge is a distinctly human emotion, or is it? If somebody hurt one of your friends over there, Miss Spencer, would you feel compelled to hurt them in return?"

I took this as a rhetorical question, even though Wild stared at me for what seemed like an eternity before returning to his lecture.

"Given enough time, the flock will attack any predator it thinks is responsible for the death of their friend."

A bird left its perch and swooped close to my head. I looked to Wild for assistance and saw that he had donned a surgical mask. Another bird came screaming right toward my face as I barely ducked out of the way. The cawing of the birds had turned into a roar.

"As the one who works most closely with these birds," Wild shouted over the birds, "I cannot take the risk of them associating me with trouble. But you, young lady, you have less to lose."

The entirety of the flock took aloft and began swooping. Feeling panicked, I ran toward the shelter of Wild's office before falling to the ground with my hands over my head. The crows were screaming as they took turns pecking at my body and biting my hair.

"Professor!" I heard Warren shout out.

"Silence!" Professor Wild bellowed over the noise. "Have you learned the lesson yet, Miss Spencer?"

I was about to say yes when I remembered Desmond's breathing technique. I inhaled through my nose and slowly let out a long exhale through my mouth. I did it again and again. Suddenly, I recalled the pelican and pigeons that I had communicated with before.

After a few moments, I calmed my breath, stood up, and walked back to the body of the dead bird. A crow buzzed by my ear and another skimmed just over my head. I knelt next to the dead bird as its fellow crows continued to dive bomb at me.

I closed my eyes and focused on having compassion toward the soul of this little creature and any other creature that may have loved it. Slowly, I could feel the crows connecting to me. I began to hear the individuality in each specific crow caw, to understand the sadness and acknowledgment they were seeking.

There was one other mental connection I was making in the room, a human one, but I ignored it and concentrated on the crows.

Before I knew it, the birds stopped their attacks and, one by one, they landed next to me. All sixty birds. We formed a circle around the body of their fallen friend. I could feel their thoughts in my head. I knew that they didn't consider me an enemy anymore. They only wanted to honor the dead and move on. After a few moments of silence, I stood up again and turned to Wild.

"You're correct, these are amazing creatures, Professor Wild. They will remember me, but not in the way you thought."

I returned to my seat. Focusing my eyes on Wild, I saw a smile of approval cross his face.

Out of the corner of my eye, Warren held up a fist for me to bump. Our fists met first and then our eyes. Warren smiled the same charming smile he always did. I could tell he had no idea that our minds had just connected.

CHAPTER 24

An uneventful week of class and training had kept us all busy and too tired to do much else. We welcomed the weekend and a Saturday night at the pizza joint on the promenade. A flyer promoting next month's 'crew showcase' was posted above our booth. Everybody on the SOS had to perform a routine of their choice at least once a year. I was up next at the end of the month.

I didn't want to do it.

"That's the whole point, Akela. Do something you've never done before. Expand your comfort zone," Leo said while fidgeting with a modification to his drone controls.

"And humiliate myself in front of the entire boat?" I asked.

Warren looked up from a mouthful of pizza. "So what? Leo and I did a juggling act a few months back."

"How'd that go?" I asked.

"Well, let's just say the bruises have faded, but not the memories, unfortunately."

I couldn't think of anything I wanted to perform. I took a bite from my pizza and sketched quick pencil outlines of me kneeling with the flock of crows.

Warren peeked over my shoulder. "Why don't you show off your art? It's really good."

"Thanks." I'd been doodling and drawing scenes of my experiences in a notebook since arriving on the SOS. Maybe Warren was right, and I could present my art somehow.

I thought to ask Warren about the connection I'd sensed during Wild's class, but I decided to wait.

We finished eating and sat on the grass underneath the giant Eucalyptus trees. These Saturday nights in the park made us feel almost like normal kids again. We had freedom, food, and plenty to talk about. What we talked about was anything but normal though. I looked up into the trees and saw a few crows perched together on a branch.

"So, what do you think of Professor Wild?" I looked from the birds to the boys. "He seems a little edgy?"

"You think? If you inspected dead animals and tried to figure out how they died or who killed them, you'd probably have an edge, too," Leo said.

"I don't think anybody on this ship loves animals as much as Wild. He just sees things from a different perspective. A darker one," Warren somberly added.

"I wonder if he's the mole?" I asked.

"Could be. Supposedly, Wild was the last person to see Dodd alive," Leo said.

"Professor Wild and Akela. Right, Akela? You told us that you saw Dodd when you were getting into the helicopter," Warren said.

"Are you saying that I could be the mole then, too?" I asked sharply.

Warren put his pizza down and tilted his head like a questioned puppy. "C'mon, Akela."

"Sorry," I was getting used to being skeptical now. It was a hard habit to break. "Tell me what you guys know about Wild." I closed my journal.

Leo put his project aside. His eyes got wide with excitement before he spoke. "Well, before the SOS was constructed, Sam was working to stop a worldwide bird smuggling operation. Many species of bird were on the brink of extinction. Sam recruited Professor Wild. He eventually found Dodd at the center of it."

Leo took a swig of water. "Wild infiltrated Dodd's operation disguised as a broker of rare birds. After years of undercover work, Wild finally earned Dodd's trust, and he agreed to have Wild deliver one of the few birds outside of Dodd's collection. Once inside Dodd's compound, Wild alerted Sam of the coordinates, and an attempt was made to capture Dodd."

"And?" I asked.

"Dodd disappeared somehow. Maybe like he did with you, Akela, or like that whaling boat did, and the kraken did," Leo scanned the room as if he were searching for a ghost. "Nobody knows how he did it. His compound was surrounded with no way out. Dodd vanished into thin air. Wild and Sam brought back everything they could from Dodd's hideout. Live and dead specimens."

"That's where all of those stuffed birds came from," I said.

Leo nodded. "A single feather has been plucked from each wing." Leo held up a finger.

"Why?" I asked.

"Well, there's only one way of finding out." Warren leapt up from the floor so energetically that both of his feet lifted off the ground. "Anybody have interest in a little night expedition to get a peek at Wild's 'rare' birds?" His brown eyes sparkled with adventure.

"Seriously?" I shook my head at Warren. The last thing I needed was to get in trouble. I had enough to worry about.

"Akela, what's the worst thing that could happen?" Warren reached his hand down to me.

Leo slowly stood up. "I usually don't side with Warren's ideas, but we aren't going to find out anything by waiting for Sam to tell us."

Leo was right about that much.

"You really think they'd punish us?" Warren pulled his sea glass out from beneath his shirt. "C'mon, we're kinda a big deal around here. At least to Sam," he said and gestured for me to take his hand.

Leo reached his hand out to me as well. I remembered my dive off the deck and the anxiety I'd felt beforehand and the exhilaration afterward. I took a deep breath and reached out a hand to each of them.

"Let's go bird watching, boys."

We huddled around Leo's handheld remote drone display and watched as Leo navigated the tiny flying device down the corridor to the open atrium. The coast was clear.

"People work all hours on the SOS of course, and it wouldn't be abnormal for us to be out, but…" Leo paused to emphasize the exception. "But us being in a teacher's office would be definitely considered out of bounds and could get us in big trouble." He clearly was having second thoughts and eyed both of us for our reactions.

I was having second thoughts as well. It wasn't too late to turn around, but Warren thought otherwise.

"Big time," Warren chimed in. "BUT…" Warren mocked Leo's dramatic pause, "But what if Professor Wild turns out to be the mole and we uncover that? We'd be heroes. You think of that, gadget boy?"

Leo eyed his control screen. "Okay. Let's go."

We followed the path of the drone as it buzzed through the atrium, down into the university quadrant. Warren opened a door and we began scaling the long stairway to Wild's classroom.

I was with them step for step, but my mind was elsewhere, caught up in the idea of rare birds, prophecies, and moles. That and getting busted.

Lost in my thoughts, I tripped and bumped into Leo.

"Hey, don't mess with a pilot while he's in flight." Leo shook his head at me.

A clear-headed question came to mind. "Wait, how are we going to get into Wild's office?"

Leo smiled as if he was waiting for me to ask. "This is how." The drone was hovering at the top of the stairs, right in front of the retinal scanner.

He pulled up an image on the display as we peered over his shoulder. As he zoomed in, I could see that it was a shot of Professor Wild standing in his classroom. The image started moving as he hit the play button.

"Did you really take a video during Professor Wild's class?" Warren asked, incredulous.

"What's the difference between that and taking notes?" Leo responded in all seriousness.

Leo zoomed in on the video of the professor's face, then even closer on his eye. He then cropped out the rest of the video so that the only image was an extreme close-up of Wild's moving eye.

Up the stairs, the drone hovered in front of the door. As Leo hit select, the recorded image of the eye was now in front of the scanner.

"Do you think this is really going to work?" I asked just as the door opened. Leo and Warren executed a perfect no-look high-five as we all started up the stairs again. The drone, far ahead of us, flew into the classroom.

The classroom was dark except for moonlight coming in from the skylights. We slowly moved around the perimeter of the room with the drone flying only a few feet ahead of us. I bumped into a table holding a stuffed ostrich. The bird started to teeter toward the ground, before I barely caught it.

"My eyes are taking a while to adjust," I said as a light shot out from the drone and lit up the outstretched wings of a huge, menacing eagle directly in front of us.

We all let out a scream before covering our mouths.

"Sorry, I programmed headlights." Leo dimmed the drone's light.

We made our way toward Professor Wild's office with the drone flying out in front of us. The door was slightly open, and a light appeared to be on in the room.

Leo turned the drone microphone all the way up, but I could hear the voice without the help of the machine's speaker.

"It's him. Wild's in there," Warren said with his eyes wide open. "Let's get out of here."

Wild's voice got louder. "Here, kitty, kitty. Here, kitty, kitty." Suddenly the door opened wide, and Leo's flying robot disappeared.

He held his hands out and showed us that he didn't have control over the drone anymore.

We watched the image on the controller as the drone landed in Wild's hand. He held the camera to his face. "Aloha, children."

"Let's run," I said just as all the lights went on and the front door slammed shut. Wild appeared in his doorway holding the drone in his hands.

"Well?" Wild said expectantly, then turned around and walked back into his office.

As far as I could tell, we'd nothing left to lose at this point, so I started walking toward the office. Leo and Warren stood frozen, until I gestured for them to follow.

Wild's collection of dead bird specimens was amazing, but what I saw now in his office took my breath away.

"Come in," he said as he put Leo's drone down on the table and held his arm up for a magnificent, multi-colored Osprey to land on. The bird had a different vibrant color on every single feather.

"Professor Wild, this bird looks like it flew through a rainbow carwash." Leo walked up to the table, while subtly placing his hand on his toy.

Wild moved his gaze from the bird to all of us and then right back to Leo. "Yes, yes it does, somewhat." Wild gestured for Leo to put the drone back on the table.

Leo sighed and did as requested.

Wild placed the bird in a large, comfortable cage. "I hate keeping any animal in captivity, but this one, this one is too important to be flying free right now."

"Is that because of the prophecy?" Warren asked.

"It's probably because a rainbow bird can't hide itself from predators," Leo said.

Wild locked the cage and smiled with a glint of mischief in his eyes. He didn't appear angry that we broke into his classroom. He almost seemed happy that we had. "You're both right. This bird is special. Incredibly strong, but equally vulnerable while Dodd is still around. And yes, there are many elements to the prophecy, young man. Which do you speak of?"

Warren cleared his throat, then cleared his throat again and seemed to be gulping for air. I glanced at Leo.

"He does this when he's nervous," Leo offered.

"Spit it out, boy. This isn't a test. Consider us colleagues discussing a matter of business," Wild said before changing his tone. "We will address your breaking and entering into my classroom later. Fair enough?"

We all nodded, and Warren finally began to speak. "Well, Sam has told us about the main prophecy of course, the one we're all fighting to win with the sea glass, but when Leo hacked—"

Leo made a loud grunting sound.

"You did what?" I asked.

Wild gave a small shrug, walked around his private office, and stood in front of an old oil painting of a man.

"Charles Darwin," I said.

"Very good, Akela," Wild said as he looked over at Leo and then pressed a button on his watch. The drone powered up and slowly flew toward our teacher.

"Tractor beam button. Leo, your Uncle Gadgis installed it on my wrist piece." Wild grabbed the drone. "Leo, pull my eyes again. I want to see what further changes I need to recommend to our security team." The image of Wild's retina appeared, and Wild held it directly in front of Darwin's eyes. Nothing happened.

"Interesting," Wild said to himself. "Okay, all of you spin the other way for a moment." Seconds later, Wild told us we could turn back around.

I blinked and Wild was comfortably seated at the table with a manuscript open in front of him. How'd that happen so fast?

"Come sit." He waved us forward.

Professor Wild delicately untied the seal to a large leather binder and opened it wide on the table. The inside cover was labeled 'Osprey of Good Hope.' He handed me a laminated black and white photo of the beautiful bird.

"That's her name?"

"Yes, but I like to call her Hope," Wild said fondly to the majestic bird.

I stared at the black and white photograph of Hope. There was something about the background, the foliage and the sky that gave me the feeling of a bygone era.

Professor Wild pulled out a detailed map of Central and South America, with images of different birds over the various regions. "Here is where I found Hope." Wild pointed to a mountainous region deep in Guatemala and then to Peru. "And here is the excavation site, the sacred place where Sam and your parents found the tablet of the prophecy."

"About Htmalo and Chixtal's war," Leo said.

"And about the sea glass map," Warren said.

"And?" Professor Wild said, expecting us to have more to add. "You did say you hacked into the prophecy database?"

Finally, Leo spoke. "Yeah, well, much of it was encrypted, but from what I could access, I saw that Chixtal created a weapon. One constructed from the feather of every known bird on the planet. Dodd has all of the feathers except for one."

"Had, Leo. Dodd *had* all of those feathers." Wild stroked his beard.

"Dodd is without Hope, but he is far from hopeless in this war," Wild said, studying the map. "I rescued Hope and many other birds from Dodd. She is safe here."

"How'd Dodd escape? I heard you and Sam had him and he just vanished into thin air?" I asked Wild. My mind flashed to visions of Dodd appearing in Bonita Fields and in my dreams.

"Dodd did vanish, but with help from the prophecy. Remember, Htmalo and Chixtal were spirits of unlimited power. Your sea glass is proof of their strength to reach across centuries to influence the fate of our planet. You should know that your glass pieces are not the only magical tools in this war." Wild pointed to Hope. He then unfolded the map further, not noticing as a photo slipped out onto the floor. Another photo of the Osprey of Hope. This time there were two young men standing with Hope.

"Hey, that's Sam." Warren pointed to the man on the right.

I leaned in closer to examine the photo and picked it up off the floor. It was Sam. The other man's face was faded beyond recognition.

"I don't understand," Warren stammered as he grabbed the photograph from my hand. "This photo looks like it's over a hundred years old, but Sam looks exactly the same?"

"Time is very mysterious. Some believe it moves in a circle like a clock, and others believe it is a one-way street to a destination that varies based upon your beliefs, and for others..." Wild seemed to get lost in an unfinished thought and then deftly swiped the photo back from Warren.

Leo took advantage of Wild's moment of distraction to put his hand back on the drone, and then motioned to all of us to move toward the door, but it was too late.

An SOS security officer was standing at the door, blocking the exit.

Wild stood up. "Sorry kids, I've said too much. It's past my bedtime now. I'll have the officer here to escort you back to your quarters."

"Would you like me to report this incident, Professor?" the officer asked.

Professor Wild looked at each of us as if trying to decide our fates. "No need, officer. I'll make sure they work it off. I want all of you here every Sunday for the next month. I have plenty for you to do."

Great. There went my one day of sleeping in.

CHAPTER 25

The boys were wrong. Our sea glass didn't protect us from detention. Our once treasured Sunday leisure time was now taken up by Professor Wild putting us to work in his lab. Chores ranged from cleaning up after living specimens to categorization of dead ones.

The boys were suspicious that Wild was the mole. I had some concerns, too, but I liked him, and he seemed to have taken an extra interest in me after the crow funeral. Most importantly, I had larger unanswered questions and Professor Wild liked to talk.

"He's fishing us for information, Akela. Be careful what you tell him," Warren whispered to me during a snack break.

"And be just as careful with what you believe. He may be feeding us fake news," Leo said.

"Well, he's telling us more than Sam is, that much I know is true," I said. "Leo, you had to hack the server to find out about The Osprey of Hope, right? Sam didn't tell you about that, and definitely didn't tell us that the spirits placed more than just our sea glass on the battlefield."

"You're right," Leo said. "There's definitely more to the prophecy than Sam wants us to know… I just don't know why," he said and snuck a quick glance at Wild's office over his shoulder. "Still, be careful, AK."

I ignored him.

"It was only an old photo. Nothing more, Akela." Wild said, when I asked him about the photo we saw of Sam in his office. I didn't believe him, but I didn't want to press the issue. I had other questions.

"You mentioned there are more clues and magical weapons as part of the prophecy?"

"Yes." Wild looked up from his work. "Sam and Dodd are both acquiring weapons in order to outpace the other and eventually win the war."

He spread his arms out and made two distinct bird calls. A crow landed on his right arm and a dove landed on the left.

"Or to achieve peace. There are two sides to this coin, and two sides to every war." Wild made another whistle. Each bird flew to the opposite arm, switching sides. Wild raised a bushy eyebrow. "Sometimes more."

Leo was cleaning up after the crows and shook his head at me. Warren was painting the opposite wall. He held a finger up to his lips. Cryptic comments like that from Wild weren't going to help with the boys' suspicions.

But I ignored them. We needed to find the Isle of Green, and I needed to keep Wild talking. I had faith the Isle of Green would be a resource. Possibly even a sanctuary if Dodd was able to launch his virus bomb. But first, we had to find the last two sea glass pieces. I had a hunch Wild could help.

"Right, and Dodd appears to want the sea glass to prevent Sam from forming the Isle of Green?" I asked while dusting off an ostrich that was taller than I was. "Are there any clues to help us find the other pieces?"

"Yes and no," Wild said. He slowly lowered his arms, letting the dove and crow fly off. "One would expect to find the glass and their holders on the continents that they are shaped after, right?"

"Yeah, that's logical. I mean, that's how all of us got here."

"It is, except for the 'no' part of my previous answer, which stems from a belief that one of the pieces is like you."

"Like me?" I asked.

"Yes, born to be in the sea, but permanently and always—a moving needle in the world's largest haystack: our ocean," Wild said. "Htmalo hid it there for a good reason."

"Because it'd be next to impossible for Dodd to find?" I asked.

"Yes, but also because it would be next to impossible for anybody to find. Anybody, except someone with the right talents, somebody born for such a mission." Professor Wild grinned when he said that, but it wasn't a happy smile. He said it almost like a challenge. I liked challenges.

We finally had a clue. One of the two remaining sea glass pieces was in the ocean. Great, but where would I start?

Professor Wild spoke softly. "Fortunately, we have you kids and two other sea glass holders on board. We are safe for now, but we must remain vigilant. Dodd will not stop until he gets what he wants." He turned to look back at his office. The door was open, and Hope was visible in her cage.

We finished up our chores in silence and started to head out the door. Wild called out to us, "Don't ever forget, young lady, that Sam is our benefactor and our leader, but to Sam you are a weapon, I am a weapon, and so are you two boys. Sam will do his best to protect all of us, but the mission is his primary goal." He paused. "And what good are weapons if they aren't brandished or expended?"

CHAPTER 26

Four more oil spills had occurred across the world's oceans, all just like our attack by Dodd's kraken. An undetectable beast appeared from the depths and tears the ships apart and then disappeared all over again. To make matters worse, we had further evidence that Dodd was getting closer to developing his virus bomb.

News of a kraken or a bomb would send the public into hysteria. But Sam and the SOS team managed to keep the media uproar down to a low scream versus a fever pitch. The goal was to allow the public to go about their daily lives without panic. Whatever Sam's methods were, they'd worked so far.

The operations team and Sea Swarm bots were deployed to clean up all four spills. The only bummer was that I wasn't utilized on any of those missions. Sam was determined that I needed more training before I got back into action.

"C'mon, Mik. I've been working hard. I survived Dodd once and I can do it again. Check out these guns." I flexed my new muscles. "I can do this!"

"No," Mik said bluntly. "Listen, kid. It's not just about being stronger, and it's not all about you. Dodd and Octavius are master tricksters, just like Chixtal. You gotta become more aware of yourself and your surroundings or you'll be fooled again." She tapped her forehead lightly. "You're too caught up in your head."

I wanted to plead my case to Sam, but he was nowhere to be found. Mik said he was at one of his factories scattered around the planet, attempting to ramp up Sea Swarm production, or the halls of Congress lobbying to combat climate change. That or looking for the sea glass piece in Antarctica. He could be anywhere, doing anything, but if I were him, I'd be chasing down Dodd, his bomb, and his destructive ghost of a sea monster. We needed to stop Dodd. That's what I wanted to do.

Unfortunately, I wasn't allowed to, so I researched. This time, I went after Sam, but I found nothing. He either blocked or deleted all references of himself. Outside of his S.S.-penned columns in Global Alert, I couldn't find a single sentence about Sam Shipman. It was like he didn't exist at all unless he was right in front of you.

He'd said there was a mole on board the SOS, yet it was Sam who I felt the least comfortable about. He was a mystery to me. I was grateful that he'd rescued me from my landlocked life in Bonita Fields, but I was starting to have those uneasy feelings again like I had back there. I was fighting in a war against mythical and powerful forces. I had new friends, new teammates, and I wasn't sure who I could entirely trust.

My stress level was running on overload, and apparently I wasn't the only person who noticed. Desmond, true to his word, offered to help me create a daily meditation.

We met in a converted storage closet that Desmond had transformed into a sanctuary of calm. It was the quietest room on the ship, with one soundproof window that let in a soft glow of natural light. The room was empty save for pillows on the floor and a small table with candles. Sitting on comfortable cushions with our legs crossed, Desmond and I faced each other.

"Akela, stress, fear, and anxiety will always be there at some point or another in everybody's life."

"What about Dodd nightmares, krakens and virus bombs? Will those be in everybody's life to deal with or just mine?" I was worked up and not quite hearing Desmond.

"What we can't control, like those things you just mentioned, we let go, Akela. What comes in, how we will deal with it, process it, and move forward is why we meditate," Desmond instructed. "Breathe. Make space for those feelings in your body. You are the ocean. That feeling of unease, it is only a wave passing through your boundless ocean."

We breathed together. As I took one deep breath, then another and then another, the feelings of anxiety slowly diluted.

"Better?" Desmond smiled.

"Yes, a little bit. I mean, the kraken is still out there." I tapped my chest. "It's not here with me now, but I'm still worried it will return."

"As Achcaan Chan, the great Tibetan master, said, 'The leaves will always fall'," Desmond said softly and clearly. "When we come to accept that every day will bring challenges, more leaves, and we do not fight it, we begin to let go."

"Let go of what?"

"Everything, Akela. When your mind is free of desire, you become free. Shall we practice?"

At first when I'd try to meditate, I'd take a few deep breaths, focusing on the inhale and exhale like I was taught, but soon my mind would be off like a butterfly, chasing thoughts of dolphins, my parents, missing operations, moles, prophecies, Dodd, the kraken, the virus, Kaipu, Alana, where Sam was, whether Warren liked me, if I liked Warren, why I was here, why were any of us here, Johan's man bun, what was for lunch that day, and on and on and on!

I told Desmond that I was failing at meditating.

"Do you return to your breath after losing your focus?" he asked.

I nodded.

"Well then, you are practicing meditation," he said with a smile. "My guru said, 'Meditation is just like your gym training. Every time you lose focus, you put the weight bar down. Every time you realize that your focus was lost and return to your breath, you pick the weight bar back up'," Desmond said. "You are working out and training your brain."

I liked that visualization. "At this rate, my brain is going to get really buff. There's a lot going in this head."

Desmond tapped his bald head. "In everyone's head, Akela. Remember, that voice in your head, that voice is not you. It's your thoughts, and you are not your thoughts. Do not try to eliminate the voice. You can't. Just watch, listen and let it go."

"If it's not my voice, whose is it? What if it's telling me good things, should I let go of those, too?"

Desmond smiled and his eyes sparkled. "That voice is an echo from long ago. One that moves through all of us. And yes, you can still nurture and grow your own positive voice. Develop a positive mantra and use it when you need it most. Can you think of one?"

I thought of one and I was going to use it. *You're a badass, Akela Spencer.*

More weeks had passed, with each day different, but I had started them all the same. Sitting. This morning I ended my meditation and sat silently for a few long moments. Loss was on my mind. Not just my loss, but Warren's and Leo's as well.

We all had sea glass. I had North America, Warren had Europe, and Leo, Asia. It couldn't have been a coincidence that we all had similar experiences of losing our parents. Sam and Desmond also had sea glass. If my theory was correct, both men were just like us. They'd lost somebody they loved.

The odds of me being able to ask Sam directly were slim to none at this point. He was rarely to be seen. How he was able to travel so far and so fast was a mystery to me.

I pinged Desmond on my watch and asked him to meet me in the cafeteria. When I arrived, he was already seated at a table with a coffee in one hand and my favorite smoothie in the other. In the background on the room's stage, a duet was working out the vocals on The Band's famous song, 'The Weight.' My stomach knotted up just thinking that I had to perform tomorrow.

When I returned to the moment, Desmond was waiting there, staring at me with his benevolent smile.

"Sorry, Des. I'm trying VERY hard to stay present, but it's not always easy," I said as I put both my hands up near my eyes, mimicking horse blinders. "I'm all ears and eyes."

"Akela, just being aware that your mind wanders is mindful. There is no sorry, there is only now. Here and now." He stroked his salt and pepper beard. "What would you like to talk about?"

I reached out and touched his hand. He reacted by placing his other hand over mine.

We sat there, silently, as I searched for the words, but for some reason I couldn't locate them, until I realized that Desmond and my mind were connecting. Without speaking, he began to tell me his story.

Des grew up in the Ivory Coast. His father was the leader of his village, whose existence was sustained and surrounded entirely by Mother Earth. He and his sister, Ayala, grew up never wanting anything more than the freedom to work, live, and play.

And, of course, to swim. Desmond and Ayala were twins, both of the ocean. Inseparable siblings, they would spend hours patrolling the coastline with the whales in the area. It was a peaceful existence until an oil company discovered a large reserve directly offshore from their tribe's land.

Desmond's grip on my hand tightened as he continued relaying his story to me. Our eyes were locked. I felt as if I was there with him, in his mind, in his memory. I knew this wasn't a happy story, and I braced myself. Desmond shook his head and told me to remain open. I did.

Desmond's family, his community, and other local villages, all banded together to stop the oil drilling. At first, they tried roadblocks, but the government and the oil drillers were all corrupt, and their concern for the local people was limited to just trying to keep news of their plight to a minimum. The government and oil company, a Dodd-owned corporation, displaced many, including Desmond's family.

In a move of desperation, Desmond and Ayala snuck out one evening into the water. Dodd's oil company had begun construction on the underwater foundation of a large oil rig. Massive boats with heavy equipment to drive steel pylons deep into the ocean floor were anchored two miles off the coast. Des and Ayala thought they could sabotage the operation by strategically placing large rocks into the drilling engine.

Des stopped for a moment and a tear fell from his eye. Ayala had moved in first. Both she and Desmond, only kids, had grossly miscalculated the lengths Dodd would go to protect his operation. Ayala was quickly snared into a practically invisible and unbreakable net. Trapped and unable to reach the surface, Ayala drowned as Desmond frantically tried everything to free his sister.

Eventually, the mechanism operating the net was released and Desmond was able to return his sister's body to the shore. On land, he carried her back to his parents and tribe, where she received a burial ceremony of a fallen warrior.

I was crying now, too, lost once again in the thoughts of sorrow. Then I saw Desmond smiling at me, and my heart filled with compassion.

"Ayala is with me every day. Her love and passion fill my heart and drive me forward." Desmond tapped his heart.

Coming out of our trance-like state, I realized that a small crowd of crew members had drawn around us while we had tele-communicated. It must have been a strange sight for them.

Ahimsa and Johan were in the crowd watching us, as well as Warren. Ahimsa came and put her hand on both of our shoulders. She had tears in her eyes.

"What'd you say to each other?" Johan asked before Ahimsa smacked his wrist and gave him a look to stop.

I glanced back to find Warren, but he was gone. I turned to Desmond. "You want to go find Mik and practice not getting our butts kicked?" I asked.

"Yes!" he roared with a laugh. "But not too much. Remember, you're performing tonight, too."

Right, my performance. Ugh.

Chapter 27

While I'd secretly hoped for a very fleeting painless sickness to leave me or the crew unable to attend tonight's Sunday dinner and talent show, sadly I was out of luck. I'd have preferred to go a few rounds with Mik kicking my butt instead of performing.

Also, I wanted more time to think. After hearing Desmond's story, I was sure that Dodd had a hand in all our past losses. I mean, Desmond's was clear as day. The logging operation in Poland that killed Warren's parents had a high probability of being a Dodd-owned company. My best guess was the loss of Leo's family was somehow not an accident at all either.

Most importantly, I needed to find out exactly how and when my parents had died.

I walked back to my room. I had a few hours before my performance to get prepared and I really needed to shower. When I turned the corner to my hallway, there sitting on the floor outside my door, was Warren.

"Hey, AK," he said without getting up. "Good workout?"

"Mik worked me over again. I'm getting better, though." I smiled, waiting for Warren to say something, but he just sat there. Finally, in a flash of movement, he sprung to his feet. He put his head toward his armpit and pulled his face back.

"Sorry, if I stink. I was running," Warren said and took a step back.

"I think we cancel each other's stenches out." I took a step forward. We both had abnormally powerful noses.

"Hey, um, I know how nervous I was before performing, and I wanted to tell you not to be. Nervous that is," Warren said as he inspected his shoes before bringing his eyes up to mine. "You'll do great."

"Thanks, I appreciate it." I had a feeling he'd come here for other reasons.

I dropped my gym bag to the ground and stalled for a moment as I tried to mentally connect with him. I could sense him there, but no attempt from his end to connect back. "You know, I was thinking about how you said you lost your ability to mentally communicate, you know, connect with the wolves."

"Yeah. And?" Warren kicked at an invisible ball.

"Well, I was thinking that I could work with you on it. Desmond has been working with me on mindfulness. I never knew I could train my brain. Maybe we can retrain yours? If you wanted to?"

"That'd be cool. When do you want to practice?" Warren replied quickly.

I checked my watch. "How about now?"

"Now? Don't you need to practice for tonight?" Warren asked.

"Just a little. And this is more important anyway. Sit." I grabbed his hands, and we sat right there in the hallway.

"Right here? Why not in there?" Warren tapped on my bedroom door.

"It's not appropriate to have a boy in my room, let alone a wolf boy," I said. "Besides, Desmond says to 'start from where you are'. So here we are, let's do it."

"How does this work? I don't remember how I used to make it happen. It just happened, you know," Warren said and nervously shifted his weight from side to side.

"It's in there, Warren. I can sense it. I bet the wolves can sense it, too. We need to work on a way to reopen that door."

"I saw you and Des holding hands, and here we are holding hands," Warren said.

I realized I'd forgotten to let go, but I didn't want to. I had never held a boy's hand before. Desmond didn't count, as he was old enough to be my uncle or father and that's how I thought of him. Holding Warren's hands, though, was different. I felt a buzz of excitement.

"Sorry, we don't have to hold hands. Although, it may help kick-start things," I said.

"I'm good with it if you are?"

I smiled.

"Let's practice," Warren said.

We sat there for another thirty minutes, holding hands, sometimes talking, other times silently staring or with our eyes closed. Warren said he could faintly sense my presence telepathically. It was a start.

I checked my watch again. "Now I have to go." Warren popped up and helped me to my feet. "I'll see you at the performance?"

"Of course. What are you doing?" Warren asked.

"You'll see."

Warren smiled and sped off down the hall.

I closed the door and leaned up against it.

That evening I stood in front of all the crew and teammates. Desmond was the easiest to pick out of the crowd, and not just because of his height; he just had a presence about him that drew people in. Next to him was Mik and the boys. Ahimsa, Ericka, and Johan were seated at a different table further from the stage. I scanned the room, but couldn't locate Sam. Big surprise.

I was the first performer of many and was happy to get mine out of the way early. I asked Leo to help with the audio-visual component of my three-minute show.

Leo nodded that it was time to start. The lights went out, along with the projection of the solar system high above. In its place was a three-dimensional projection of the front page of my notebook floating over my head. The beginning notes of Van Halen's classic rock song 'Jump' started to play as my virtual notebook opened to show the first page of my project. "'Welcome Aboard' by Akela Spencer."

During a free period at school, I'd used the time to draw pencil sketches of my dive from the balcony and swim with the pod. I drew hundreds of single pages, took photos of them all and, with Leo's help, created a stop-motion movie of my dive, re-introduction to the pod, and meeting Desmond and Johan. As the video started, I watched the crowd to see their reactions. Everybody was super into the show, except three who were watching me: Warren, Professor Wild and Johan.

In a dramatic twist, in one segment, my drawings showed the pod quickly molding together and transforming into the shape of the kraken swimming beneath me, before returning to the shapes of individual dolphins again. The crowd gasped, then applauded. I could tell from Mik's expression that she wasn't pleased.

When my video stopped, silence momentarily filled the room. My heart felt like it was creeping up into my throat when suddenly the crew erupted in applause. By the end of the night, my cheeks were sore from smiling.

CHAPTER 28

Later that evening, I sat on my deck and turned off the balcony lights. I was relieved my performance was over and wanted to meditate.

It was a cloudy night with no moon or stars to add any light. Desmond had worked with me on my fear of the darkness and had suggested exposing myself to it more, so I turned off the deck lights.

I breathed deeply, keeping my eyes open. My senses slowly became more alert. The wind brushed my face, and I could hear the ocean murmuring below an endless song of welcome, menace, and mystery. The sea had played a key part in taking my parents lives and was now playing an instrumental role in my life, hopefully with a better ending.

Closing my eyes, I continued breathing deeper and slower until I found myself swimming alone. There was nothing but light above and the infinite ocean around and below me. I was an astronaut floating in deep space, except there were no planets or stars, only water. The lack of objects for points of reference was disorienting. Still, I kept swimming straight down, the light receding with every stroke. I could hear Dodd's voice calling my name and my parents' names as well. I wanted to stop, but my arms disobeyed my brain. I turned to swim back to the surface, but I couldn't tell up from down anymore. Everything was fully black.

Why couldn't I find the surface? Why was Dodd calling my family? A rush of movement and water flew past me, spinning me around. Something was in the water with me, something huge. I needed to swim back to the surface, back to the light, but there was none!

I opened my eyes to pitch black night. Awakening into more darkness sent me into a panic.

"Lights, deck lights!" I yelled and was instantly able to see again.

I was on my deck, in my chair and all alone. I was hyperventilating and put my head between my knees to catch my breath. Again, Desmond's teachings helped me regain control.

Inside, I grabbed my iPad. The news story of the death of Desmond's sister was easy to locate because it was well publicized at the time of the incident. Dartivion's offshore oil drilling operation was clearly involved. Warren's family history took more research, but I'd zeroed in on a logging accident in Poland that killed two park rangers. The timber company owned by Dodd was the one clearing the forest. Bullseye.

Narrowing down the year of Leo's family accident, I landed on the theory that Leo had lost his mom and Aunt Gadgis in a super typhoon in Japan. A freak result of the storm. That'd be hard to peg on any specific companies owned by Dodd, but the fact that it had happened so far out of season, most meteorologists blamed the event on global warming. I was gonna chalk that one up to Dodd again.

Finding out about the specifics of my parents' incident was proving to be much tougher. Mik had said it was a Japanese whaling vessel that capsized our boat. Dodd owned whaling fleets in Japan, so I had to assume it was one of his whaling boats that took out my folks. At the time, he probably thought he got me, too. It was a leap to pin all the deaths on Dodd, but I couldn't help but feel like it was true.

This search into Dodd's role in so many deaths of friends and loved ones was starting to bum me out.

I pulled out my phone and group-texted Warren and Leo.

"Can't sleep."

"Me neither," Leo replied.

"Ditto," Warren agreed.

My iPad screen started ringing. Leo set up a three-way FaceTime meeting.

"Sup guys," I said.

"Yo," Warren said as he mowed a hand through his wild mass of hair.

"Evening," Leo said.

I told the boys what I'd been able to dig up on Dodd's involvement in all our loss.

"Wow, that's super messed up," Warren said and suddenly punched the wall next to him. "We have to stop him."

"Hey! You'll need those hands to fight," I said.

Warren shook his hand in the air as if to wave off the pain. "I'm fine," he said, "just angry."

"Me, too," Leo said while furiously typing on his laptop.

"What are you up to, Leo?" I asked.

"Hacking something, I'm sure," Warren said.

Leo stared at the screen, shifting his eyes from Warren to me and back to his computer.

"You're right. I'm hacking—actually, is it technically hacking if you just figured out somebody's password?" Leo asked in a whisper.

"That's the definition of hacking, Leo. You know that," I said. "Whose password did you figure out?"

"Professor Wild's. I set up an algorithm that delivered every combination of the words Wild, Hope, and bird names. I also used his birthday," Leo said with a smile.

"Very cool," I said.

"Thanks. Everybody uses their birthday, so that part was easy," Leo said.

"Crap, I gotta change my password now," Warren shook his head.

"So, it appears Professor Wild's been accessing the prophecy database," Leo said quickly. "I'm in it now."

"What's in it?" I asked.

"Let me share my screen," Leo said, and in a second we were watching Leo navigate through password protected folders. There was one named 'Portals', another titled 'Objects', and a third called, 'Fountain'.

"What do you think Fountain, Portals or Objects mean?" Warren asked.

"I can't get into any of them. Believe me, I've tried," Leo said.

Finally, he stopped on a folder titled, 'Sea Glass.' In each folder, there was a sub folder named after each continent.

"All these folders are locked, and I can't access them, even with Wild's password. All of them except one." Leo clicked on the folder titled, 'Lost to the Ocean/Australia.' This was the sea glass Wild had told me about, the one Htmalo hid in the ocean. The file opened to a photograph of words carved onto a stone tablet.

"Whoa, I've never seen this before," Leo said.

"You able to make anything out, AK?" Warren asked.

I scanned each word and tried saying them out loud.

"No," I said, as I kept trying to pronounce the words. "I can't make anything out, other than there are a few words that are repeated a lot."

"Good eye, Akela," Leo said as he typed away. "This is the top word, AK.: 'Mathias'. Does that name mean anything to you?"

I wrote the word down in my journal. "I'm sorry guys; I don't know what any of this means. I'll sleep on it, maybe it'll make more sense in the morning," I said while stifling a yawn.

"Yeah, I'm hitting the wall here, too," Warren said with a laugh. "Get it, hitting the wall?"

Leo and I both sighed.

"I was hoping there'd be more to go on. I'm hacked out for the night. Get it Warren, hacked out." Leo shook his head and signed off.

"Well, I'm no help with computers or languages other than my own. I'd ask the wolves if I could, but I can't, so I'm going to sl—"

"Wait, what did you say?" I asked.

"I was going to say that I'm going to sleep." Warren rubbed his eyes.

"No, before that, you said you'd ask the wolves." I paused and closed my eyes. Why hadn't I thought of it earlier?

"Wild had said, 'somebody born to it'. I can ask the pod." I sat up straight and suddenly felt wide awake. "If I was born for any reason, it had to be this, right?"

"I hope you're right. Just be careful, AK," Warren said.

"I will. Night,"

Tomorrow, I'd start my search for the needle in the world's largest haystack.

CHAPTER 29

The next morning, I woke up with the sunrise and walked out to my ocean deck. The sun crested above the horizon as if it were released from an underwater anchor.

Grabbing a smoothie from my mini fridge, I threw on my favorite bathing suit, shorts, and sandals, and then beelined down to the Aqua Hold. The whole way, I repeated my new mantra in my head. *You're a badass, Akela Spencer.*

As usual, Johan was up before me attending to the scuba gear, his hair, and taking water samples.

Desmond and Johan were working on my scuba technique to improve my breathing as well as my recognition of species and their patterns. Like Mik said, I needed to be more aware in and out of the water so that I wouldn't get tricked by Dodd again.

"Well, well, well, not used to seeing you so chipper this bright and early, AK." Johan looked up from his gear.

"Early bird gets the…" I started to say, but remembered that Kara used to call me 'worm'. Akela, the bookworm. *Well, look at me now.* Akela the bookworm was about to go swimming with her dolphin friends.

"The badass gets the worm," I said.

"What?" Johan turned around with a shocked expression.

"Sorry, did I say that out loud? I meant Akela gets the worm." Yikes. That wasn't too awkward.

"Right, of course you did." Johan shook it off. "So, are you going to practice your scuba today or just swimming? Today would be a great day to take the Zodiac to that diving spot I've been telling you about."

"Don't we need Mik's permission to leave the SOS?"

Johan dramatically tossed his long blond hair back and pulled a mask over his eyes. "Not today. She's off the boat, Antarctica I think with Sam, do you know?"

Antarctica? How'd she and Sam travel so fast? I shook my head.

"Figures. Anyhow, with Mik gone, I can make the call as to whether we leave the SOS." Johan tightened his mask.

I didn't know about that and didn't care. Today I was on a mission, and I didn't want to waste time fiddling with my scuba gear. I didn't want Johan around either. "No, I'd rather stay in the hold today, with the pod if that's cool. Also, no scuba gear."

Johan smirked in disagreement and fell backwards into the water. He quickly resurfaced.

"Can you at least wear the mask I left out? It's new gear, and I need you to test it out." He smiled wide.

"Fine." I grabbed the mask, kicked off my sandals and quickly followed him in.

I watched Johan swim off toward the kelp forest before I turned the other direction in search of the pod. The Aqua Hold area was enormous and ever-changing. Except for the kelp and coral attached to the ship, the sea life came and went as it pleased. The sea forest and coral served as an attraction for some of the smaller sea life to gather in the research area. The presence of larger mammals, dolphins, whales, otters, and other creatures depended on where the SOS was in the ocean.

Gadgis and Leo had created a sophisticated sensor system that would alert the staff of any potentially dangerous or abnormal creatures entering the SOS space. While the ocean was enormous, the thought of the kraken making another appearance was always nearby. I looked at that fear from a distance and put it aside for now.

The dolphin pod didn't fit into either category of dangerous or abnormal. They were unique in the sense that they never traveled far from the SOS. At least that was what I'd learned in my swims with Dolphin Jon, Dolphin Ana, and the gang. They'd been connected to Sam and his crew as far back as Grandpa Dolphin could remember, which was very far back.

Maybe they knew something that could help the SOS in its battle against Dodd. It's possible that they've known something all along, but up until now, they'd nobody to communicate that knowledge to. That is, until Dolphin Girl came along.

My ability to communicate with the dolphins had already created a whole new curriculum aboard the SOS. The pod told me many stories about how environmental changes were impacting their lives and I realized that others on the SOS needed to hear their experiences. The partially submerged bubble classroom was where we started working more closely with the dolphins in learning about the oceans and Earth's problems from their perspective.

We'd have class and, if the timing worked out, as dolphins didn't have watches, one from the pod would come in for a chat. Of course, I'd translate for the class. Yes, Dolphin Girl to the rescue, yet again.

Sometimes Desmond would join our class sessions and do some translation for a passing whale, but it was apparent that while his underwater abilities were unparalleled, his language skills were very limited compared to mine. So, I was kind of a big deal to the researchers on board. Just saying.

Regaining my focus from my self-congratulations, I swam in and around the perimeter of the area in search of the pod. I saw rooster fish, dorado, a thresher shark, a ton of tropical fish, but no dolphins. After about five minutes of swimming, I came up for air. Stay present, Akela. I submerged again and focused my thoughts on calling the dolphins into the SOS.

I closed my eyes and let myself feel the weightlessness of the water, the sea current caressing and moving around me. Focus, listen, wait, I told myself. I'd open my eyes every few seconds, but each subsequent time I found I was able to close them longer and trust in the ocean around me. More importantly, to trust in myself.

After what I thought must have been at least a few minutes, I opened my eyes. There in front me, nose to nose, was little Rhino.

"Well, hello, sleepy," Rhino squeaked just as Jon poked me in the side of my belly and startled me out of my staring contest with Rhino.

"Hello, my friends!"

"Catch me if you can," Rhino said and quickly dove beneath the water. I followed in pursuit as Rhino led the pod, weaving in and out of the kelp forest. It was exhilarating feeling my body react in ways that I didn't know it could move.

Jon trailed closely behind me, occasionally pushing my feet with his nose to encourage me to go faster. Faster and faster we went, weaving a dizzying trail.

"Hey, I need to talk to Grandpa," I quickly said between breaths.

Jon sped up and was now by my side.

"I thought maybe he could help me and the SOS," I said. *"What does the pod know about Jarvis Dodd?"* I slowed my pace as I needed information more than I needed more exercise. Rhino was well ahead and turned to come join us.

"Ha, slow poke." Rhino laughed and sped off while Jon and I slowly glided up to the surface. On the way up, Jon let out a large squealing whistle.

Grandpa appeared from the kelp bed and slowly made his way toward the two of us.

"Yes?" Grandpa said sternly.

"Akela has some questions for you, if that's okay?" Jon asked.

Grandpa looked disapprovingly at Jon. *"Humans never cared to ask us any questions before they started ruining our home."*

"Grandpa, I'm sorry," I replied. *"I can't explain or justify what we've done to the ocean. All I can say is that I'm trying to help fix that."* I smiled, hoping it'd help.

Grandpa stared at me.

"*Fine. Let's swim.*" Grandpa quickly set off toward the side of the ship without waiting for either of us. Jon nodded and we started to swim after him.

We passed underneath the far perimeter and entered the open ocean waters. I knew I was supposed to ask permission or at least let somebody know that I was technically off ship. Johan said we had approval to leave today, but I assumed that was with him watching me. Oh well, we shouldn't be too long. I hoped.

We swam fast for another few minutes until the ship's cloaking system kicked in and it disappeared. My mind couldn't help but think about the risks of being this exposed in the open ocean. The rest of the pod appeared in the distance, circling us for security, and much of my nervousness calmed. Still, I was on guard.

"*I feel more comfortable talking out here,*" Grandpa finally said.

"*You know the SOS is your friend, right?*" I asked.

"*I know that. I know many other things as well. But it's what I don't know that gives me pause.*"

"*Do you know about Jarvis Dodd?*" I asked.

Grandpa looked hard at me and then Jon before back at me. "*I know he is the enemy, or at least one of their leaders. I know his ships fish with large nets, killing not only fish, but other mammals… baby mammals,*" Grandpa said through gritted teeth. "*I know his inland companies spill pollutants into fresh and salt waters, killing the fish and disturbing our already sensitive ecosystem. I know that this is probably only a small percentage of the destructive behavior that is done at his behest. I believe these are things you know as well and probably far more deeply than me, Akela.*"

"*You're correct, Grandpa. But do you know about him? Where he came from? Anything that might help me, and the SOS find him and fight him? Anything?*"

Grandpa thought for a while. "*Akela, I'm forty-five years old. That's a long life for a dolphin. I have heard Dodd's name since I was a baby that was afraid to swim too far away from the safety of my mother.*"

"*Hmm, that's a long time ago. Whatever Dodd was doing, word traveled fast, on land and sea about his evil ways,*" I said.

"*Yes, that could be true. And that Dodd is much older than you believe.*"

"Well, I've searched far and wide on the Internet looking for any clues to that effect."

"I don't like the sound of this Internet thing," Grandpa said.

"Nets in general aren't good," Jon agreed.

I nodded and realized that I was taking this conversation way off course. *"You were saying that Dodd could be much older than his listed age?"*

"There is one way to find out," Grandpa finally said.

We waited for Grandpa to continue. He was taking his time as if debating whether to tell us something. Finally, he spoke. *"You should visit Mathias."*

Mathias, that was the name from the file Leo hacked.

"Who is Mathias?"

Jon spoke up. *"Mathias is a Greenland shark that is rumored to be close to five hundred years old."*

Grandpa swam up so close to me that his nose was almost touching mine. *"Mathias is more than just old. It is said that he is an oracle. One who knows all."* Grandpa started swimming and circled me while he talked. *"There is an endless geyser located on the ocean floor, protected, and hidden from sight. Mathias is believed to reside there. If any ocean creature would know more about Jarvis Dodd, it would be Mathias. Go to Greenland and ask for him."*

Finally, I had a clue toward finding the sixth sea glass piece and finding the truth about Dodd. My mission was clear. I had to go to Greenland and find Mathias somehow.

"I've told you all you need to know. Go, Akela," Grandpa said sternly.

I looked at my watch. It had been almost thirty minutes, and I wasn't wearing any communication device. Johan would be looking for me, and I had to get back to the SOS.

My excitement over my new lead into the mystery of Jarvis Dodd and the lost piece of sea glass was bubbling over to the point that I found myself running through the corridors of the SOS in search of the boys. I immediately texted them. They were in the Mountain Biodome.

I weaved my way around my crewmates as I sprinted toward the dome. Pausing briefly at the entrance to the Mountain Biodome, I steadied my breathing so I could scan my eyes. The glass door slid open and I jogged in.

The Mountain Biodome was the largest on the ship behind the Ocean Biodome. The highest peak was only four hundred feet, but the quick rise of the mountains still had a dramatic effect. A freshwater river flowed between the tallest and second tallest peak. The river weaved down into a grass valley and then out into the prairie plains of the adjacent dome.

Jogging in the direction of the valleys, I figured I'd start at the lowest point before climbing. A small flock of sheep and a few deer passed by as I made my way through the increasingly tall grass. Eventually, I passed through a gateway of large boulders which served as the entrance to the valley floor. The view was breathtaking. I paused momentarily to take it in when I noticed quick movements from the corner of my eye. I'd been so caught up in my head over Mathias and going to Greenland, that I'd let my guard down.

I sniffed the air and then heard the rustling of the grass to my left and above me. Mountain lion. Great. I was going to be the first dolphin in the history of the planet to get eaten by a cat.

I stayed statue-still, judging how far the river was from my current position. If I could get in it, I'd be safe. But could I outrun a mountain lion?

The lion jumped down. It was the size of a small bear. It stood there, crouched, its lean muscles rippling and ready to explode. I took a small step backwards and the lion roared, its mouth opening wide enough to easily hold my neck with her two-inch-long fangs. Mik's practical motto of fighting engagement came to. 'Fight or run, don't hesitate'.

I thought about fighting, but I'd no choice except to run. But first, I screamed as loud as I could, "HELP!"

My scream startled the big cat and gave me a head start toward the safety of the water. As I ran, I focused on connecting with the lion and Warren at the same time. The cat's mind was in predator mode, so I couldn't break through; she was too far gone.

The lion was only a few feet behind and the river was still out of reach. I was running for my life, but not fast enough to save it. I thought to turn and fight when, from the other direction, a blur of fur and human skin flew by, followed by a loud impact of flesh colliding, and a cry of pain. I didn't stop running or turn to look. Instead, I dove into the river and went deep just in case the cat followed me in.

When I came up, I could see that the wolf pack of the Biodome, led by Warren, had come to my rescue.

Warren offered me a hand as I got back to the river's edge.

"Thank you," I said as he lifted me out of the water. "Where's the lion?"

"She went back to her cubs. You ran past her den, Akela. She was only protecting her family. Are you okay?" Warren asked.

"I'm fine, thanks to you." I smiled and gave him a big wet hug.

"I heard you, Akela. I heard your scream, but I also heard you calling before that, in my head. It wasn't clear, but I knew you needed help. So did the pack," Warren said. He walked over to the wolves. The lead wolf slowly lowered its head to Warren. Warren did the same, and the pack turned and trotted off. "I've been practicing. I'm still not all the way there, but I could hear you today, Akela. The door is opening."

CHAPTER 30

Later, we all sat down in the Mountain observation room. Leo, who'd been practicing his drone skills by filming Warren and the pack, pulled up the video incident on the big screen. I watched in amazement as Warren, running with the wolves, had come flying across the valley floor to intercept the mountain lion right before she pounced. The mountain lion turned and fled back behind the boulders to her home.

"What made you come running all this way in your bathing suit anyhow?" Leo asked as he sat down next to me and handed me a hot cup of tea.

I took a sip and started to tell them about Mathias.

We went for lunch on the promenade and took our pizza underneath the big eucalyptus tree.

"Thanks again for saving me back there," I said.

"You'd do the same for me, Akela. Someday, you might have to," Warren said. "You know, watching that video, your running form could use a few pointers. I could speed you up in a lesson or two."

We smiled at each other.

"Oh, man." Leo sighed. "Guys, can we get back to Mathias?"

"Right." I reiterated to them what Grandpa had told me about Mathias.

"Whoa. Dodd may be way, way old." Warren gasped.

"Way old is right," I said.

"Guys, if Mathias is the key to finding the sea glass lost to the ocean," Leo said and checked his watch. "We have to get to Greenland, and at the present, we're thousands of miles away."

"That's a long swim. Maybe we can ask Mik to fly us? She and Sam seem to be able to get anywhere on the planet ridiculously fast." I looked around to the boys to see if that was a reasonable option.

Warren stood up and stretched. "Sam and Mik might be gone for another few days. Maybe we borrow one of the planes?"

"You know how to fly a plane?" I asked.

"Not me, Leo. He can fly a drone better than anybody. I can't imagine it's too much different, right Leo?" Warren looked at his pal.

Before Leo could answer a voice boomed from behind the tree and startled us all. "Don't be silly, kids."

Professor Wild walked past the eucalyptus tree. One of his hands brushed across the bark of the tree, while on the other hand a female robin sat peacefully.

"The robin is a fascinating bird. As with almost all of nature's creatures, the males have the vibrant plumage and the females more subdued." Wild stroked the bird's head.

I checked my matted down wet hair versus Warren's wild mane. Yup, humans, too.

Wild went on, "Yet the better half of our species is always programmed to do the majority of the hunting, gathering and caretaking."

We sat looking up to him as he walked to the dead center of our circle as if he were giving a class lecture.

"I heard your conversation, kids. I can help. Follow me."

Professor Wild walked away without turning back. We followed him through the park. The robin left his hand as we exited. He led us through the main corridors and eventually into an area of the ship I'd never been to before. A gated access point stopped our progress.

"No funny business, Leo," Wild said as he scanned his eyes and the door opened.

Leo mouthed the word 'mole' to me as we followed Wild through the door, but I couldn't see Wild being a spy for Dodd.

"Won't the security system register that we all came through with you?" Leo asked.

"Yes. I'll deal with Sam about it, but I think he'd support this move in the context of our larger battles."

"And so do I." Johan bolted through the open door with us.

"Johan. What are you doing here?" I asked before noticing that he was wearing a full thermal wetsuit and carrying his scuba gear.

"I'm going with you, Akela," he said in a serious tone.

Was Johan in the park with us? And how had he geared up so quickly? I dismissed the thoughts, as I was happy to see him. If I was going somewhere, I could use an operations teammate who was comfortable in the water to join me on my trip.

"Uh, where exactly are we going? I said, glancing around the windowless room.

Professor Wild straightened himself out. "Ahem, you are going to Greenland."

Now it was Leo's turn to ask the obvious questions. He bit his lip. "Professor Wild, I don't mean to be rude, but I don't understand how Akela is going to go from this room all the way to Greenland."

Wild quickly answered. "Not from this room, Leo. Obviously not."

We all nodded, but clearly still not understanding.

"You will be traveling through the Portal Way," Wild said.

"Oh, the Portal Way," I said with a micro-shrug. Warren and Leo responded with raised eyebrows. What the heck was Wild talking about?

"Sam hasn't told you about the Portal Way yet?" Wild asked. "I find that very surprising."

"I don't find it surprising at all," I said. It was par for the course for Sam not to tell us what was going on.

Leo leaned over to me and whispered, "Guys, one of the files we saw last night was labeled 'Portals'."

Professor Wild walked to the wall and put his index finger against it. Slowly, he started writing with his finger while quietly talking, no, singing to himself. It was too low for the others to hear, but I could. He was using an ancient language I couldn't pinpoint, yet it sounded familiar.

He then stood back and reached into a small pouch tied to his pocket. He grabbed a handful and tossed what I believed to be gold speckled dust against the wall. The dust vanished, and a moment later, the wall transformed from a solid object to a wavy, translucent moving image right before our eyes.

We all stared on in stunned silence.

"That's how Dodd escaped from you, isn't it?" Leo said as he connected the dots faster than the rest of us could.

Wild nodded and spoke. "Htmalo and Chixtal, the warring spirits from the prophecy, created pathways and portals for their warriors to use throughout the world. Some of these portals are fixed, and others we've learned to recreate by reciting words from the ancient transcript."

"And with gold dust," I said while staring at the wall.

"Yes, gold, Akela. The prophecy and treasure of the ancient cultures allow us to travel to any destination on our planet," Wild finished.

"Whoa," Warren said. "How does it work?"

"How does any magic work?" Wild replied with his own question. Nobody answered.

"Exactly. The magic disappears when you know the trick," Wild said.

"So, that's how Sam moves around so quickly," I said.

"Yes, it's one way, Akela," Wild continued. "If we add coordinates to the ancient words, the portal will take you to the frigid waters of Greenland, in search of Mathias, the Shark."

"Is it true that Mathias is almost five hundred years old?" Warren asked.

"The five-hundred-year age number is just an estimate for all Greenland sharks. Mathias and his species are the longest known living multi-cell organisms on our planet," Leo said.

Professor Wild nodded to Leo. "Right as always, young man." He then turned to Johan and me.

"The piece of sea glass, the one lost to the boundless ocean, Akela. If the dolphins are correct, Mathias will know. Mathias will know many things." Wild choked up and wiped a tear from his eye.

"I'm sorry, kids. It's just that we could've spent lifetimes searching the ocean for the sea glass and never come close to finding it. That is until now. This could be a pivotal point in the battle!" Wild said excitedly. He stared at the portal.

I shuffled my feet nervously and looked to the boys for reassurance, but they were fidgeting more than I was. I inhaled slowly through my nose and exhaled. *Stay calm, Akela.*

"So, I'm broadly interpreting some loosely written rules by allowing this mission," Wild spoke to the wall. "But sometimes you must make executive decisions, even when the chief executive isn't around. If Sam was here, he'd most definitely approve. Fortune favors the bold, right?" Wild looked right at me.

"Right?" I said, but I did not feel very confident or bold with Wild's decision.

"He'd also be very upset if we didn't take the opportunity to find Mathias right away," Johan added.

"There is no 'we', Johan. It's too dangerous for you to go," Wild said.

"Wait, so it's not too dangerous for me, but it's too dangerous for Johan?" I asked. "I could use some company."

Now I was starting to get worried. Warren was standing next to me. I reached down and squeezed his hand. He squeezed it back.

"I'll go," Warren said in a voice that didn't match the bravery of his idea.

We stole a look at each other from the corner of our eyes. It wasn't a good idea at all. He knew it, I knew it, we all knew it. But still, I felt my heart beat a little faster. I squeezed his hand harder.

"No, you won't," Wild and I said at the same time.

Wild walked over and stood directly in front of me. "It's just that you, Akela, are of the sea. I believe getting back home will come naturally for you," Wild said while running his hand through his unkempt, black beard.

"What's so hard about that?" Leo asked.

"On land, it's a challenge, but possible, but underneath the water, it's almost…" Wild stopped. "It won't be a problem for Akela. Take this." Wild handed me a neoprene zipper bag.

"Gold dust?" I asked.

"Yes. Even in water. When you are at the re-entry point, just pull some out. You'll be fine, Akela," Wild said, putting his hand on my shoulder. He looked me in the eye. There was concern and care in his gaze. "You remember the words I said to open the portal?"

"I do," I answered.

Johan walked toward the melting wall and reached out to the portal. "How do we go in?"

Wild evaluated Johan for another long moment. "Fine. If you insist on going, don't leave Akela's side. You won't get back otherwise." Wild's voice rose as he walked closer to the portal entrance.

"You are landing directly in the water. Johan, you'll have a breathing apparatus in place, and Akela, you must do whatever it is you do that allows you to breathe underwater," Wild said.

"For the record, I don't have to do anything." I put my hands on my hips. "It's just who I am."

Johan gave me a look and suppressed a laugh. There was something new in his expression. He grabbed a wetsuit off the floor and tossed it to me. "Put this on. You'll need it in Greenland."

We stood motionless in front of the portal wall wearing our thermal suits. Johan put his mouthpiece in.

"Be safe guys," Warren said, looking directly at me. I could only muster a short nod. I was so nervous.

"Remember," Wild said in the most serious tone I'd heard him use since first attending his lecture, "to re-enter the portal, you must not only be at the right longitudinal coordinates, but also at the proper depth, since you are portaling to an underwater destination."

Wild said the coordinates out loud and Johan and I repeated them. Johan repeated them a second and third time.

"Ready," I said to Johan.

A loud beep came from Wild's watch.

"Well, hello, Sam," Wild said into his wrist piece.

Sam's voice came through. "Track, sorry to skip the formalities, but I got an alert that you are in the Portal Room?"

Wild looked quickly back and forth and put up his hand to gesture that we should wait.

"Yes, Sam, we are in the Portal Room. Akela has uncovered a clue to the sixth sea glass piece! We were just about to call you for authorization to use the portal," Wild said with a smile, still holding a hand up for us to wait.

Suddenly, Johan grabbed my hand and yanked me through the moving wall with him.

"Wait!" Wild yelled.

As we passed through, I could faintly hear Sam's voice. "I know what you're thinking, but everybody must stay there. Don't use the portal. It's not safe!"

It's not safe? I tried to think, but I was caught up in the oddest sensation of incredible speed, yet without moving. I couldn't really tell if my eyes were open or closed, as it was pitch black. At first, fear gripped me, but then the darkness took on an oddly familiar quality, like I'd been there before. I had heard people describe out of body experiences before, and I hoped this was as close to having one that I might ever get.

Then, in a flash, we were in water. Warm water, oddly enough. And what was that smell?

CHAPTER 31

The reek of chlorine engulfed my nostrils and my eyes instantly stung. Pool water. I closed my eyes tight again, trying to flush out the burning sensation. I was about to ask Johan how he was doing when I realized that I was no longer holding his hand.

"Johan!" I called out and opened my eyes. There was nothing but blue water and the borders of cement. Maybe Johan didn't make it through the portal with me. "Johan?" I asked again, starting to worry.

There was only sky above me, but below was only cement, not ocean. Slowly I stroked toward the surface. As I neared the top, I could see three silhouettes standing over the ledge. One of them had the exact stature of Johan. I paused a few feet beneath the water line. Was Johan a hostage already?

"Come up already, Akela," I finally heard Johan's voice say, but something was different.

I poked my eyes barely above the water and saw Johan standing with two men in black. My heart sank. Johan wasn't being restrained. More than that, it looked like he may be in charge. Sam's words came back to me, 'It's not safe'.

"Welcome to the other side. There's nowhere to run or swim to now, Dolphin Girl," Johan said in a mocking tone. "You're in a fish tank where you really belong."

I tried not to show any reaction, but it hurt to feel betrayed. More than that, I was angry, and not just for me, but for the entire SOS. Ahimsa, especially. When Mik found out about this, she'd kick the living blond out of this pretty boy's hair.

Taking in my surroundings, this wasn't a big ship, maybe more like a luxury yacht in size, but the vessel was armed to the teeth. The Dartivion Corporation logo flew high above the deck like a pirate's flag.

I took a deep breath. "So, you are one of Dodd's men after all. I should've figured; you always seemed a little under qualified. How'd you infiltrate the SOS?" I figured I'd at least try to get some useful information if I could.

"Wow, you are dumb as you are gullible to think I'd tell you anything. Anything other than you shouldn't have worn that mask I gave you," Johan said while one of the men in black grabbed a long pole with a sharp hook on it to pull me out of the pool. His silhouette looked like that of the Grim Reaper.

That mask must have tracked me and the pod leaving the SOS. Johan knew I was up to something and followed me. How could I have been so careless? It didn't matter now, I was trapped. I took the mask off and flung it at the men, catching one of the goons flush on the nose.

"Get out of the pool, now. Or I'll have my boys fish you out. Ha, get it? Fish you out?" Johan laughed a super irritating laugh. He was starting to remind me of my cousin.

My blood was boiling at a level I hadn't experienced since Kara and her buddies tossed my books into the school pool. Screw it. Ducking back underwater, I started swimming as fast as I could in the tight space. Round and round the pool I swam, increasing my speed with each lap.

Johan screamed, "What's she doing?! She looks like a fish being flushed down the toilet. Grab her!"

The pool water began to move with me, like a whirlpool, further projecting me faster and faster.

The long hook stabbed in and out of the water trying to snag me, but he was way too slow and I was way too quick. *You're a badass, Akela, and badass fish don't get flushed.*

With a last push of energy, I launched myself out of the water. Adios, nasty pool! I crashed my foot into Johan's face at full force as I propelled over him, but I wasn't going to clear the railing. My fast reflexes kicked in and I grabbed the pole from the man in black, planted it on the deck and used it to vault myself up and toward the side to escape.

Looking down, I only had to carry another ten feet to clear the deck of the boat and into the open ocean. Instinctively, I stretched my limbs as far as they could go and then quickly tucked into a somersault to clear the outer railing. Before I knew it, I was falling from the deck down to the water. I opened out from my rotating tuck and gracefully pierced the water headfirst. If there were judges watching, they'd have given me a perfect ten. I did it. I was off the boat… and man was the water cold!

Still, it felt good to rinse the layer of chemicals from the pool water off my body. My eyes adjusted quickly and I started to get my bearings back.

I suddenly remembered the bag of gold dust and felt for it in a panic. Luckily, it was still there, attached with a string to my waist.

Desmond's voice came to me and I returned my focus to the present, and to the soft whirring of an engine coming from above. A shiny vehicle was slowly getting bigger as it moved in my direction. Johan and Dodd's goons were coming for me.

I was a few thousand miles away from the SOS and the help of my teammates. Even with all my training, taking on Johan and the Dartivion men would be a tall challenge. *What to do Akela, what to do?* I couldn't just retreat to the SOS and leave Mathias to Dodd. No, I only had one reasonable option.

Find Mathias.

If I could find the ancient Greenland shark, not only could he possibly help us in our fight against Jarvis Dodd, but if he was that wise, he could help get me home.

At least that's what I hoped, as I swam through the crystalline frigid waters.

The submersible was gaining ground on me from the increasing noise from its engine. Like Sam, Dodd had almost unlimited financial resources and access to his own high-powered toys. Johan's sub wasn't any normal sub, and while I'm not any normal underwater-swimming, dolphin-talking, environmental-crusading girl, I was still human, and my legs were getting tired in this cold water.

The water was so clear, I could see for what seemed like miles. In the distance, I spotted sea-life and headed that way. As I got closer, I recognized the distinctive unicorn-like horn of narwhals. They saw me and swam in my direction. I hoped they were coming to my aid, as their horns looked menacing.

"Peace, my friends," I said in a mental tongue that came to me naturally.

The two horned beasts looked at each other and then back again at me. I realized that I might be the first human they'd ever encountered, an unfamiliar or alien species to them.

"I'm a friend. I'm looking for Mathias, the Greenland shark. You know of him?" I asked.

The smaller and bolder of the two narwhals approached me.

"I am Marjorie and this is Malachi. Not everybody knows Mathias, but Mathias knows everybody." The narwhal spoke slowly and with a hint of doubt in her voice.

"Don't tell her anything," the male narwhal rushed.

"Well, I'm in a big hurry." I gestured behind me. *"You don't have to tell me, but if you could just point me in his direction before these Dartivion guys—"*

"Did you say Dartivion?" Marjorie asked.

"Yes, they're after me."

"Malachi, that's the company that Mathias has been preaching to us about. And you, you must be who Mathias said would come to help us! He's been telling us for years that some humans were on our side and that a girl would come. I didn't believe it until now," Marjorie said.

"It's true. There's more of us than you know. We're all in this together!" I said.

Malachi spoke. *"Together, eh? I don't see many humans having to swim around islands of plastic. At what point did you decide that the ocean was your waste basket?"* He shook his head and horn at me.

"You're right, Malachi, but it's only a small, but very powerful minority that is intent on taking advantage of Mother Earth, your ocean, our ocean, to enrich themselves. And to fulfill the other end, the evil end of the prophecy."

"How are you, *a little human girl, going to help us?"* the male narwhal said, no longer jousting his horn while he spoke.

The female narwhal swam closer and playfully bumped her mate out of the way. *"Can't you see? She is here, swimming, talking, communicating with us. She's not afraid. I can see that in her eyes, and I can also see that she believes every word she is saying. There are enemies out there who've hurt us, Malachi. She is not one of them. She is fighting to stop them."*

Malachi circled around me as I stared forward at Marjorie. I trusted he wasn't going to hurt me. He stopped directly in front me and spoke. *"And so are we. We will fight with you."*

"Thank you, Malachi! I need to find Mathias to do that. He might know something that can help us in our fight," I said, quickly looking over my shoulder at the sub that was getting closer.

The two narwhals turned to see the submersible headlight beaming through the thick glacial water. Malachi spoke again. He pointed to the ocean floor with his horn. *"You see that ridge running north to south? Follow it. Mathias will be where it stops."*

"Thank you! Are you coming with me?"

The beasts both shook their heads simultaneously. Malachi started to joust his horn rapidly back and forth again. *"If the machine that is following you is from Dartivion Corporation, well then, I think it's time we introduce our horns to them."*

"Go, Akela. Go find Mathias!" Marjorie yelled.

I took off, following the ridge line to find the oracle Mathias.

CHAPTER 32

The ridge on the ocean floor led to an odd formation of boulders cropped together. The pile of rocks rose almost fifty feet up from the depths.

I sensed a presence, a strength or force, something very powerful, as I approached the rocks. From a distance, the tower of volcanic matter seemed haphazardly placed. Just a mound of big rocks on the ground, but as I swam near them, I could see that they were intricately linked together in a helix-like spiral structure that allowed water and light to pass through the center. I got within a few yards of the formation when I heard the rushing sound of water, but I couldn't see where the noise was emanating from. How could water be moving so quickly underwater?

As I swam closer to the spiral structure, a bright, multi-colored light appeared as if it were coming through a prism. It was projecting from halfway up the rocks. I swam within touching distance and slowly put my hand through the light beam. I felt a shock of energy.

Quickly, I withdrew my hand back and then cautiously pushed it into the ray again. This time the sensation was even stronger. Not only could I see and hear the ocean, but I felt more closely connected to it than ever before. As if the sea water coursed through my veins and pumped the blood in my body.

I kept my hand in the light as I swam up toward the origin of the beam, but I was only doing so semi-consciously. It was as if the light was guiding me. I lost track of time and distance as my whole body became engulfed in the underwater rainbow.

Simultaneously, I was swimming with the pod as a child, falling from the pelican into warm Hawaiian waters and riding the crests of the SOS. Every moment or instance in which I had connected to the ocean was playing out through my mind and body in a cascade of images and emotions.

I was taken back to Kara's swim team and car washes where soap and pollution fed into the storm drains. I witnessed sea creatures, strangled by the waste taking, their last breath. There was an overwhelming feeling of sadness for what the contamination of plastics had brought to the ocean and all its creatures. Still, there was a feeling of opportunity to restore harmony, beauty, and peace. The presence of hope was real.

Suddenly, I awakened from my trance-like state, and realized I was only a foot away from the light source: a beautiful, eye-shaped hole in the rock. Was this a portal too? I reached my hand out closer to the source and was about to touch it when the hole blinked.

I pulled my hand back.

"I'm not entirely sure of your human customs, but I thought a handshake was more appropriate than an eye poke," a deep voice said.

The eye blinked again and then I noticed the silhouette of a large, shark-like body that was attached to it. It had been camouflaged against the gray surface, but now it slowly separated itself from the rock and started to swim. The body was more than twice as long as I was and looked beyond old, more like prehistoric.

"Mathias?" I telepathically whispered.

"Hello, Akela," the Greenland shark said as he slowly circled me. *"Follow me."*

Mathias swam past me, down to the ocean floor, and stopped at the base of the formation. The sound of the water was loudest at the bottom.

"That light coming from your eye, I could… I could feel everything," I said, trying to communicate an almost indescribable sensation.

Mathias's eye was now only gray, bright, and intelligent, not showering out rays of magic.

"The light that shines in me shines in you and shines in all of us," Mathias spoke as if he was not just talking to me, but to the ocean. *"I've only found a way to channel this font of energy."*

"Where does the energy come from?" I asked.

"From the center. The energy is the life force for our planet. It is everywhere if you know how to look for it. Here, this underwater fountain, is one of those places. Here, I can help others see what I can see," Mathias said while gesturing one of his fins toward the formation. *"I've been waiting for you, Akela."*

"Is it also a portal?"

"Only inward," Mathias said. *"Not in the way you arrived to me."*

"How'd you know how I came here?" As soon as I said that, I realized that Mathias also knew my name before I gave it to him. Maybe Grandpa had been right.

"You came to me, Akela, because I know things."

"Yes, the dolphins said you are the oracle. That you're able to see and can help us find—"

Mathias moved his body, and I noticed a shiny object around his neck. It was sea glass!

"And for this, my sea glass," Mathias said.

"Yes! I am looking for that!"

The glass was in the shape of Australia. My sea glass moved underneath my wetsuit in the direction of Mathias's piece. I couldn't believe it. The sixth piece of sea glass, lost to the ocean, was now found. I needed to get Mathias back with me somehow.

"Like yours, Akela, it holds power. And like everything, it is stronger connected than alone. Everything is connected, Akela. There is no separateness. Do you see?"

"Like the Isle of Green?" I asked.

"Like everything."

"Where'd you find your glass?"

"Not everything is known, even to me," Mathias replied. *"But I know that mine was meant for me, as yours was meant for you."*

"And ours are meant to be together," I said.

Mathias nodded slowly. *"Everything is connected."*

"Can you tell me about Jarvis Dodd?" I asked before I heard a loud crashing behind me.

The submersible appeared in the distance, closely followed by the narwhals, who were taking turns trying to pierce the underwater vehicle's outer casing with their horns.

I turned back to Mathias. *"They're coming for me."*

"Yes, they are coming. The narwhals will turn them back." I spun around again to see that the submersible was taking on water. One of the men in black pulled a release valve and the submarine started to rise quickly to the surface.

Marjorie and Malachi high-fived each other with their horns in a victory celebration.

I was in desperate need of oxygen.

"Go to the surface. I will be here when you return. Hurry."

I quickly swam upward, soon breaking the seal between water and sky. I treaded water lightly as I tried to catch my breath. The wetsuit was helping, but I was cold, and my muscles were tired.

I reached down and touched the gold dust pouch. Good, I could still get home. I'd have to bring Mathias back through the portal with me somehow.

Far off in the distance I could see the Dartivion vessel on the horizon. The smaller submersible was now on the surface, with the two men in black sitting with the top open, using paddles to row it back to the larger craft.

Wait a minute, where was Johan? Why hadn't he pursued me along with the men in black? I mean, I was the prize. Dodd had used Johan to lure me away from the SOS so that he could capture me. Or had he?

A shudder ran down my body as I took a deep breath and swam as fast I could back to the bottom. My heart was in my throat as I pushed myself to a speed I didn't know I could achieve.

I saw the rock formation and a shadowy figure swimming around the backside of it. Bubbles were coming from his back. Scuba gear! It was Johan. I had to get back to Mathias to warn him.

I'd inadvertently directed Dodd's goons to Mathias. How had I missed that Johan was the mole? He always followed me around asking questions. I should've seen it! *Focus, Akela.* This was not a good moment to beat myself up.

As I neared, I lost track of Johan as he moved behind the boulders. Then, I saw the light again. The rainbow beam poured from Mathias's eye, illuminating a wide area of the ocean floor. A rush of panic hit me. Johan would be able to find Mathias now.

When I rounded the corner of the boulder formation, there was Mathias with that beautiful kaleidoscope of light flooding out of him. In the center of the beam was Johan. What was Mathias doing, allowing Johan to share in this vision?

I swam directly up to Mathias.

"Mathias! Johan works for Dodd. He's not here to help, he is evil!" I mentally yelled, knowing that I was probably telling Mathias something he already knew.

The spotlight of colors continued to flow from Mathias's eye. I was again momentarily hypnotized by the sight.

"He's not evil, Akela. His beliefs are evil. At his core, like all of us, Johan is good," Mathias said calmly.

Johan was moving toward us slowly. He was clearly under a spell, but soon, he would come to and then most likely resume his attacks.

"It's too late, Akela. At least for the fountain. I only wanted to show Johan that he has a choice before it is gone. We always have a choice," Mathias said.

Gone? It was only then that I heard the beeping noise that came from the bottom of the boulders. I bolted toward the sound. Explosives. My stomach flipped and my pulse quickened. Johan had wired the entire base of the helix structure with enough TNT to blow up a formation ten times it's size.

Think, think fast. The timer on the explosive read 90… 89… 88… 87…

The bomb was a mess of chains, wires, and buttons. I couldn't make any sense out of it. *If only Leo was here; he'd know how to dismantle these bombs.*

He wasn't there, though. Up close, I examined each wire and where it was connected. This was a waste of time, as I knew absolutely nothing about bombs or wiring. The timer read 70… 69… 68…

Okay, I can't disarm this device, but maybe I can remove it. Moving around to the back of the bomb, I saw that it was secured with thick, titanium chains. Despite tugging on them with all my strength, they didn't budge. My hands began to shake with both fear, cold and exhaustion. I couldn't save the font, Mathias, and myself, but maybe I could get us back to the SOS.

55… 54… 53…

Johan continued slowly gliding up the rainbow toward Mathias. He was only a few feet away from the oracle now. I wasn't sure what would happen first, Johan killing Mathias, or the bomb blowing us all up. I momentarily froze, as I watched Johan reach Mathias. He faced the ancient shark eye to eye. Slowly, Johan took his mask off. He wiped his eyes as if he were crying.

33… 32… 31…

That was it! Johan was my only chance to save it all.

I quickly swam up toward Johan and grabbed him by the arms. *"You are good, Johan. You can still do good. Please help us."*

Johan looked at me and mouthed the words, "I'm sorry, Akela."

"Go, Johan," Mathias said urgently.

"You, too, both of you!" Johan mouthed as he swam toward the explosive. He removed a key from his pocket and unlocked the titanium cable.

Mathias pushed me away from the fountain as the light went out from his eyes. We swam in the opposite direction of Johan, who had detached the bomb and was swimming away from us. He looked back in our direction, and for a brief instant, our eyes met before he continued away with the explosives.

Seconds later, a shockwave ripped through my body and sent me spinning. The blast knocked the wind out of me and left me unable to swim. Still, my body moved toward the surface.

I looked down to see Mathias helping me upward. *"Did Johan survive?"*

Mathias shook his head.

I reached for the pouch of gold. The blast had knocked it loose and now it was gone. We had to get back through the portal, but how?

"The gold! Mathias, how are we going to—?"

"Relax, Akela. Allow yourself to return back home," Mathias said.

I wasn't sure what that meant at first, but Mathias said it as if it was simply true, so I had to trust him. Closing my eyes, I went to the meditation room in my mind. Desmond was there, but he only smiled and bowed. I then pictured myself swimming with the pod back at the SOS. They were family now, as was the operations team. The ocean was my home as well as the SOS. Was that the home Mathias was referring to? Yes.

I felt my body relax right before the time and weightless sensation of portal travel took over me again. The darkness didn't bother me this time; it felt even more familiar, and I allowed myself to breathe through each uncomfortable feeling, each moment, one at a time.

Before I knew it, I opened my eyes and saw the outline of a vessel above, and I could sense the pod nearby. Mathias was by my side. We were back in the SOS Aqua Hold. I didn't know how we made it, but we did.

A voice whispered in my ear, "Akela, you did it. We see you coming up from below. Congratulations." It was Sam's voice.

This was my real family and the only home I was meant to return to. I smiled and passed out.

PART II

CHAPTER 33

It was low tide, and the temporary expanse of sand was pocketed with scattered tide pools, like oases in the desert. The inhabitants of which—mostly hermit crab and tadpoles—were now exposed to the threat of ever vigilant and always hungry seagulls. Would they survive until the safety of the ocean's cover returned? Would I be able to find the last piece of sea glass before Dodd destroyed the planet?

In the distance, the wind gusted, creating moving lines of sand that blew, shifting and writhing like beach snakes, down the shoreline in my direction. I stood motionless, leaning into the wind, hypnotized by the dancing beach. The sand swirled around me, until I joined it, spinning joyously, without a care. It was a feeling I only felt when I was in the ocean. But this wasn't the ocean, or a beach I'd ever been on before. Where was I?

In a sudden movement, the playful reptilian sand lifted higher into the air, blending into a giant circular shape. With every passing second, the shape became more detailed until I recognized familiar markings. Continents. It was the Earth! This was a map, but not of sea glass, only sand. I walked closer to the globe, hoping, and almost expecting to find a critical clue to help in my quest to stop Dodd. But then the orb dissolved back into the beach

In its place, rising from the sand, was Jarvis Dodd. The ground below my feet went from firm to soft and then to liquid in an instant. Before I knew it, I was up to my neck and sinking in quicksand.

"You may be able to breathe underwater, Akela, but what about underground?!" Dodd laughed maniacally.

The more I struggled, the more I sank. Panic had set in. Where were my teammates, Warren, and Leo? What was I going to do?

Dodd squatted down next to me. "Join me, Akela. Why die in vain, when there is so much we can do together, like rule the new Earth."

Dodd's laughing became muffled in my ears as they began to fill with sand, only my mouth and eyes above ground. This was it.

I reached out to take Dodd's hand and woke up in a pool of sweat.

It took a couple of days to recover from the events in Greenland and make sense of everything that went down there. The expedition and explosion had taken a lot out of me, psychologically and physically, and I wasn't sure which was worse.

I was still in the infirmary with no visitors except medical staff, when Mik showed up with a smoothie and coconut water. She filled in the blanks as to what happened while I groggily slurped away.

"Where are the boys?" I asked.

"The boys are fine, and you'll see them soon enough. Mathias, too. He's with the pod." I was relieved to hear that Mathias was okay.

"Sam and I need to debrief you before you speak to anybody else." Mik patted my arm gently before I pulled it away

"I get it. That's just in case I don't spill any secrets to the wrong people, right?" I brought my voice down to a fake whisper. "There could be another spy on board."

"No, Akela. There are no other spies. And it's a mole, not a spy. Spies are unseen, moles hide in broad daylight, just like Johan did," Mik said.

"When did you know Johan was the mole?"

"We'd narrowed down the list of possible suspects to two, before we got notice of your portal jump," Mik said.

"Professor Wild was the other suspect, wasn't he?"

Mik nodded. "But that doesn't matter now, AK. It only matters that you made it back safely."

"Yeah, so, how in the heck did we get back? I lost the gold pouch and Mathias told me just to, 'return home' and we did somehow," I asked just as Sam entered the room. He was always dressed the same—shorts, Hawaiian shirt, and a Lakers hat.

I finished my smoothie as Sam took a seat in a chair next to me.

"Mathias guided you home, Akela. I'm not sure how, but he did," Sam said, avoiding eye contact.

The blast had left me dazed, but I remembered feeling more like I guided Mathias home, I just didn't know how. Mathias would tell me the truth when I got a chance to see him. For the first time, I noticed a pouch hanging from Sam's belt. His eyes followed mine to the pouch and then back up.

"I will tell you about the portal soon enough. Once you're healthy. All that matters now is that you and Mathias are both here, along with your sea glass. Because of you, Akela, we're one step closer to the Isle of Green!" Sam clapped his hands.

I ran my thumb along the western coast of my sea glass. A light bulb flickered on in my brain. "Wait a minute, did you guys know I'd find out about Mathias?"

"Well, we didn't know about Mathias specifically, but yes, we did expect you to find something, and you didn't let us down." Sam sat up excitedly and looked at Mik.

"We knew that the clue to the sea glass, the piece lost to the ocean, resided in you and your abilities," Mik said. "Amazing job, kid."

They both spoke as if they were complimenting me, but inside, I couldn't help but feel used. Professor Wild was right. Sam had used me as a weapon in his war with Dodd. When would he use me again?

Mik noticed the irritation on my face. "It was a miscalculation on our part, Akela. Especially us not being on the SOS to help you. Johan and Dodd were a step ahead of us, and they would have succeeded if it weren't for you. I'm proud of you."

"I wish I felt proud. I was fooled… by Johan." I was going to say *by you guys, too*, but thought better of it.

I felt lost. My new world wasn't as stable as I had once thought; it was more like quicksand. I unsuccessfully tried to stop my eyes from filling with tears.

"You weren't the only one fooled, Akela. We all were," Mik said, wiping a tear away from my eye.

"What happened? I mean, was Johan always working for Dodd?"

"We're still trying to piece that together, but no. Johan wasn't always with Dodd. I can't believe that, and I won't believe that. Somehow, Johan was compromised," Sam said, looking away and out the window at the dark ocean waters. "Dodd is more powerful than we realized."

I wondered if Dodd had visited Johan in his dreams and had convinced him there to join the side of Chixtal.

I couldn't help but feel sad. Sad and angry. Besides Kaipu and Alana, I hadn't spent time with anybody who had died before. The reality that Johan was there with me, with us, swimming, breathing, and living only a few days before, but would now never set foot in this world again, was tough to comprehend.

"Tell me, Akela, what did you learn about Dodd from Mathias?" Sam leaned in closer. Whatever emotion he'd had for Johan was now gone from his voice.

I told him that I'd learned nothing about Dodd from Mathias. It was true, as I hadn't had the chance yet. He seemed surprisingly content with no news about Dodd and stood up to leave.

"We have the sixth piece now," Sam said. "That means Dodd will accelerate his bomb plans and ramp up his hunt for the last sea glass piece."

"And probably hunt the sea glass holders, too," I said.

"Not probably, Akela. Dodd won't ever give up, that is the only certainty," Sam said and left the room.

CHAPTER 34

I couldn't wait until I was out of the infirmary to talk to Mathias, so I pretended to fall asleep. When Mik left the room and the doctors took their lunch break, I bolted down to the Aqua Hold. Mik had said that Mathias had joined Jon, Ana, Grandpa, and the rest of the pod there. I needed to see him. The doctors told me that I wasn't strong enough to swim yet, but they didn't know how strong I was becoming.

As I rounded the corner and ran onto the dock, I saw Desmond's unmistakable silhouette. I casually and quietly walked up next to my big, sweet friend.

He put his hand on my shoulder and squeezed me against his side. "Oh my, Akela. I am so glad to see you," he said. He turned me to him and gave me a big hug. I didn't realize how much I'd missed him. He pushed me away to arm's length. "Look at you, you're becoming a true warrior of the ocean. I worried, but I shouldn't have."

I didn't know what to say, but with Desmond I didn't have to talk. I knew he loved me, and he knew I loved him, so we just smiled at each other. He knew why I was there.

"The pod is making sure Mathias is well taken care of and comfortable," Desmond said.

"Good, I need to speak with him about Dodd," I said.

Desmond lowered himself to meet me eye to eye. "Listen here, young lady. You cannot go back in the water until the doctors and Sam clear you to swim again."

"Can you speak to him?" I asked, knowing Des only spoke broken Whale, and that he hopefully wasn't aware that Mathias had the ability to communicate across all ocean species. It was a gamble.

Desmond paused for a moment. "You're right. You do need to speak with Mathias. Follow me."

I followed Desmond off the floating dock, back into the SOS and downstairs to an underwater observation area. This was the room the ship's marine biologists and other researchers used to monitor and study all subsurface activity. One side of the room was a giant bubble reaching out into the ocean biodome. With the movement of the boat at times, the room gave a sensation of being suspended in a giant air pocket floating in the sea.

We walked past the few scientists in the room, who all parted for Desmond and me. I saw Ahimsa and went right for her and gave her a big hug. I don't know how long she and Johan were together, but his actions and death had to hurt her in many ways.

"I'm so sorry."

"Well, I feel a little better that I wasn't the only one fooled," Ahimsa said. "I'm glad you're safe." She pointed toward the end of the room with the glass protruding out into the water. She knew why I was here.

As I walked through the room, all eyes followed me. The scientists had watched and documented almost every single underwater movement I'd made since coming on board the SOS. To them, I was a subject of fascination and scientific wonder, maybe even more so than the other creatures they studied. My greatest fear of becoming a scientific experiment was now my reality, yet it was okay.

Leaning against the glass, I scanned the water for the pod and Mathias. One by one I telepathically called their names until a connection was made and the pod, one at a time, all swam into view. The scientists started whispering behind me.

Mathias and Grandpa were the last to come. The dolphin pod opened to let the elder statesman come in and surrounded them in a semi-circle in front of the viewing bubble. Mathias nodded when he saw me. We began to communicate telepathically.

"I knew you'd be alright, Akela," he said.

"I'd be better if I were swimming with you guys, but yeah, I'm good. Thank you for helping me," I glanced around the room. *"How'd you know I could get back through the portal?"*

"Because you had done it before, Akela. Many times before."

What was he talking about?

"You were too young to remember. You traveled with your parents everywhere, including portals," Mathias said and then swam in a small circle away from the pod and then came back.

Wait, they did what? Sam had said that my parents took me everywhere, but I never considered that I'd been in a portal before. My head was spinning.

"Where'd we go?" I asked.

Mathias was now directly in front of me again.

"That you will find out soon, Akela. You came here to ask me something else, though. You wanted to know about Dodd." I paused, deciding whether to ask a question or to just see what Mathias had to say. He knew why I was here and what I'd ask, so I waited.

Mathias bowed his head as if to acknowledge that I was understanding his ways. *"Dodd, or at least what he calls himself today, has had many names through the years. He is at least as old as I am, and possibly much older."*

I knew it. I wanted to ask more, but again I waited and listened. Just like Desmond, Mathias was teaching me to listen.

"And so is your friend, Sam Shipman," Mathias said slowly.

Wait, what? That ancient photo in Professor Wild's office, it was real? I put my hands up to my head.

"What's going on, Akela?" Desmond whispered. "Everything okay?"

I quickly composed myself, at least on the outside, and gave a thumbs up, remembering that I was the only one hearing this information. This was a communication link between me and Mathias.

This news would wreak havoc aboard the SOS. According to Mathias, Dodd and Sam were both at least half a millennium old. Maybe more. My god, what if they were immortals?

Right then and there, I resolved to keep this news to myself until I figured out the best path to take with the information.

Mathias gracefully bowed his head at me. I returned the gesture and waved to the rest of the pod. The youngsters, Jon and Ana, wiggled their tails and all followed Mathias out of sight.

CHAPTER 35

The next morning's meditation practice was especially difficult. How could my thoughts not wander back to the idea that both Sam Shipman and Jarvis Dodd had somehow been alive for hundreds of years? Possibly much longer. As hard as I tried, I couldn't help but cut my session short.

I checked my daily schedule. Hmm, that was odd. I had a new class added after my Ocean Studies and my martial arts training: Home Economics.

The syllabus listed the class location as the kitchen of *Chez Shipman*. I walked in to see Sam standing alone in the kitchen. He'd donned a cooking apron and was working a knife back and forth across a sharpening stone.

"Where's everybody else?" I asked.

"It's just us," Sam said while looking up from his blade. He wasn't smiling.

Now if I'd been watching this scene on a movie screen, I'd have been yelling at the character being played by me to RUN! I'd just learned some critical information about Sam, and now I was alone with him and he was holding a knife. It was a textbook setup to silence me.

But I wasn't watching a movie, this was my life. Why was I the only student in this ridiculous class? Maybe Sam really had found out I'd uncovered his secret and now he was going to off me. I mentally went through some of the knife defense exercises Mik had shown me. I was confident I could handle myself.

Sam smiled. "Relax, kid."

I was working myself up. I took a deep breath. "So, home economics. You've already got me pegged as the stay-at-home mom type, eh?"

Sam chuckled as he put the knife down. "What's wrong with that? Raising a family isn't for the faint of heart. Especially when you're doing it on the open seas while fighting an environmental war, like how your parents did."

"I hate to state the obvious here, but clearly that didn't end well for them or me."

"Not everything is as it seems, Akela," Sam said. "Like this."

With a sudden movement, Sam picked up his knife, turned and threw it in my direction. My heart almost stopped, as it took a moment for my brain to register that he wasn't throwing it at me. I could hear the knife zip through the air and hit right in the middle of one of the many rectangular patterns on the wall behind me. I didn't know Sam could move so fast. I felt naive to think I could easily defend myself against him.

The knife hung ominously from the wall as I gathered myself. It was a good throw, but I wasn't quite sure why he was showing off.

"My turn?" I started to ask when the struck wall panel began to withdraw inward, which was soon followed by the surrounding panels. Within seconds, a door appeared where the wall once stood. Sam moved toward the door, but I was frozen.

"Close your mouth, Akela. It's time to take the next step."

As I stepped from the kitchen into the hidden room, the door quickly closed behind me. The new space looked about the size of a basketball court and was just as wide open. Sam walked to the middle of this empty room and gestured for me to follow. My eyes scanned the walls, floor, and ceiling, looking for a hint of anything that might show me what the purpose this room served and why I was in there, but the room was devoid of anything. White walls, white ceiling, white floor.

"Am I being committed to the loony bin?"

"The walls aren't padded, but I can see what you mean."

"Are you saying that you actually know what the inside of a mental facility looks like?"

Sam seemed like he was a very well-adjusted and successful environmental crusader, but living hundreds of years could drive anybody mad I would think.

Sam laughed a little as he watched me size him up. "I might be a little nuts, but no, I've never been committed. Evaluated, yes, but not locked up."

I watched his face closely for any indication of deception in his eyes, but I saw nothing. He was taking in the room as if he were seeing something that was invisible to my eyes.

"This room is the most dangerous room on the ship if it were to fall into the wrong hands. As much research as I've put into developing solutions that will keep our planet safe and healthy, I've also had to prepare for the inevitable—the time when Chixtal's and Dodd's forces, the forces of destruction and desecration, will reveal themselves and bring the battle to us. That time is now."

"Now?" I looked around at the empty room.

"Yes. This room is hardwired to respond to only one thing: my voice." Sam scanned the room before his eyes stopped.

"Access Weapon Pod One," Sam said in a commanding voice.

A panel in the floor folded into itself, allowing for a large banquet-sized table to appear in the space where Sam had been looking. On top of the table lay a variety of items and devices, none of which I'd ever seen before. I picked up the one closest to me, a yellow wetsuit.

"Try it on," Sam said.

I zipped it up over my clothes, "How do I look?" I started to say, but stopped as Sam grabbed another large knife off the table and threw it at me.

I screamed as I watched the knife stop an inch short of my suit and fall harmlessly to the floor. I'd had enough knife throwing for one day.

"Force field technology?" I asked.

"You got it, AK. That suit will protect you from all non-ballistic and nuclear force weaponry," he said and lent me a hand back up.

"It sounds like we're going into a real war?"

"We're already in one, and we're close to winning a crucial battle. We are one final sea glass piece from forming the sea glass map and finding the Isle of Green."

Sam pulled his green sea glass piece necklace out from his shirt and examined it closely. It was the exact shape of South America.

"Dodd will bring out all of his heavy artillery to stop us," he said, tucking away his glass puzzle piece.

I dusted off my suit. "I like the suit, but you got any other colors?" I asked, evaluating my bright yellow suit. "Canary yellow seems a little conspicuous, don't you think?"

Sam nodded. "Point taken."

I moved down the table and grabbed a ten-inch pipe of sorts. I spun around pretending it was a lightsaber and I was Luke Skywalker to Sam's Darth Vader. As I moved with the pipe, I felt it activate in my hands. It vibrated quickly and made a loud thudding sound.

Sam dove out of the way as a gust of air flew out of the pipe, past him, and made a dent in the far wall.

He pushed himself back up to his feet. "Be careful with that, please."

I looked down at the pipe in my hand.

Sam stood up and took the weapon out of my hands. "Gadgis developed it, along with most of everything here. It's the world's smallest and deadliest air cannon. It'll stop almost anything under ten tons right in its tracks. Non-lethally."

"How many tons is the kraken?"

Sam looked at me solemnly. "More than ten tons. A lot more. It might slow it down, but it wouldn't stop it." Sam put the air cannon back on the table. "What do you believe, Akela?"

I thought for a second. "I believe that you haven't told me everything about my parents, this ship, you, the prophecy and many other things," I answered. It was true, Sam was withholding information.

"Fair enough." Sam folded his arms across his chest. "But when you first arrived, you were skeptical about the prophecy and its powers. Do you believe now?"

I'd seen and experienced more fantastic events in the past few months than I could've ever imagined. I guess I just accepted them more than questioned how they happened.

"I believe in what I can see, feel, touch."

"That is not belief, that's just experience. Do you believe in your heart?"

"I guess so… sometimes," I answered. Where was Sam going with these questions?

Sam walked past me to the wall.

"There are powers at work that defy science, physics, and chemistry. I have the resources to build things within the clearly defined confines and rules of those disciplines. But if you add a little thousand-year-old magic, for lack of a better word, anything is possible."

"Like how Professor Wild used a portal to get me to Greenland?"

"Yes! Track's portal came in handy there. That's a portal I built," Sam said.

"You built that? That's impossible?"

"Things are only impossible until they are not, Akela. We built it with a combination of the prophecy's magic and the top minds in modern science," Sam said.

"And gold dust," I added.

"Yes, that portal uses Mayan gold. It can only move you laterally, though, across the same time dimension. There is another more powerful portal that can go further, and in more directions," Sam said.

"Like back in time?" I paused and waited for Sam to tell me his secret, but he waited me out.

A wry smile crossed Sam's face. "We are all time travelers, Akela. From birth to death. Most do nothing with their life and still travel across time. Exceptional lives, though, lives led with adventure, infamy, achievement, or simply with so much pure love that generational memories are created. Yes, those are the only ones that can transcend the linear plane of time."

"That's a poetic thought, but not an answer to my question," I said. "You've done a lot for me, Sam, and I appreciate it. You've given me a new life, but you aren't telling me everything, and I'm getting tired of it."

Sam shifted his head back and blinked at me. He seemed momentarily caught off guard by my candid comment, but quickly recovered. "Stop thinking for a moment, Akela. Let me show you something. Something that only arises from belief." Sam closed his eyes and started breathing in and out very slowly.

Soon he started singing in a low deep voice. It was almost like a chant, but it was in a language I felt familiar with; I couldn't place what it was though.

As he sang, writing started to appear on the walls. Slowly and deliberately, the words he sang, as if they were being written, flowed across the blank walls perfectly in synchronization with his singing. The words were starting to click with me, the syllables and tone, it was like a picture coming into focus.

It wasn't only words on the wall, though. Soon numbers began to materialize, calendar dates to be exact. Sequences of days, near, far, and ancient past, moved along the walls in swirling circles that would collide, merge, and then break from each other, only to form new sequences.

The sun soon appeared on the walls. The blazing nuclear explosion that keeps our planet alive, would rise from the floor, travel across the ceiling, and set on the opposite wall. It did so every few seconds, each time shifting ever so slightly with each cycle.

Our tide-controlling moon did the same, changing through every phase, from new moon to full only to start again and again. The light in the room synchronized with the celestial movements.

The dizzying movement of objects, data, and light made my head spin. I closed my eyes and focused on the words Sam was singing, the moving puzzle of patterns of information still imprinted on my mind.

I was beginning to understand the language. Opening my eyes, an image appeared on the auditorium wall. At first it was blurry, like trees moving in a mist, but slowly, the form became clearer and clearer until a cave opening appeared against the far wall. The words, numbers, sun, and moon all froze in place.

Sam was silent then. My head was still spinning, but slower and slower, until like a recently abandoned playground carousel it came to a stop. I felt comfortable that I could speak without throwing up. I hoped.

"You said, 'raising kids' isn't for the faint of heart. My parents took me in there, didn't they?" I pointed toward the portal.

Mathias had told me that I'd been through a portal before. Sam couldn't say the opposite. I needed to hear something, anything to give me faith that he was a leader I could fully trust.

"They did," Sam said, studying me for a moment. I stared him down, hard. "Remember, Akela, I told you that your parents took you everywhere. I never lied to you."

"Yeah, you did say that, but you left out a minor detail about them taking me through a portal to another dimension," I said angrily. Not telling somebody the whole truth was pretty much a lie in my book. "Tell me everything."

He smiled slightly. "You are very similar to your mother in many ways… Not just in your looks and intellect, but sometimes in your poor ability to hide your true feelings."

I blushed, yet I wasn't embarrassed that my anger showed. It was justified, at least to me.

"Why didn't you tell me about this before?"

"One word. Focus, Akela. Focus is the only reason I didn't tell you about your parents and the portals earlier. If you had known, you may not have followed the path that led us to Mathias and his sea glass. I couldn't risk that possibility."

Sam was right about my lack of focus. So was Mik. Professor Wild, too. I was Sam's weapon of choice, and he was using me perfectly.

Sam looked past me into the portal. "Your mother was brilliant, Akela. A master linguist. But it was more than languages. Your mom was a cryptographer, a puzzle solver of extraordinary abilities. She could see patterns where others could only see words or numbers." Sam's eyes grew wide. "She discovered a secret subscript within the ancient writings."

Sam moved closer toward the entrance of the cave and I followed. The warm, moist, tropical air caressed my skin as I neared. He kept speaking as if he was trying to communicate with somebody through the portal.

"The text within the script your mom deciphered, it explained how the gods believed time, days and years to move simultaneously in congruent circles," Sam explained as he drew rings in the air with his hands. "Past, present and future, all encircling and orbiting just above and below each other. Your mom identified the pattern to determine where in the time portal it would take you."

"Wow. She figured out how all those numbers, dates, the sun and the moon and lights changing made sense?" I asked.

Sam hesitated before answering. "Yes, and you may be able to as well. Someday. You have to be sure, though, because if you don't know where you are going, you definitely won't know how to get back."

Sam looked me in the eyes. "That part is critical to remember, Akela. Getting back. Critical. Do you understand me?"

"I think so," I said.

"You must *know* so, Akela. The first step is to believe in the prophecy. Belief transcends everything else. If you believe, then sing the words of the song."

"You call that a song?" I couldn't help but joke. I was nervous.

The power and magic of the prophecy was far more than I'd ever imagined. Whether I'd been in a portal before or not, the idea of going back in time scared the heck out of me. Getting stuck there scared me even more.

Sam laughed, a real bellyacher that echoed off the walls. "Music was never my strong point, but it's not the tune as much as the lyrics that matter. The words are simple, but very meaningful. Your mom transcribed them for us. 'If your heart lies still and you let go of everything, if your mind is free and you let go of everything, if you believe that everything is one, then you can come in'. Your mom sang those words and everything you saw today appeared for her. You understood those words, didn't you?"

I nodded. The language was already in me, stashed somewhere. Upon hearing it, that hidden door was opened.

"Your mom was so brave. She went first. I was hesitant, but of course we all went. We followed your mom on our quest to find Ht-malo." Sam paused and looked up at the ceiling. "They died before we ever found him."

The mention of my parents' death redirected me back to my recent portal experience, Johan's death, and his attempt to kill Mathias and me.

"How'd I get back with Mathias? I had no gold dust and was barely conscious?"

Sam took his hat off and patted his hair down before putting it back on. "Part of me thinks that you were so young when you went with your parents, that, like a language, the ability to move through the portal was second nature to you."

"Maybe I did remember the way?"

I walked directly in front of the cave entrance and shot my arm out. Instantly, the cave was gone, and my hand smacked into the wall.

"Ouch! What made it go away?" I wiggled my hand to shake off the pain.

"You did, Akela."

"Are you saying it closed because I don't believe?" I asked Sam, but I was asking myself the same thing.

"Only you know that," Sam said as he walked out of the room. "Re-gardless, our mission is in the present, not the past. We need to stop Dodd, and to form the sea glass map to preserve our future."

"Why'd you show me the portal if you don't want me to use it?"

Sam stopped. "Dodd has a portal, Akela. I need you to be prepared for anything and everything going forward." Sam continued walking. "That's why."

We walked out of the chamber, through *Chez Shipman* and back out on the main promenade.

"Thank you for telling me about my parents, Sam." I smiled. It felt good to know the whole story, even if it took me pulling teeth to get it. Sadly, the outcome remained the same; my parents were still dead.

Sam's watch beeped. A hologram appeared. It was Mik, but she was muted to my ears. "Gotta run," he said.

"Wait, how old are you?" The portal and information about my parents had completely distracted me from asking Sam his age. I couldn't believe I got distracted again. Or did Sam distract me on purpose?

"Too old for this," Sam said as tapped his watch and started to jog toward the door. "Stay on alert, and remember the words of the song, Akela. You'll need them someday."

CHAPTER 36

I went back to my suite, sat on the balcony, and stared out at the sea.

Sam talked about magic, and he pulled a trick of sorts on me. With the opening of the portal, my mind lost focus on the question of his past. He could open a portal into other dimensions. So, yes, he could travel through time. I'd even traveled through time with my parents. Maybe that's where I got my sea glass? I had so many questions.

At least I knew then that Chixtal, Dodd and their side had similar portals. That's how Dodd showed up near the helicopter in Bonita Fields. Maybe that's how he's getting into my dreams, too.

The photo of Sam and the Osprey of Good Hope appeared in my head. A flash of excitement and adrenaline sprinted through my body and propelled me out the door. I needed to tell the guys.

Forgetting again that the automatic door, I slammed into it. *You gotta be kidding me.*

I slumped to the floor holding my head. There was a knock on my door.

"Come in."

And there they were, Warren and Leo.

"Why are you sitting on the floor?" Warren asked.

"I have an idea about that," Leo said, holding in a laugh and placing a hand on my head. "Mik has me working on a program to speed up the automatic doors. Low priority. Obviously."

"For you it is, for me, it's a big deal. Pull up some floor guys." I patted the ground next to me. "You're gonna want to sit down for what I'm about to tell you.

I told the boys everything that I'd learned from Mathias and Sam. They sat there quietly for what seemed like an eternity.

"Well?" I asked.

"So, you think that Dodd and Sam are time traveling immortals?" Warren gasped.

"Maybe," I said.

"I suppose," Leo said. I could see the gears in Leo's mind turning. "Or it could just mean that Mathias had become aware of them through their time travels."

"That could be true, too," I said.

Leo nodded. "Yeah, it's just a lot to wrap your head around. But that'd be the most logical explanation."

We all sat there in silence for a minute.

Warren stood up and walked back and forth. He stopped and looked at the sketch Kaipu made of me swimming with the pod as a baby.

"You were a cute baby, AK," Warren said.

"Thanks," I replied. He was a cute teenager, too.

Warren's eyes lit up with an idea. He spun around at us like a courtroom lawyer making a point to a jury. "And, since you've clearly aged between that drawing and today, we can rule you out as being an immortal."

"Thanks, Detective," Leo said as we exchanged dismissive looks. "I'm going to take another run at hacking the prophecy database. There was a file titled 'portals' in it."

"I may be able to translate it now—" I started to say when all our watches simultaneously let out a loud beep.

"Sam wants us in the operation room now." I moved toward the door and stopped. "So, how do we handle this information? Do we confront Sam directly?"

Leo shook his head. "No, definitely not in front of the rest of the team."

Our watches beeped again, louder this time.

"Guys. Double beep. We need to go now." Warren started for the door in a flash of speed that would be impossible for any of us to keep up with. "Leave it to me. I'll get Sam to admit he's an immortal," he said confidently with a smile and bolted out of our sight.

"Oh no." Leo rolled his eyes. "Detective Wolf Boy and his plans."

Leo and I were the last to arrive in the operations room. The whole team was huddled around the surface table.

"What took you so long?" Warren asked with a wink. I liked when he winked.

It was the first time we'd all been in the same room since Johan's death. I couldn't help but look at Johan's assigned ops chair and feel pangs of sadness and anger.

Apparently, I wore those feelings openly on my face. "It's alright to miss him, Akela," Desmond said from the head of the table. "What he did doesn't make him a bad person."

That's what Mathias had said also.

"It doesn't? I mean, he destroyed the underwater fountain, he tried to kill me and Mathias, and in turn, give Dodd the power to win this war we're fighting."

Desmond smiled. "There is no arguing that. What Johan did—his actions—were filled with anger and hatred. His deeds were reprehensible, all fueled by Dodd and Chixtal. But at his core, like all of us, there was good. That good saved your life. All I am suggesting is that you let it go, Akela."

"Look! The kraken," Leo said, pointing at the giant image shown from a satellite video.

"Is that the SOS?" Warren asked, pointing at a larger image directly in the path of the moving kraken image.

"You're looking at a satellite video from midnight last night. The kraken was on course to attack the SOS, but then changed course for some reason." Sam clicked a button, and a new satellite image showed the kraken moving away from the SOS.

"Wait. The *Spirit of the Sea* isn't detectable by radar, sonar, or satellite." Leo pointed at the image.

He was right. Our ship was a ghost ship. As big as the SOS is, we were able to move throughout the ocean without detection.

"How's it possible that we're seeing the SOS or the kraken? Both aren't visible." Leo looked around the room at everyone.

"For as endlessly inquisitive and investigative as some of you are," Sam paused and looked at the three of us, "I'm surprised it never occurred to you to try and figure out what made the SOS stealthy."

Mik swiped her hand across the screen to bring up the image from our mission to stop the oil spill and where we first encountered Dodd's creature.

"Ericka and Ahimsa were able to take a sample from the tanker attack. They discovered that whatever had attacked us was plastic. With help from the computer team, they were able to reprogram our satellite software with the ability to detect plastic anomalies." Mik pointed at a huge mass on the map.

"A plastic kraken." Sam snapped his fingers. "It only makes sense that Dodd could harness the most damaging elements of the ocean and then use them against us. Just like we used recycled plastics recovered from our clean up efforts to build the SOS." Sam looked down. "The answer to the kraken was always right under our feet."

Leo slapped his forehead. "Literally! The *Spirit of the Sea* is made of plastic. Wow. Why didn't I think of that?"

"Yes, reused, old plastic," Warren said, turning toward Sam. "I wonder what other old—I mean really, really old—mysterious things or people live on this ship."

Everybody looked at Warren like he was crazy. Probably because he had a crazy look on his face. I tried making eye contact with him to discourage any further left field attempts at bringing up Sam's immortality.

Desmond stepped forward. He spoke quietly, but his baritone voice still carried tremendous weight. "Dodd wouldn't call off his monster unless it was for good reason. Do we know why the kraken shifted its course?"

"No, we don't, but there is somebody who will," Sam said. All eyes turned to me.

"I'll find Mathias," I said and took off running.

Chapter 37

I dove into the water and swam as fast as I could in the direction I thought the pod would be. I telepathically called out for them, but didn't receive any reply. They'd left the SOS.

The underwater light shifted brighter as I crossed beneath the outer edge of the ship's hull and entered the open ocean.

I was wearing the new suit Sam had shown me in the weapons room. It was canary yellow, a huge fashion faux pas in the world of underwater covert operations, but the upside functionality of the suit offset the style issues. It felt awesome, and to be honest, I looked good in yellow.

"Nothing yet," I heard Mik's voice in my comm. "I've circled the SOS while increasing the radius."

Above, I could hear the rotors of the JetCopterBoat whirring as Mik attempted to find the Greenland shark and the family of dolphins from the sky.

Desmond had swum off looking in the opposite direction. "I've got nothing either."

"It's Mathias. He knows," I said with the sudden realization that I probably should've never left his side. "The kraken shifted his target from the SOS to Mathias. He knew the kraken was coming and left the SOS before we did. He's luring the beast away."

"Find him. If Dodd has Mathias, he'll control his sea glass piece as well as whatever other secrets and knowledge Mathias has. We can't let that happen," Sam said.

There was a brief pause on the other end. Leo's voice popped up. "Let's assemble the caterpillars."

"Do you think they're ready?" Warren asked.

"It's about time we find out. Call Professor Wild," Leo said.

"Hey, guys," I chimed in. "My communications might be cutting out, but it sounded like you said something about caterpillars. Come again?"

Leo came back on. "Just keep heading north by northeast. That's where Mathias and the kraken are heading. Oh, and find the pod. We're going to need them."

Mik lowered a rope and picked me up in the JCB. We flew off in the direction of Mathias, and it wasn't too long until we saw the pod.

"Get out in front and drop me."

Mik accelerated and then lowered the copter above the surface.

"Go! I'm heading back for Desmond and Sam," Mik said.

I jumped, penetrated the water, and let myself submerge to where I thought I'd intersect the pod. I could see the shadow of the chopper pass over as I stopped descending. I called out for the dolphins.

Ana was out ahead of Jon and the rest of the family. She saw me first. *"Akela! Thank goodness!"*

Jon stopped next to us. *"Mathias, he left last night and told us to stay behind, but—"*

"We got worried and took off after him," Ana said, completing Jon's sentence.

I started to swim slowly and gestured for them to follow. *"Mathias is luring the kraken away from the SOS. I don't know what his plan is, but he's still out ahead of us, and the kraken is closing in."*

"Mathias swam away to protect us, didn't he?" Ana asked.

I nodded. *"We've gotta find him."*

Swiftly and silently the pod and I raced through the ocean after the kraken and Mathias.

We swam at full speed for an hour before I heard the humming of an engine nearby. My comm unit beeped, and Professor Wild's distinctive voice materialized in my ear.

"Most scientific research follows a logical progression, Akela, with one experiment following up on the findings of another. Every now and then, however, good fortune plays a part. Such is the case with a paper just published in Current Biology, which reveals to the world a moth capable of chewing up plastic. Are you following what I'm saying?"

"Nice to hear from you as well, Professor Wild," I said. I could hear Warren and Leo chuckle in the background. "I assume you're explaining why caterpillars might be part of our plan?"

"Yes, yes, yes. Bright girl. So, anyhow. This brilliant researcher noticed caterpillars chewing holes through the wax in some of her hives while they lapped up honey.

To identify them, she took some home in a plastic shopping bag. But when she got around to check on her captives a few hours later, she found that the bag was full of holes and the caterpillars were roaming around her house."

"Aha!" I exclaimed. "The caterpillars may help us remove plastic waste from the Earth."

"More importantly, or timely," Leo added, "they can help us defeat the kraken!"

"You can't spell defeat without spelling eat," Warren joked, or at least tried to.

Professor Wild cleared his throat. "As I was saying, when Sam and I read this report, we developed some unique, shall I call them, hybrid caterpillars for the purpose of helping clean the oceans."

"Very cool," I said. "What now?"

"Surface now, Akela," Wild said.

The pod and I slowly started rising to the surface. I tried to visualize an army of little mutant plastic-munching insects taking on the massive plastic kraken, but I couldn't see it.

I popped my head up and the pod followed me. We all turned our heads to see the approach of an SOS auxiliary boat. As it slowed down, a door opened just above the water level and a smaller Zodiac inflatable zoomed out from underneath the larger vessel. I could see Warren, Leo, and Professor Wild on board, heading in our direction.

Warren was driving and cut the Zodiac's motor as it drifted to us. The dolphins cleared a path while staying on the surface.

Leo pulled a glass jar out of his pocket and handed it to Wild. I could see a little caterpillar squirming around in the jar.

"Umm, where's the rest of them?" There's no way that little caterpillar was going to damage the kraken.

"That's it," Wild said. "Actually, there are two of them, but the other's personality is a little unpredictable, so she's still on the boat."

"What's one little caterpillar going to do?" I was about to say, when off in the distance the kraken let out a blood-curdling scream as it breached the surface. Everybody turned to see the multi-colored patchwork of a monster before it submerged.

Desmond's voice came over the comm. "Guys, speed this up. The kraken is gaining on Mathias; you must hurry."

Wild quickly unscrewed the lid of the bottle. "I suggest you all step back," he said as he gently placed the caterpillar onto his hand, briefly inspected it and then tossed the furry little guy into the ocean.

"Don't eat him," I said to the dolphins who all gave me a not-so-funny look.

We all slowly waded backwards. Wild had a mischievous smile on his face and gestured for me to move further back. Warren sparked up the Zodiac motor and smiled my way.

I was nervous, but I was starting to learn how to calm that energy. One way was to get out of my own head and focus on something or someone else.

I called out to Warren over the engine noise, "You ready for your swim lesson, Wolf Boy?" I figured this was an appropriate time as any to start flirting.

The kraken breached again.

"I think I'll take a rain check. Dinner and a movie is starting to sound a little more like my speed."

"Look!" Wild pointed at the insect.

The caterpillar was starting to grow. Slowly at first, but then rapidly. I blinked and rubbed my eyes to make sure I was seeing clearly. In a few seconds, it was the size of my fist. A second later, it was the size of a car, then a larger car, a bus, a plane and oh my goodness, it was massive.

"Everybody get back!" I dove down and the dolphins followed me. We surfaced a hundred yards away and looked back upon a gigantic, fifty-foot-plus tall caterpillar floating on top of the sea!

Wild's voice popped into my ear. "Even I didn't think he'd get that big."

"Now what?" I asked while staring at the humongous floating insect.

The kraken resurfaced with a scream, waking us up from our awe-struck caterpillar daze.

What do you want us to do?" Ana asked me, and I relayed to Sam.

"The caterpillar can defeat the kraken, but not without your help, Akela. And the pod's help. The insect needs direction. Literally. It can fight, but it's very slow. You must be its motor. We need the pod to propel and maneuver the caterpillar in the fight against the kraken."

"And you need me to direct that fight?" I asked.

"Yes, Akela. But from above the water," Sam said.

"Okay. Is Mik coming to pick me up again?" I asked.

"No, you're going to direct the fight from up on top of the caterpillar," Sam said.

Warren brought the Zodiac back around and tossed a large rope harness to me. I looked at the rope in my hand and then up at the building-sized caterpillar. I didn't see this coming.

"You can do this, Akela," Sam said slowly and calmly. "Actually, *only* you can do this."

I swam around to the front of the floating mass of fur and craned my neck to look up into its eyes. *Hello, Furball.* I focused all my efforts on messaging that I was a friend and that I'd like permission to ride him.

Furball returned my stare and tilted its neck to mirror mine. Then, just as I was about to give up on this idea for being ridiculous, the beast lowered its head all the way down to the water, bowed forward and waited.

Shocked, I looked around at the guys on the Zodiac and then the pod. I expected everybody to be in awe of my powers.

"Get on with it already, Akela!" Bingo yelled at me.

"Whatever he said, Akela. Go!" Professor Wild added.

So much for my adoring fans. I grabbed the harness in one hand and then some of the fur of the caterpillar's neck, hoping I wasn't hurting the beast. Slowly, I pulled myself up on his head and then eventually onto his neck. I turned my body to where I was facing forward. Furball's neck was way too wide for me to straddle, but as I roped the harness around, I noticed that it provided foot straps that allowed me to stand up. I felt around with my feet, trying not to look down. This caterpillar was HUGE—it was like looking out the window of a five-story building.

Finally, both of my feet found the harness straps and I comfortably settled into a position that allowed me to look around without fear or vertigo.

I looked down. The Zodiac, along with Wild and Warren, was only a little rubber ducky in a giant bathtub.

"I am the caterpillar princess!" I hollered as a strange feeling of excitement and confidence overtook me.

Sam's voice returned to my earpiece. "Settle down there, AK. There's no time to waste. Get the pod working to move you and the caterpillar to the kraken."

I took a deep breath. Never in a million years would I have thought I'd want to try to find and fight the kraken, but I knew what I had to do. I remembered Desmond's training on positive self-talk. I repeated my mantra. *You're a badass, Akela. You can do this.*

I communicated to Ana. *"Guys, gather the pod and propel us toward the plastic monster. It's the only way we will catch up."*

The pod submerged, and shortly thereafter a swirling movement surrounded the caterpillar.

"Remember, Akela, the caterpillar can fight on its own, but it needs propulsion and direction from you," Wild said quickly. "Get the two beasts in proximity. If my calculations are correct, the caterpillar's strength, if proportionally expanded along with its size, should give him a fighting chance against the plastic monster."

I felt Furball lurch forward. We began moving quicker and quicker in the direction we last saw the kraken.

A fighting chance. I heard Wild's words over and over in my head as we moved toward a vacant horizon.

"Any idea where the trash heap has gone?" I asked into my comm.

"Away from you, AK The beast is fast, but we've got a chance if you can get that caterpillar moving," Leo said.

"Team," I heard Desmond's commanding voice boom in my ear. "Trash heap… those coordinates, I know where it's going."

"The plastic gyre of the Great Pacific," Sam said solemnly.

"Come again? Getting a lot of static up here on Furball," I said.

"It's called the Great Pacific Garbage Patch," Desmond continued. "There are five plastic gyres in our oceans—collections of plastic and floating trash that are trapped by the currents and accumulate to form islands of debris."

Warren chimed in. "They say the Great Pacific Gyre is the size of Texas!"

"And the kraken will be undetectable if it gets to it," I said with a sudden realization.

Mik's voice joined the conversation. "I haven't been able to locate Mathias. I think the kraken might have him."

"That or he's under the gyre already."

The patch must be where Dodd was launching his operations from. If Dodd was there, why would Mathias willingly swim to him? His capture would be devastating. And what else was Dodd hiding down below? Was his virus bomb there as well?

I had the entire SOS pod propelling the caterpillar, but we still weren't going fast enough. We needed more sea life to aid our mission.

"Desmond," I said. "We need you down here. I need more horse-power. Actually, I need more whale power to be exact!"

"On my way, Akela," Desmond said.

Mik circled the chopper around and Desmond dropped into the ocean. I had no idea if there was a pod of whales in the vicinity, but I did know that we'd find out soon enough. While I could communicate with the whales, I wasn't confident that I could simultaneously guide them and the dolphin pod. Not to mention hold onto a giant cater-pillar and lead it into combat against an equally giant plastic kraken. I mean, it wasn't like this situation popped up frequently in everyday life to train for.

In the distance, the ocean seemed to change color and consisten-cy. If I didn't know that the Great Pacific Gyre existed, I might have thought we were racing toward a massively big, yet impossibly flat is-land. The thought of Dodd and all his companies, cronies and cohorts contributing to the gyre made me angry. Dodd's virus bomb came to mind, and that anger shifted to fear.

I felt like a pawn in an ancient environmental chess match between two warring spirits and their modern-day generals, Sam and Dodd. The only female piece on the chessboard, the queen, was also the most powerful, though. Dodd and Chixtal couldn't get Mathias and his sea glass; The Isle of Green was our only protection against Dodd's virus.

I remembered my mantra and pulled on the reins as if I could push the caterpillar to move faster. With a surprise, I felt a sudden burst speed. Leaning and peering down, I could see the giant outlines of gray whales and orcas that had joined the dolphin pod. The pod had welcomed in their brother whales.

Turning my focus inward, *faster, faster,* I chanted internally.

"We are going as fast as humanly and oceanly possible, Akela," Des said. *"Are we going to catch the kraken?"*

I could see the back of the beast now. Just the shadow of it really. It was giant and moving very fast toward the safety of the plastic gyre.

Leo checked in. "AK, you have just over a minute. If my calculations are correct, which they almost always are—" A collective sigh from the team interrupted Leo. "—well, they *are*, and that sigh just cut into the approximate seventy-one seconds we have before we lose Mathias to Dodd!"

"Faster!" Sam demanded.

Desmond's voice came next. He was almost yelling at us through his exhaustion. *"We are giving everything we've got down here!"*

Closing in on the monster, I could now see the millions of discarded bottles, cans, trays, straws, bags, and other debris that were all connected to form his body. The kraken was a colorful moving mass of our waste coming back to haunt us.

I patted Furball on the shoulder. "I hope you're hungry, buddy. Prepare to attack!" I screamed at the top of my lungs. I could feel Furball's stomach rumble underneath my harness. I followed up with a mental yell to my underwater friends.

"Let's go!" Desmond yelled.

We were within ten yards of the plastic beast. *Now,* I thought. *Now!*

With a massive surge of energy, I felt Furball's body lift out of the water. The dolphin and whales pushed toward the surface with all their collective might. I wrapped my wrists around the caterpillar harness.

We were flying! Airborne caterpillar! I looked down and saw that we were directly above the monster. I jumped up and drove the neck of my caterpillar friend down toward the back of the kraken. The sound of Furball's teeth gnashing into the plastic monster was music to my ears.

As we landed down on the kraken's back, the beast bucked forward, sending me high into the air. Fortunately, I was strapped in and landed back down in the harness. We were behind the creature again. I could see the hole we'd left in its back.

Pieces of plastic started to fly off the gyre and replace the wound in the kraken's back. Faster and faster the trash pieces moved in and reassembled into the body. Whatever damage we had done was quickly erased.

"Uh oh, that's not good," Warren said.

"Understatement of the century," Leo said.

"Strike again, Desmond!" I yelled.

The caterpillar picked up speed and again we launched into the air. As Furball's head angled down toward the monster, I looked up to see the approaching gyre.

"Akela! You're going to land in the gyre!" Warren shouted.

Before I could reply, a hissing screech drowned out all other sounds. The kraken rose from the water, rotated its body, and bared its fangs at us. I didn't care if they were plastic, those teeth looked like they could cut through metal. With a shudder, I remembered that they could.

I pulled hard on the caterpillar reins and tried to maneuver us away from a direct head-to-head confrontation. My caterpillar was long and tough. The kraken was not quite as long, but way denser. I could sense that its power was far superior to mine.

With another pull, the caterpillar started to turn sideways. As we rolled through the air, I could hear the kraken's plastic teeth clanging together and missing a chance to sink into us. I breathed a sigh of relief, but it was short lived, as I fell free from the harness. I looked down. I was about to land directly on top of Dodd's garbage isle.

CHAPTER 38

So, that is where it all went. It didn't get recycled, buried, or shot off in a rocket to the moon. It was right there, floating and suffocating our primary source of existence on this planet.

My body hit the gyre and I waited to penetrate through the trash into the ocean, but I didn't. The Great Pacific Gyre was so thick that I remained on the surface of the floating garbage heap. I tried to stand, but it was like trying to get to your feet on an inflatable raft. I could get up for a second or two, but I always wound up on my hands and knees.

There was no sign of the kraken or Furball. I swung my head around and scanned the horizon, but I couldn't see the edge of the gyre. Either I'd flown in further than I thought, or the gyre had reorganized itself around me to better keep me from the safety of clean water. I reached up and felt my sea glass still hanging from my neck.

I was trying so intently to get my bearings that I didn't realize my communication's piece had become dislodged during impact. Lifting my arm, I noticed blood running down my hand. I looked down at the mass of cups, cans, and trash I was standing on and noticed my feet were bleeding, too. Not only was this rubbish island a plague on the planet, but it was also a floating Swiss army knife of sharp edges of old metal cans and plastic.

Realizing that with every movement I was slicing myself further, I froze and concentrated on putting my intercom back into my ear. Slowly, very slowly.

Once the intercom was back in place, voices flooded my ear.

"Hey guys," I said, trying to hide my fear.

"Akela!" a chorus of my teammate's voices called out.

"I'm alright, guys." I tried to keep my voice steady. "Where are the beasts?"

Sam's voice appeared in my ear. "The caterpillar and kraken both penetrated the gyre. The gyre covered up the holes immediately. We can't detect anything underneath its surface."

"Mathias, Desmond, the pod?" I asked.

"No sign of any of them. They all appeared to have gone down below the surface of the gyre. None of our systems are working with them," Leo said.

I took a huge breath and tried to slow my breathing. I was scared. "Okay, you mind getting the chopper over here and getting me out?" Tilting my head slowly while not moving my feet, I noticed the SOS chopper hovering in the distance, but not moving any closer to my position. It was moving lengthwise around the fringe of the world's discarded trash.

There was a pause in their response. Too long of a pause.

"What's going on guys?" I asked impatiently. "This gyre isn't exactly a bed of roses. More like a cheese grater."

Sam finally spoke. "I've got the submarine en route, Akela. ETA twenty-five minutes. But we can't pick you up with the chopper."

Leo jumped in. "You see, there's something jamming our comm systems and overriding the flight computers as well. Some sort of electro-magnetic pulse that starts to short the chopper out as soon as we get more than a few yards over the surface. We're working our way around the edges with no luck. This trash heap is just gigantic, and somehow it's getting bigger by the minute."

"Dodd," was the only word I could get out of my mouth. I noticed my breath was short. I started to extend my inhale and exhale.

Another deep breath and another, then another. Desmond's voice came into my head. *"Keep breathing Akela, just like we practiced."*

Wait, was this me remembering his voice, or was he communicating with me?

I focused my thoughts. *"Des?"*

"Akela! There you are! Are you near me? Can you get us out?" Desmond asked.

"I'm on the surface of the gyre. Are you okay?" I asked quickly.

"I've been swimming down below since you went down. I'm okay for now, but at some point, I'm going to need to come up for air." He sounded tired.

"How much time do you think you have?"

"Thirty minutes, max. We were all swimming full force and the oxygen in the water is much lower underneath the trash," Des said.

"Any sign of Dodd or Mathias?" I asked.

"Nothing yet, but there is something down here. I sense a different vibration in the water, something inorganic that is not on our side, Akela. Something evil."

I switched back to the team. "I just contacted Desmond. He's okay, but running out of air. Thirty minutes approximately. He hasn't seen Mathias, Dodd or the kraken, but confirms that there's something else besides trash causing interference with the chopper."

"That's about the amount of time until the sub arrives. We need to do something sooner. Dodd and the kraken aren't just going to let everybody hangout down there and have a trash picnic," Leo said.

"Oh, no," I heard Mik say.

"Oh, no, what?!"

"AK! Run!" Leo shouted.

A forty-foot wave of garbage was roaring in my direction. Something underneath the surface of the gyre was generating it.

I tried to turn and run, but the giant floating trash pancake made my legs feel like Jell-O. Like a toddler in a bouncy house, I took two steps forward and half a step back before starting to tip over. Next time, I tried one giant step and was launched back in the opposite direction and onto my face, landing on a bag of Doritos.

I righted myself off my stomach and into a sitting position.

The wave was growing by the second. I looked up at the now six-story swell of garbage. I wasn't sure if the wave would land on me, or if it'd sweep me up and eventually pass me. Either way, I didn't want to find out. With all my energy and focus, I stood up. Taking a wide stance, I was able to balance, but not much else. If I was going to surf some garbage, I was going to do it standing up.

Desmond had to be close. I tried to communicate with him. My mind was racing in a million different directions, but I breathed just like he'd taught me.

There I stood on the world's largest floating island of trash with an avalanche of garbage about to crush me. And I was calm. I thought about all the training, all the progress, and the friends and family I'd made since leaving Bonita Fields. It was all there in that moment with me. Soon, there was only one road, one path that I could focus on.

"Desmond, if you can hear me, I need your help," I communicated repeatedly.

Again, I called out for Desmond. Why wasn't he responding this time?

"Akela, brace for impact!" Sam said. "Use the wave if you can. I think you'll have a better chance of getting out from below the surface. We'll do everything in our power to get you out safely. I promise."

I heard Sam's voice, but I had all my focus on Desmond. I could sense that he was close. I could sense that the pod was close, too. It was more than a hunch. I could hear them!

"Akela, open your eyes! We're coming right for you!" Desmond and Leo yelled at the same time.

I'd closed my eyes for what seemed like a minute, but it must have only been a few nanoseconds. I opened them.

Holy giant-surfing, trash-guzzling caterpillars! Leo and Wild were right in front of me, both wearing scuba gear and holding onto the harness of an even bigger caterpillar. The furry giant was eating through the giant wave. Above the roar of the fight, I could hear the chatter of dolphins and whales. They were propelling our caterpillar forward. Right next to the beast was Desmond riding Furball! Both caterpillars were taking big bites out of the tidal wave of trash.

I was still balancing awkwardly as the bottom of the wave hit my feet.

"We're going to eat our way out of this mess," Desmond said calmly. "You need to grab onto me, so we can get you out of here."

I climbed up the giant wave, which now had water seeping through parts where the caterpillars had done their damage. Desmond was scaling down the neck of Furball. He had undone part of the harness and turned it into a rope for me to grab onto.

I'd scaled halfway up the wave on my bloody hands and knees. I looked up and saw I was within a few dozen yards of Desmond. Desmond braced himself against the neck of his caterpillar and held on with one hand as he leaned outward to extend the rope. This was it! Desmond tossed the rope.

"Akela, look out!" I heard Warren's voice say just before the kraken appeared in the wave of water. A giant tentacle lashed out at Furball. It missed the giant insect, instead hitting Desmond and knocking him off.

Furball turned its fluffy head and caught the kraken's tentacle with its mouth. Simultaneously, the bigger caterpillar turned back, dipped its head into the water and pulled out another kraken tentacle. They had the beast. I was now at the top of the wave, looking down at the two caterpillars dismantling the kraken bite for bite! The kraken struggled, but it was no match for the appetites of Furball and his bigger sister. We were winning.

The two genetically engineered, trash-devouring insects had also opened a growing patch of open water. This meant that any mammals trapped beneath could breathe air!

Where was Desmond, though? I scanned the patch and couldn't see him. I heard the helicopter rotor blades and turned to see the SOS chopper hovering just off the gyre.

"The magnetic pulse interfering with our gear was using the wall of trash to generate its force field. With the hole in the gyre, the force field is down, but only partially. We still can't get to you," Leo said.

Wild's voice came in, "But my birds can. Akela, look west."

I had lost my bearings and slowly spun around until I saw them, a black flying V shape in the sky. At the front of the formation was a larger multi-colored shape. As they moved closer, they came into focus. The crows from the SOS were coming, with the Osprey of Good Hope leading the way.

"The birds are going to pick me up?" I remembered holding onto the pelican and flying off from Kaipu's deck.

"Yes, Akela. Together, they can."

The birds swooped down from the sky in formation, and I noticed they were carrying a rope. I steadied myself as my avian allies rocketed toward me. They lowered to just above my eye level and flew right at me from less than thirty feet away.

The osprey and the murder of crows pulled up inches before my face. I grabbed the rope and held on tight as I was lifted off the gyre, high above the fight and toward safety. I was flying with the birds for the second time in my life.

My feathered friends pulled me up above the trash patch. I looked down at the garbage island. Wild and Leo's caterpillars were munching away through the mess. The kraken was gone.

That was a relief, but what about Desmond and Mathias? I couldn't leave them. And what about Dodd? If he was down there, I needed to go after him right then. I didn't know when I would get another chance.

I looked up at the birds and then off toward the chopper.

Mik's voice came on, "Keep holding on, AK. The birds will bring you off the patch and I'll pick you up from there."

"Guys, I gotta help Desmond."

"Akela, don't you let go," Sam said.

I looked at the Osprey of Good Hope, thanked all the birds and let go. I smiled at the memory of Kaipu as I flipped forward and entered headfirst through the window of blue water to find my friends Desmond and Mathias. It was time to capture Jarvis Dodd.

CHAPTER 39

The salt water burned through each scrape and cut. Still, the ocean never hurt so good. I grit my teeth, knowing that it was the beginning of the healing process.

The dolphin pod and the whales were all still working with Wild's giant trash-eating caterpillars. There was no way they could eat up this entire patch in one sitting, but if the professor could create more of their kind and us humans slowed our waste, then maybe in time they could eliminate the gyre.

Desmond was nowhere to be found, though, and I called out mentally to him with every stroke I took.

I heard a loud sigh come through the comm. It was Sam. "Akela, I guess I shouldn't be surprised you went back into the water."

I started to slow my swim. "I'm sorry, I couldn't leave Desmond."

"Don't slow down, AK. Desmond, Mathias, and their sea glass are down there. You're the only one who can bring them out now. Don't let me down." Sam signed off the comm.

Without a clue about which direction to go, I listened to my intuition, which was telling me to just dive deeper. As I did, I could feel the pressure rising in my ears and body as I pushed through the ever-lessening light. The visibility was no more than a few yards ahead of me and I had a quick tinge of panic as my mind flashed to my swimming nightmare of being disoriented in the dark. Then, I heard Dodd's voice calling my name and my parents' names.

"You guys hear that?" I asked.

"Hear what?" Leo answered.

It's just in my head. I tried to concentrate, but soon began to wonder if Dodd was setting a trap for me. I started to worry about Sam, too. He'd made a point of saying I needed to save the sea glass. Was he more concerned about the sea glass than he was for me and Desmond?

As I stroked deeper, the darkness seemed to be closing in on me. My chest tightened and I screamed out.

At the same time, a light projected from a small pendant on the breast of my suit, allowing me to see ten or more feet ahead of me, like a car with headlights on a moonless night.

Leo's voice came back into my comm. "Sorry if my lights scared you, AK. Automatic headlights. Once it gets dark enough, bam, then you have swimsuit lights."

"Thanks, Leo," I said. The sound of his voice, along with the light, snapped me out of my fear. 'Do me a favor, guys, and please keep talking to me."

A projectile buzzed through the water at enough speed to turn me into fish food.

"What the heck was that?!" Another missile came at me, and I spun and twirled myself out of the way as more and more of them came into sight.

"AK, you gotta get out of there, now!" Mik yelled.

"No kidding!" I was darting back and forth now, continuously swimming up, down, left, and right in a hopefully unpredictable pattern. I remembered Mik's karate motto, 'a moving target is harder to hit.' So,

I kept moving. My yellow suit could handle a big impact, but I didn't want to test it out right now, and not this far below the surface.

Through the comm I could hear team members talking quickly amongst themselves, when Mik's voice took over. "Turn the lights off, AK! They aren't heat seekers, they're only tracking the light."

"How do you know?" I asked as I dodged another shot.

"Your suit, it neutralizes your body heat. There's gotta be too many other creatures down there for heat missiles to work. Trust me," Mik said.

I pressed hard on the pendant and finally found a switch. "Here we go." I dodged another bullet just before everything went black. I could feel a few more torpedoes zoom by me, but then the frequency of fire tapered off until the waters around me were calm again. I was safe for the moment, at least safe from those missiles. But I was again alone in the dark. *Breathe, Akela.*

"Good call, Mik. They stopped firing," I said and stopped swimming for a moment.

If Dodd could create a plastic kraken and a virus bomb, what else did he have up his trash-filled sleeves?

As if she was reading my mind again, Mik's voice appeared. "Don't worry, the kraken is kaput, kiddo."

"Track's caterpillars made a nice meal out of that wretched beast," Sam said.

"You should see it, AK," Warren added excitedly. "Our furry friends are traveling back and forth along the gyre like goats on a lawn." Hearing Warren's voice, I suddenly realized that I missed him.

Sam came back on. "Akela, listen. You must keep diving, but you'll be diving alone soon. The comm will stop working as you descend deeper and when the patch closes. Remember, we are always with you and—" Sam's words became fainter and fainter as I swam until his voice disappeared completely.

All black. Soundless. For a second, I thought I might succumb to panic again, but this time I stopped myself before it set in. I found the feeling of water on my skin comforting. I could smell the ocean water and feel its coolness in the deeper depths. Then, I heard that sound. A low, slow groan in the unmistakable voice of the Greenland shark. It was Mathias.

I wanted to call out for him, but knew that would draw unnecessary attention from whatever was down here. I heard it again and swam in its direction.

Desmond mentioned there something in the darkness, something very large. I was sensing something as well. It was inorganic, but not another plastic monster. I wasn't sure how I could detect something in this total blackness, until I realized that I was echolocating it from the movement generated by my swimming.

I desperately wanted to make a little noise to clearly map it out. Whatever it was, its size was beyond massive.

Instead, I kept moving toward the object. With my body heat neutralized, I felt confident that I was moving undetected.

The sound from Mathias came again. It was clearer now. He was moaning in pain. I swam with my hands outstretched. I didn't want to touch the sub, but I needed to get as close as possible to work my way around to Mathias. Was Desmond with him?

Then I heard the hissing. I spun around in the darkness and swam fast in the opposite direction.

Again, there were more snake-like noises. Oh, no. I remembered that sound from the Sea Swarm mission. I darted in the other direction, seeing nothing, and now spinning in panic circles.

"*Hello again,*" a voice said in Octopus. Octavius.

I felt a rush of water pressure toward my face, and I braced for impact, but there was nothing. Nothing except whatever vision I had disappeared into an impossibly darker shade of black. I was suddenly very, very tired. Everything went dark.

CHAPTER 40

When I awoke, my eyelids felt so heavy, as if they were sealed with concrete. I was groggy and tried to focus on the last thing I remembered. Something got in my eyes, then everything went black. Octopus ink. Octavius got me again. I tried to reach up to my face, but my arms were restrained.

As my mind raced, I was able to pull my wandering thoughts back into focus one by one. *Focus on the positive.* I was alive. Yes, I was a captive, but I could wiggle my hands, feet, head, and torso. I was restrained, with my arms and legs pinned down, but my body seemed to be in working order. Now, where was I? Was Desmond there, too? And how could I get out? Wait, did I still have my sea glass?

I tried to lift my arms, forgetting for a moment that I was restrained. Instead, I buried my chin into my chest and moved it left to right until I felt the necklace and eventually my sea glass. Phew.

"My, you are quick to study, Akela," a man's voice said. "Don't worry, I haven't taken your precious necklace… yet."

I couldn't see the man who spoke my name, but I recognized that voice from the helicopter and from my dreams. I could feel him smiling over me.

"Jarvis Dodd," I said, and I heard a sharp inhalation of breath from the man before he spoke again.

"Most people in your situation would be hyperventilating in panic. Strike that, most people would not have survived to even be here," Dodd said as he circled me.

"You know, Ms. Spencer, it doesn't surprise me. I'm sure Sam's team taught you many breathing techniques aboard the *Spirit of the Sea*. I would expect only so much; Sam was never much for original thinking. Most of everything he learned, he learned from me, including the power of breath."

Were Dodd and Sam once colleagues? I struggled against my restraints.

"I can see by your reaction that my former affiliation with your current boss is news to you?"

I stayed silent. Lies were to be expected from followers of Chixtal.

"It's okay, I didn't expect you to know the entirety of the story. No, Sam never tells the whole story, does he?" Dodd walked slow circles around me. "Although, if my henchman had been a little more competent, you would already know it by now, as you'd be working for me."

"Never," I said through gritted teeth.

"Ha, never is an altogether different concept when there is no horizon, my dear." I felt a cold hand touch my forehead, and I flinched against my restraints. "Calm, calm now, Akela Spencer," Dodd said quietly. "This will restore your sight, and once you are able to see, we will undo your restraints."

We? Who else was there? I felt a liquid being poured slowly over each covered eyelid. My eyes tingled and warmed as the fluid soaked into my lids and eye sockets. Slowly, light started to return to the room, and within a minute I felt the locks holding my eyelids shut slowly lift. I could only see the silhouette of Dodd. I blinked, but the blurriness did not leave my sight. Another shadow of a person, much taller, stood further in the background, not speaking, but I could hear his breath. Eventually, my sinuses further cleared as well, and I could smell the saltwater on him. It was Octavius.

"Rest a while and let your eyes recover," Octavius said. His human voice was very different from what I expected. He almost sounded kind.

Those were the last words I heard as I dozed back to sleep.

I didn't know how long I'd slept. When I opened my eyes, I was in a small, neatly arranged bedroom. The restraints were gone from the bed, only replaced by a tight metal bracelet on my arm. Quickly, I glanced around the room. There was nobody with me. I pulled hard on the metal bracelet, but it wouldn't budge.

A small bureau was against the wall. A mirror hung above it. Over the bed was a porthole, and I gingerly sat up before standing on the bed to peer through it. My body felt tired, but everything still worked. Out the porthole was nothing but the black ocean. If there was a deepest blue, we'd passed it.

I hopped down and walked over to the desk. On the desk was a black and white picture. Two men appeared in archaeologist outfits standing in front of a large vine covered cave. I squinted my eyes shut and opened them again, quickly trying to make sense of what I saw. The photo was like the one in Professor Wild's office that we'd seen of Sam, but it was taken from a different angle. The one in Wild's office had obscured the face of the man with Sam. It couldn't be, but the resemblance was uncanny. Sam Shipman and Jarvis Dodd. There they were, not looking a day older than they did today.

Maybe Warren was right, and they were immortals? Unless they made that trip recently, Dodd and Sam had stopped aging. Not only that, but they were also former friends or co-workers.

A knock came at the door and it slowly opened. Dodd was back. He looked exactly like he appeared in the photograph I held, the photo from the Dartivion website, and when he appeared next to me by the helicopter. He never aged.

We both stared at each other. I wasn't going to speak first. Finally, Dodd did.

"I take it your accommodations are to your liking?" he asked.

I sat silently.

"You do know, Akela Spencer, that Sam hasn't been entirely honest with you. He's told you only what he's wanted you to know." Dodd paced the room as he spoke. "Only enough to convince you to do what is in his best interests. Did you ever stop to think that maybe Sam's motives weren't as pure as he wants you to believe them to be?"

"As a matter of fact, I didn't." I casually sat back down on the bed. "Sam never gave me any reason to believe that his entire life wasn't dedicated to this planet and from protecting it against the likes of you."

I tried hard to keep my facial expression neutral. Dodd was right, though. Sam hadn't been entirely honest with me.

Dodd turned to look at the photo, and I took that opportunity to make a move. I jumped to my feet and lunged at him, but I was somehow stopped midair. Frozen, to be more precise. I was a foot from Dodd's face and six inches off the ground. I couldn't move. Dodd just smiled at me. Man, I wanted to punch that smile off his face.

"Ms. Spencer, you're acting very naive for being such a bright girl." Dodd looked at his watch. He then pointed to the bracelet tightly affixed to my wrist. Dodd touched a button on his watch, and I fell heavily down onto the floor. My knees hit hard, along with my elbows. I was alright, but I wasn't going to try that again.

Dodd shook his head at me. "Johan stole the plans for that technology from Gadgis. Such a shame to lose Johan. A twit, but a useful one," Dodd said with zero emotion.

It shocked me at that moment how he reminded me of Sam. He then clapped his hands together.

"Now, if you want to learn the truth, can you promise not to try anything else stupid?"

I tugged at the bracelet, realizing there was no chance it was coming off my wrist. I nodded.

"Good, now come with me."

I followed Dodd out of my room. Octavius was waiting outside the door and walked behind me as we moved down a long corridor. Along the way we passed many rooms, each with a porthole window. The rooms appeared expansive from what little I could see and were filled with thousands of varieties of plant life, something I hadn't expected to see on Dodd's vessel.

We continued walking silently. I stole a quick look at this Octavius creature that had attacked me twice and captured me. I was surprised to see a tall, handsome, teenage boy. He looked a little older than me, probably around Leo's age. His eyes were sad.

"Eyes forward," Octavius said.

I turned back around. He was of the sea, somehow, just like me, but he was on the wrong side of this battle.

The long tunnel ended, and we walked out into a giant room that belied the size of the submarine. I gasped. The open area we were now standing in looked like we were in an underwater shopping mall. The submarine must have been huge!

"It's as big as your *Spirit of the Sea*, maybe bigger," Dodd bragged without turning around.

People were hurriedly buzzing around in every direction. There was a glass elevator going upwards with lions in it. To my left was a giant domed window through which I could see a jungle-like environment with monkeys playing in the trees. Octavius noticed me taking in all the sights.

"Look below you," he said.

The floor we were standing on was made of glass. Beneath the surface, I could see an extended underwater holding area filled with all varieties of sea life.

"It's beautiful, isn't it?" Octavius said.

It was beautiful. I could see a few people in scuba gear swimming with the fish. I scanned the sea for Mathias, but I didn't notice any sign of him or Desmond. I tried to telepathically connect with either of them, but nothing happened.

As we walked, I was trying to make sense of what was going on, and I kept coming back to the realization that Dodd's submarine was an underwater version of the SOS.

Dodd stopped in the middle of the atrium and spread his arms wide. "What you see here is no different than what your hero, Sam, is doing above the surface," Dodd said with a smirk.

He gestured toward the lions in the elevator. "They are going to our African biodome. The plants and fauna you saw earlier are to be planted in each appropriate environment to replicate exactly what would be happening in an uncorrupted, unpolluted state. Jungle environment, ocean and so on. We have specimens from all corners of the world here, flourishing without interruption from mankind."

I shook my head in disbelief. "This makes no sense. The land, the oceans, the air, you are killing the planet. Why are you doing that and trying to preserve it at the same time?"

Dodd ignored my question and walked onto a circular platform. Octavius put an arm on my back and pushed me toward the platform. I tried to knock his arm off my back, but he was stronger than me.

Dodd pressed another button on his watch and the platform rose from the center of the floor and we rapidly ascended upwards toward the hundred-foot-high ceiling. I started to duck just as the ceiling opened, revealing a control room.

Dodd hopped off the platform and strode toward a wall of monitors. Scenes of destruction played on every screen. Trees burning, coral reefs being demolished, sewage being dumped into flowing rivers. Every screen, a different image of mankind slowly destroying its only home.

"Reminds you of the SOS. Doesn't it, Akela?" Dodd said as he sat down in a tall-backed chair with extended armrests. The chair was on a platform a foot higher than the other seats, which made it look throne-like. He gestured for Octavius and me to sit in two smaller chairs below him. Octavius pulled a chair out for me and then sat beside me.

"Sam doesn't sit on a throne. He never put himself above us," I said.

But that was only a small difference I could see between Dodd's operations room and the SOS. I was dumbstruck by the similarities between the SOS and whatever Dodd called this submarine.

I realized that there were other open seats. I thought of my teammates, and I could feel my temperature rising.

"Where are my friends?"

He laughed, a high-pitched cackle. "All of the amazing things you've just seen right now. The realization that yes, Sam and I are both old, very old, and yes, that we were once colleagues! As well as the obvious question as to what am I, Jarvis Dodd, doing with all these specimens.

A question that might lead you to reconsider which side you should be fighting on, and all you can think of at this potentially momentous time in your life is where your friends are?"

Octavius half suppressed a laugh next to me.

"Compose yourself," Dodd said and shook his head at Octavius.

Dodd threw up his hands and swiped his watch. Instantly, all one hundred monitors individually switched like puzzle pieces to show one giant image. It was Desmond and Mathias! They didn't look hurt, but as I looked closer, I could see the metal bars around them. They were trapped in an aquatic holding cell.

"Where are they?"

"They are here, and yes, they are okay and will continue to be if you cooperate."

I stared at the monitor and focused all my efforts on communicating with Desmond or Mathias. Nothing was happening. I turned and saw Dodd looking at me intently.

"Titanium holding cell, my dear. Your telepathic talents won't do you much good while they are in there," Dodd said. "Ah, that reminds me."

Dodd reached into his jacket and pulled out a headband. He tossed it to Octavius. "Put this on her."

Octavius stood in front of me and very gently placed the headband on me. I could hear the headband lock in the back.

"Titanium headband. Just in case you want to try your powers on anybody else," Dodd said. He looked briefly at Octavius.

Dodd switched off the monitors and the wall went black. I remembered Desmond's teachings. *Calmness, Akela, calmness.* I had to keep my composure.

Dodd stood up, walked over, and sat down on the other side of me. He turned his chair and got very close to my face.

"I'll be blunt, Ms. Spencer," he said, somewhat irritated. "I need you. You and your sea glass. Well, yours, Desmond's, and Mathias's, to be specific. That gets me almost halfway there."

"Halfway to our safety," Octavius said.

Dodd shook his head disapprovingly as he looked at Octavius.

"You know where the last piece is, don't you, Dodd?" I watched his face intently for any signs of deception.

"I know a lot of things, Akela," Dodd said. "Sit back and let me tell you the real story about the war."

Dodd stood up and started pacing.

"You see, Akela, when you've seen history unfold with your own eyes, when you have witnessed generation after generation of mankind, across all continents and ethnicities, you become aware of one undeniably consistent human trait. Destruction. It's so inherent in our human DNA that we can't save ourselves from ourselves. We are like the scorpion on the back of the toad in the parable.

"Even though the scorpion needs the toad to prevent him from drowning, the scorpion's nature is to sting. In doing so, the scorpion not only kills the toad, but also himself. Even though mankind needs Mother Earth to survive, our human nature will always prevail. We kill the Earth and ourselves."

Dodd walked over to a monitor. On the screen, a majestic lion walked proudly next to a lioness and her cubs.

"They're magnificent, aren't they?" he said as he reached his hand out and touched the screen gently as if to pet the beast. "They are perfect in their nature, calm and reserved when they need to be, and violent and assertive only when it comes to survival. But not humans. No, our larger brains have convinced us that we are the caretakers of all other life forms on this planet, but we don't have the ability to do so. It's a catch twenty-two, young lady. We're the only ones capable of saving ourselves, yet because of that capability, we are incapable of stopping our own destruction."

I couldn't tell if this was an act or not. Dodd and Octavius sat there quietly waiting for me to respond. I didn't want to argue with a madman, but maybe I could flush out his plans.

"I can't argue with you. We've screwed our planet up, but it's not too late. People, from all corners of the world, are learning to live more sustainably. Change is happening. We *can* make things better."

Dodd turned from the monitor. "Sustainable you say? A teardrop in the ocean. The tide is irreversible my dear. You ever heard the expression 'too far gone', Ms. Spencer? Well, that's what we are. Too far gone. Glaciers melting, ocean levels rising, rainforests depleting, it's all unstoppable. It's only a matter of time before the Earth is uninhabitable. Why not speed things up, and then the bet is won?"

There it was, the wager from the prophecy. Chixtal and Htmalo.

"I disagree, obviously," I said, trying to find the right wedge of a question to open Dodd's real plan. "But, if the destruction of the Earth is a done deal as you say, why are you accelerating its death and saving its creatures at the same time? I don't get it."

Dodd spread his hands wide as the TV monitors shifted to dozens of beautiful natural images of waterfalls, deserts, gardens, mountains, sea life, flowers, and wild animals.

"How could you be human and not want to preserve such beauty. You are part of that beauty, in your dolphin mode, as is Octavius as an octopus and Desmond as the whale. All creatures, except for humans, need to be preserved. Humans, well, except for the select few I'll need to pull this off, won't be necessary when the past becomes the future again."

Dodd turned to the monitors and at once, they all changed to form one cohesive giant image of an expansive view of Southern California, devoid of any sign of human development. The screen switched to New York, but without the city. Just a pristine island. On and on, images of major cities emerged on the screen, but only as they might have looked like hundreds if not thousands of years ago.

"And who is to say that at some point in time—" Dodd's eyes lit up and he stared intensely when he said the word 'time', "—yes, at some point in time, maybe we couldn't start over after the bet was won?"

"Are you Chixtal?" I asked cautiously.

Octavius straightened up in his chair next to me. I looked over at him. His eyes narrowed at me, but then darted back to Dodd. Octavius didn't know if Dodd was Chixtal or not. I had him wondering now, too. Good.

I turned back to Dodd.

I continued, "You are, aren't you? When you finally win your bet with Htmalo, you're going to take all of the animals you saved and start all over again."

Dodd walked back over to his chair and sat down. "I'll answer your question with a question. If I'm Chixtal, wouldn't that mean that your beloved Sam is Htmalo?"

Hmm, he had a good point. I was so caught up in trying to get to the truth about Dodd and his motivation that I hadn't looked at the other side of the equation. Was Sam Htmalo?

"Makes your head spin a bit, doesn't it young lady?" Dodd stood up from his chair. "Now, back to practical matters. Your sea glass, Ms. Spencer."

Dodd held out his hand. I quickly considered my options and concluded that my best path wasn't to resist, but to go along, like Mik had taught me in our Judo training sessions. Use your opponent's momentum against them.

I slowly unlocked the clasp of my necklace, not breaking eye contact with Dodd.

"I wonder if you'd found me before Sam did, would I be fighting on your side right now?" I reluctantly handed my necklace to Dodd.

"You should join us," Octavius said.

"Shush," Dodd said and held a finger up to Octavius.

Dodd then stared at the sea glass shape of North America in his hand and then held it up to the light to examine it. His hand was shaking with excitement. Octavius's eyes were fixated on the glass as well.

"You know, all you need is just one piece to prevent us from finding the Isle of Green. Why not let Mathias and Desmond go now?"

Dodd snapped out of his sea glass trance and returned his eyes to me. A slow smile came to his thin lips.

"And do what? Have them return to Sam with information on my vessel and my mission? No, that wouldn't do now, would it?"

Only now, watching the monitors, did I notice that my friends' sea glass pieces were gone as well. I stared hard, searching for any other clues from Desmond and Mathias, before the screens suddenly switched to a blinding white.

I blinked hard. The screens were showing barren, snow-covered glaciers surrounded by ice blue waters.

"Antarctica," Octavius said in a whisper.

"Quiet now, boy!" Dodd bit his lip in frustration. "You see, Ms. Spencer, I could thwart Sam from generating Htmalo's Isle of Green, but that wouldn't be as much fun as actually having all the sea glass pieces and having the island for myself. You know, a little comfortable paradise to bide my time on while my virus bomb does its work."

There it was. He didn't want to prevent us from having the Isle of Green; Dodd needed it for himself when he set his virus bomb off. If Dodd had my sea glass, Desmond's, and Mathias's, plus found one in Antarctica, that would leave Warren, Leo, and Sam.

Dodd walked over to a large black panel and pushed a button. The panel opened and a glass case rose. In it was Desmond's and Mathias's sea glass. Dodd opened the case and placed my sea glass in as well.

Dodd's plan was clear now. He was going to ambush my teammates. "Isn't that a little ambitious, Dodd? You taking down the whole SOS team?" I asked with some intentional condescension.

"Ha. You know little of ambition, girl. Ambition is persistence— hundreds of years of it. And yes, I've grown weary of this fight. Sometimes drastic measures are needed to accelerate victory. But first things first, we need to get the last piece from Antarctica."

"We?" I asked.

The screens switched again, but this time with a map showing our coordinates. We were moving from the waters of the West Pacific toward the North. But even at a record-breaking pace, we wouldn't get to Antarctica for days, if not weeks. That is, if Dodd didn't have a portal of his own to use.

Dodd saw the recognition in my eyes. "You're a quick study," Dodd said with a cackle. "I need you, Desmond and Mathias to help extract the seventh and final piece."

"And then we'll have all the pieces in one place again, finally," Octavius said.

Dodd snapped at Octavius. "Shut up already, Occy."

"Occy?" I turned toward an embarrassed Octavius. "How cute."

Octavius lowered his bright red face and looked down at his feet.

Dodd then aimed his steely blue gaze onto me. "We will be within range soon."

I knew it, we were using another portal. I wondered if I could open one myself yet.

"Octavius, return Ms. Spencer to her quarters. She'll need to be well rested for this mission. Desmond as well."

I stood up and smiled at my tall captor. "Ready, Occy?"

Octavius silently led me back down to the main level of the submarine. We passed through the sprawling main chamber and back into the narrow catacomb-like hallways.

"Why do you put up with that guy?"

Octavius didn't respond.

"You know, you don't seem so bad on land as you do in the water. It's not too late to change sides. What do you say, unlock my headband and we get out of here together?"

"Quiet!' Octavius said loudly. "You don't understand."

We walked in silence the rest of the way back to my quarters.

The size of the sub was staggering as was the length Dodd was taking to preserve each species. Yes, he's a madman and yes, as a human on this planet, my mission was to stop him from getting the sea glass and detonating his virus bomb. Still, I couldn't stop thinking about what Dodd had told me.

There was something about his plan that gave me pause. He clearly loved these animals, and, in his mind, while warped, he was going through enormous efforts to preserve them. Somewhere deep in that man's soul there was a belief, a love. Could I unlock it fast enough to make him see the error in his ways, like Mathias had done with Johan?

No. Don't be naive, Akela. In Dodd's own words, he was 'too far gone'. Maybe Octavius wasn't, though.

Back in my cell, I flopped down on the bed. There was so much to consider. Dodd was going after the last sea glass in Antarctica, and he needed me to help get it. He also needed me to draw Sam and my teammates into battle. This was all going down soon, which meant that Dodd had access to a portal. Would the song be the same?

'If your heart lies still and you let go of everything, if your mind is free and you let go of everything, if you believe that everything is one, then you can come in.'

I rolled over onto my stomach and placed my head on the pillow just for a moment. I really needed to formalize a plan, but my eyes had plans of their own. Maybe the answer would come to me in a dream.

CHAPTER 41

That night, I did dream, and it was vivid. I was back on the SOS, swimming through a maze of seaweed. Every turn I took was met with another barrier, and each time the seaweed continued to get closer and closer until I became so entangled that I started to sink. I thrashed wildly, attempting to free my limbs, but that only served to make the seaweed wrap more tightly around my body. I was a sinking sushi roll. Panic was settling in now, and my breathing became short and fast.

Dodd's voice again appeared in my dream. He was calling for me, but it was a distant call, like an echo from a massive cave or a portal. I struggled to free myself, but I could no longer move.

Then I heard another voice, at first faint, then stronger and clearer. It was Mathias's. "You are not as trapped as you think you are."

Easy for him to say; he wasn't slowly sinking to the bottom of the ocean.

"You are dreaming, Akela, but you are not as trapped as you think you are. Breathe. Observe. Your surroundings are not as they appear."

I opened my eyes to find myself wrapped up in my bed sheets. My twisting and turning had created a self-made straitjacket out of my bedding. I tried to move my arms, but they were locked to my sides.

Remembering my training, I began to breathe deeply, expanding and contracting my chest. Slowly, I started to create room in the sheets. Eventually, I was able to free one arm, then both, and then easily extract myself from them all together. I did it! I whooped to myself before quickly shutting up.

Congrats Akela, you escaped your own bed sheets. Good preparation for taking on an immortal evil genius bent on the world's destruction.

Octavius arrived and led me from my cell. We started walking down the corridor.

"Good morning."

Octavius ignored me.

"Do you really believe everything Dodd said yesterday?" I asked. After almost a minute of silent walking, I tried again.

"You know, with a little bit of re-education, you'd fit in on the *Spirit of the Sea*. You might even find that you like it. There are other kids on board. Kids like us," I said.

This time, I stopped walking and turned to look at Octavius. He stopped within an inch of running into me. My eyes were level with his chin. He looked straight over me and then turned his eyes down to meet mine.

"How'd Dodd find you?" I asked.

"I don't remember," Octavius said without taking his eyes from mine. They looked even sadder than before.

"I'm surprised you don't have sea glass, considering your powers," I said, but immediately regretted it.

"Right, I'm not special like you." Octavius shook his head.

I had a hunch and I went with it. "Did your parents die when you were young? Mine did."

We stood there for a few moments, staring at each other.

"Well?" I asked.

I wanted to try to connect with him, but my headband stopped me. Octavius was the enemy, but also like me, of the sea. I couldn't help but feel for him.

He shook his head ever so slightly, then placed his hands on my shoulders and rotated me back around. I took a deep breath.

"You know—"

"Shut up, Akela," Octavius said. It was the first time he'd called me by my name. I was making progress.

As we were walking, I heard a door close behind us. I stole a quick peak and saw Desmond following us with two armed guards. He looked healthy and unharmed. He had a similar headband on. I tried to communicate with him telepathically, but nothing happened.

As we walked, I kept hearing Mathias's words in my head. 'Your surroundings are not as they appear.'

Hmm, well they sure looked like the surroundings I'd seen before. I saw workers left and right preserving specimens and animals for preservation. I saw the water moving under my feet and the animals being cared for just as they would be on the SOS.

We were led down a long stairwell and into an enormous open room with a small lake in it. A chill swept through the room. The water must be freezing. In the middle of the lake was Dodd standing on a floating circular platform where he was manipulating a holographic image As we neared the water's edge, Dodd's platform engine kicked in and he was at the side of the pool in seconds.

Octavius directed me onto the float and then attempted to push Desmond, but Desmond didn't budge. He only looked down at Octavius and shook his head. Octavius was tall, but Desmond was a giant. Octavius stepped aside and Desmond stepped onboard without assistance.

As soon as we were all assembled, the circular vehicle shot back out into the icy lake. Eventually, coming to stop directly in the middle.

A shadow moved through the waters and circled us twice before surfacing. It was Mathias.

I wanted so badly to jump into the water and greet my dear friend, but I had to be content just to see him alive and unharmed.

Dodd slapped his hands hard on the table. "Alright my friends, now is the time for you to help me save the planet."

Desmond slowly closed his eyes. Dodd was blocking our ability to communicate, but he wasn't aware that my powers extended to Mathias as well.

Dodd hit a button and a holograph view of Antarctica appeared in front of our eyes.

The display showed the ocean level view of multiple large icebergs with their above sea level peaks and how far the bodies of ice plunged below.

"There are more than just icebergs down below the surface, team." Dodd's eyes rested on me as he said the word "team".

He then manipulated the hologram so that we were now looking at the bottom side of one of the icebergs.

"What is that?" I asked, pointing to what appeared to be a wooden chest embedded within a body of ice.

"That's what we've come all this distance for." Dodd pushed a button on the table and a video image appeared on top of the hologram.

The video showed a quick black and white sequence, Dodd narrated. "Dr. Horatio Terence—explorer, scientist, Antarctic pioneer and conservationist. He lived with his wife on the continent, studying how global warming threatened polar bear habitats. Dr. Terence was an expert on atmospheres and the first scientist to identify and lobby against the impact of CFC, Chlorofluorocarbons, on the ozone layer. He understood atmospheres better than anybody."

The video ended. Dodd seemed to speak of this man with reverence. Was it an act or the sincerity of a madman?

"Is that his coffin?" I asked.

"Good guess, but that would've required somebody to be there to bury him. In his last correspondence, Dr. Terence wrote that he wanted to walk off into the wild as free and uninhibited as when he arrived. He sent this image of himself before he was never seen again."

"He sent it to you?" Desmond asked suspiciously.

"Why yes, Desmond. I funded much of his research," Dodd said with a smile and a nod.

I glanced at Desmond, who shook his head ever so slightly.

Dodd pressed the monitor again and brought up a selfie of a man in nothing but his underwear. He had a big smile on his frozen face.

"Okay, I think we've seen enough," Octavius said with a laugh.

"Be respectful," Dodd said. "He was a true warrior, for all of us."

Dodd reminded me of Sam when he spoke like that. He brought the holographic image back into a closer resolution.

"That wasn't all Dr. Terence wrote in this letter." Dodd's eyes gleamed as he spoke. "The good doctor said he left behind all of his worldly possessions in a chest. Included in his list was a map of Antarctica."

Dodd zoomed in on the photo. Hanging around Dr. Terence's neck was a piece of dazzling light blue sea glass perfectly shaped in an exact image of the Antarctic continent.

Dodd switched on the hologram and brought up a step-by-step sequence of how he expected Desmond, Mathias, and I to extract the frozen doctor. It was straightforward, but crazy dangerous. The operation required dry suits, an auxiliary breathing apparatus, and, like I suspected, no digital communication. Dodd didn't want to alert the SOS of our whereabouts. He knew we could communicate telepathically.

I remembered Professor Wild's words about Sam using me as a weapon and chuckled to myself that I was now about to be put into service by Dodd as well.

Desmond spoke up. "Dodd, if you expect us to train and operate successfully together, I'll need my titanium headband removed. Akela's, too."

Dodd paused for a moment, then nodded to Octavius, who got up and inserted a small key into the band, unlocked it and removed it from Desmond's head and then mine.

"Hello again," I said to Desmond without speaking.

"We will get through this, Akela. Trust me, not Dodd."

I hoped so. *"He has the virus bomb on board,"* I replied.

Desmond took a deep inhale and slowly nodded.

Desmond looked at Dodd. "You know, Jarvis, we will need our sea glass back in order to complete this mission," Desmond said.

Dodd paused. He looked at each of us and then back at Desmond. Desmond spoke again. "You know that we've never completed a mission without them. You've come too far to have us fail now."

"Don't tell me what you need or how far I've come!" Dodd yelled back and quickly turned away. He appeared to be talking to himself before slowly turning to face us. "I've come very far," he said in an eerily calm voice. "Now, start training."

All day we practiced our mission. This extraction of Dr. Terence and his sea glass was the equivalent of a well-timed bank heist. Everything had to go as planned, or Desmond and I would become ice cubes.

Mathias, on the other hand, had evolved over his centuries in the ocean, and was able to adapt to massive temperature changes.

We'd made three practice runs in the pool so far, and none of them had been completed with enough time to spare. In each instance, we were able to quickly rise to the surface to avoid any danger, but we knew that wouldn't be the case if we had a half mile of iceberg above us.

On land, the plan was rather simple: Desmond and I would exit the portal directly onto the outer edge of the iceberg. It was an easy target since it was over three miles long, one mile wide, and a half mile deep. Once there, we'd navigate to the southwest corner and quickly submerge. Mathias would enter and exit the portal separately at that position. Terence was frozen directly at the bottom center of the slab, and Mathias's role was to lead us to the spot for extraction. For that, Dodd would give us enough underwater explosives to loosen the doctor then tether him to Mathias, Desmond, and me. Then we'd swim to the surface and back through the portals.

After our third failure, Desmond and I sat on the platform snacking on the lunch provided. I took a bite of the tasteless goo that Dodd's people had prepared for us. For a submarine with so much fruit and vegetables, it was shockingly bad. Almost synthetic tasting. Mathias's head popped up in front of us.

"You knew where the last piece always was, didn't you?" I asked Mathias.

"I know many things. I know of Dodd's bomb as well," Mathias answered. His head disappeared and then bobbed on the surface again. *"I also know your powers aren't tied to your sea glass, but Dodd is unsure."*

"That's good. Dodd will have to give us our sea glass back for the mission," I nodded in agreement. *"He needs us with our sea glass to find the doctor. It also means that he's planning on ambushing the rest of the SOS sea glass bearers."*

Desmond calmly stroked his beard. Clearly, he'd already made all those calculations. *"Is Dr. Terence alive?"* Desmond inquired.

"That depends." Mathias swam in a fast circle as if taking a moment to think. *"Akela, is there a reason to doubt our mission?"*

I looked at Mathias. His eyes, his soul, knew all. He knew that my time with Dodd had planted a tiny seed of doubt. The fact that Sam and Dodd were old comrades and the reality that Dodd cared for the planet in his own destructive way, yes, it had created some doubt. Not in the SOS or our mission, but in our ability to win.

Mathias nodded. He was aware of everything I was feeling and thinking. *"You are not your thoughts, Akela. Remember that, and that your surroundings are not as they appear."*

Mathias swam off. His dorsal fin slowly sank out of sight. Maybe my dream last night wasn't a dream after all.

Desmond and I finished eating our lunch in silence. We both knew that not only our lives depended on the success of this mission, but that if we pulled it off, the negative consequences were potentially catastrophic. We were the bait to lead our teammates, our best friends, our family, right into Dodd's trap.

Still, we had no choice. Recovering Dr. Terence and his sea glass needed to happen one way or another; we were just doing it for the wrong team. And with a virus bomb waiting to go off.

We resumed our practice, and I resumed screwing it up. We got close to pulling it off twice, but in both instances, I got distracted by elements planted by Dodd. Elements that were meant to throw us off. One time, it was a projection of a dolphin passing by. The fact I fell for it again, just like I did when I was retrieving the Sea Swarm unit, made me angry at myself. The few seconds I lost focus were enough to throw off the entire operation.

"Remember your practice, Akela," Desmond took my hand and looked into my eyes. "When your mind is adrift, return to your breath and return to the present. When you see, hear, and feel your environment, you can't be anywhere else except in the here and in the now."

Desmond tapped his hand above his eyes, then his ears, and then his heart.

"See, hear, feel. Here, in the now. In the now." I repeated the words quietly to myself as I dried off. Desmond looked over at me and bowed his head with a smile.

Soon, Octavius appeared. Practice time was over, and I'd failed my teammates. Octavius put our headbands back on.

As we exited the chamber, I turned to see Mathias one last time, but he was gone. His words swam around my head as we walked back to our quarters. 'Your surroundings are not as they appear.'

Everything was swimming around my head, for that matter. I missed my friends, my teammates, and the pod. I wished they were here to help. This mission for the last piece of sea glass was a tricky one, and success didn't even mean anything positive for our side. Dodd's virus bomb could still be launched.

"Breathe, Akela," Desmond said from in front of me.

"No talking," Octavius said from behind.

I hadn't realized I was holding my breath. I started slowly and deeply expanding my inhale and exhale. Calm breath in, ease breath out. Calm and ease.

I was starting to focus again as we walked past Dodd's various bio-domes and crew members. How had Dodd recruited Octavius and all these people to his cause? Were they here by their own choice? Had Dodd convinced them all that his cause was just? No. Dodd was a madman, and I just couldn't accept that these people were just as mad. That or they were enslaved, but they appeared to be happy going about their work. What was really happening here?

I wanted to reach out and stop one of them, but they were always just out of reach. Not only that, but I also noticed none ever made eye contact with me. Ever. It was like they were staring through me.

And that's when I saw it. It wasn't totally clear at first, but I experienced the deepest sense of déjà vu. The two lions in the elevator. I'd seen this all play out before.

I watched closely as the elevator passed the second level. The lion on the left was going to roar. On cue, the lion roared. I looked down to the left where I'd seen a handler leading a rhino from an African biodome earlier in the day. Bam. Just like the lion, the rhino and the handler did the exact same thing they did before. Not only that, but everybody there was moving in sequence. These people weren't real. The animals, the biodomes, the entire operation. It was a projection—a holographic representation of what Dodd wanted me to see! Mathias had been trying to get me to see, 'your surroundings are not as they appear.'

I uprooted the small seeds of doubt growing in my mind. Dodd wasn't creating his own version of the SOS. It was all a trick, and I was tired of being fooled.

"Dodd!" I yelled as my voice echoed off the submarine walls.

None of the supposed workers or animals on the ship even flinched. Holograms.

I felt a sharp poke in my ribs. "You don't want to see this, Akela. Please," Octavius said.

Desmond was smiling for the first time since I'd seen him here. He had an expression that read 'finally' all over his face. I smiled back through my grimace of pain.

"I know, Dodd. I can see it now. It's all fake, you're a fake!" I hollered again.

This time Octavius gave me a sharp punch in the stomach. I doubled over as Desmond lunged toward him only to be stopped short in midair.

"Enough," a voice came from high above. It almost sounded like a whisper, but it came with enough force for all of us to turn instantly.

I noticed Dodd slowly descending from his operations room on a podium. Octavius shook his head at me.

The podium stopped above us. "So, you want the charade to stop, Ms. Spencer? Are you sure?" Dodd said mockingly as he touched his watch and Desmond fell with a slap on the floor.

At the same time, the lights went out and the submarine went black. A chill swept over my body. The fabricated sounds from the holograph were gone, and it was momentarily silent except for our breathing. Then the lights shot back on. I was blinded. I blinked away the spots from my eyes, and when they were finally clear, I wished they weren't.

❖

The submarine was illuminated by only a few scattered hanging spotlights that kept moving and flashing every few seconds. It gave the sensation of lightning flashes. In those bright moments, I could see shadowy figures moving in the background. They wore all black and their movements were quick and swift, like rats scurrying across the ground.

I could hear the unhappy sounds and smell the musky smell of animals as their hooded captors moved them into small cages. Moving closer to the cages, I saw that they were small, unkempt, and the animals looked miserable.

A roar sounded from a nearby cage. I turned to see one of the hooded lab technicians taking a blood sample from a Bengal tiger.

"You see, my dear Ms. Spencer, it's not necessary or economically feasible to preserve all life in its current form. Hence we are extracting DNA samples, so that when the Earth is rid of us destructive humans, well at least the unenlightened ones, all will be good with the world again. Yes, and maybe on the seventh day us enlightened survivors will bring back all the species we choose. Yes, when I unleash my virus, no human shall be saved. Well, except those safely in the sanctuary of the Isle of Green."

Dodd planned to ride out the virus on the Isle of Green and then return as the sole ruler of the Earth.

He then started singing in the same tongue that I'd heard Sam use on the SOS. His voice was hauntingly beautiful as it reverberated off the walls of the sub and created a wave of sound that enveloped us.

On the walls of the submarine, text began to materialize. This time, in a different font and style than the SOS. Numbers, circles, stars, the sun, and the moon all appeared as well. They moved in a similar fashion to Sam's portal, Htmalo's portal. The movement didn't disorient me anymore. I focused on it and started to see patterns. I also understood the song. These were the words of the followers of Chixtal and I understood them. They chilled me to the bone.

"If you believe that the world must come to an end, in order for us to begin again, then you are welcome to come in."

Dodd's song came to a finish and all the spotlights moved to the newly formed hole in the wall. Everything else was black except the portal.

Dodd's voice whispered in my ear and I jumped up in the air. He placed his hand on my shoulder. "We could've been great together."

CHAPTER 42

Back in my room, I couldn't sleep. First thing tomorrow morning, Desmond, Mathias, and I would be in the Arctic Sea attempting a mission so dangerous that even the slightest misstep could kill us. The fact that I had failed every time in our practice sessions to pull off our goal wasn't helping my state of mind. Nor was the reality that if the mission succeeded, it would make Dodd stronger in his fight against Sam and the *Spirit of the Sea*.

I returned to my breathing with more focus and patience than I had ever experienced to date. There were no doubts about Dodd anymore. My conviction for the cause was iron. Saving our oceans, saving my family, and saving the world, was my only path, and it was crystal clear.

I woke up that next morning well rested and ready to go. Octavius led Desmond and I to the chamber where we would port onto the iceberg. We silently put our gear on as Octavius watched us.

"You don't like what Dodd is doing, do you, Occy?" I asked him, trying to catch his eyes, but he only looked away.

At the center of the room was a table with the case holding our sea glass. Desmond and Mathias were correct that Dodd would return them to us. One by one, Octavius gave our pieces back to us. I tried to hide my relief.

Finally, Octavius unclipped the bands from our heads and we were once again able to communicate our thoughts. Desmond spoke out loud instead.

"Piece of cake, Akela. You've been through far harder times and challenges. Breathe, see, here and feel. Stay present. You'll do fine."

"You'd better. Ready for portal," Octavius said.

"What about this?" I held out my arm, the bracelet Dodd had put on me, was still on my wrist. " I won't be needing this in Antarctica."

Octavius paused, he seemed to be considering his options.

"If that bracelet somehow interrupted our mission, who do you think it's going to be in trouble?" I added.

"Fine," he said and pressed a button. The bracelet fell to the floor.

Octavius then pulled a pouch out of his pocket. Gold dust.

"It's not too late, Occy." I turned to him just as Dodd's singing echoed throughout the chamber, but he wasn't there. Or was he? It wasn't the same song I'd heard him sing before. He was opening a portal like Professor Wild's.

"It is now," Octavius replied without looking at me.

Octavius tossed a handful of gold-speckled dust into the wall, and it slowly melted into a stream of moving shapes and colors. Desmond reached out and took my hand.

"Ready?"

"Ready," I said.

We stepped through the wall and in an instant, time and space seemed to wrap themselves around me. I couldn't tell if my eyes were open or closed, but I saw the movie of my life project before me again. My story was getting better, and I was just getting started.

I opened my eyes, and the polar glare forced them shut again. Over and over, I slowly blinked my eyes into a state of adjustment.

"You okay there?" Desmond was sitting beside me, still holding my hand.

"I'm good."

I stood up and checked my surroundings and coordinates. We'd landed on the glacier in the intended spot. The glacier steeply rose hundreds of feet to its summit. Desmond and I walked toward the edge where the icy blue Arctic Sea surrounded us.

We stared at the water until the silhouette of Mathias appeared. He surfaced briefly, then disappeared below. We both inspected our gear and checked our watches. I gave Desmond a thumbs up. *Here we go.*

The drysuits worked as intended. I wasn't the slightest bit cold as we entered the frigid water. We followed the underwater taper of the glacier deeper into the sea. The visibility was remarkable. It was difficult not to look around, but I reminded myself of how distractions had contributed to our failed practice sessions. Focus, Akela. Focus.

Mathias led the way, with me in the middle and Desmond following.

"Three minutes," Desmond communicated telepathically. We were almost to the center of the glacier and exactly on pace. He engaged a headlamp, and I did the same.

Mathias stopped. *"He's here."*

Mathias slowed his pace and edged closer to the floor of the glacier. We followed, Desmond and I both using our hands to push off the ice every few yards.

The light had faded to the point where I could only see Mathias directly in my spotlight. Desmond had affixed a line between the two of us as a safety precaution. It helped. I was still nervous, but my nerves hadn't gotten in the way so far.

Shining my light up into the glacier, first I only saw the doctor's storage chest. I craned my headlight further up until I finally found Dr. Terence's frozen body.

Desmond gently elbowed me and pointed.

There it was—the seventh and final piece of the sea glass map was here, frozen around the frozen scientist's neck. And it was starting to glow! Mathias faced us now, his sea glass necklace was lighting up as well. I looked down to see my necklace, forgetting that I was wearing seven millimeters of neoprene wetsuit on top of it.

"Take out your sea glass," Mathias said with a sense of urgency I'd not yet heard in his voice.

I paused and started to panic. *"We don't have time, we need to extract the doctor now, or we won't have enough air to resurface!"*

I felt a warmth coming from where my necklace was pressed against my body.

"Trust me, Akela. Trust yourself." Mathias swam directly up to me and nudged me with his nose.

Desmond and I locked eyes. Shining our flashlights at each other to provide light, we used our free hands to delicately unzip the front of our suits. The cold shock of arctic water was almost enough to knock me out.

"Focus," Mathias demanded of me. I went to reach for my necklace, but it released itself on its own. Desmond's shape of Africa did the same. Both pieces became aglow with so much light and color that our flashlights were no longer needed.

Our sea glasses all reached out for one another, forming a prism of color and light between each point. Then, with a flash, a burst of light shot out from the prism through the ice and to Dr. Terence's sea glass of Antarctica. They were all connected!

"Htmalo's chalice was once shattered in order to create the map to the Isle of Green," Mathias said forcefully. *"The pieces want to be united. They need to be united."*

A stronger beam shot out from the triangulated pieces and the ice around Dr. Terence started to quickly thaw. Within seconds the ice around him was gone. We tethered him to us, along with his chest. Our sea glass pieces were all still shining together, forming a halo of color that surrounded us like a bubble.

I began to swim away, but Desmond paused.

"Quick, detonate the explosives. Dodd will believe that the mission is still on course."

The explosives fell to the safety of the ocean floor, where we detonated them.

We then swam swiftly back toward our entry point, with Mathias out in front like a lead sled dog. Only Mathias knew which way to go.

I was swimming hard and fast. My endless training had given me the endurance and power to keep up with Desmond now, and we moved together like a living engine. The light of the sea glass extended behind us to where the frozen scientist and his trunk were being towed along.

Was he alive? I wanted to look back but didn't. I could feel the tension in the rope and knew he was still there.

We'd been underneath the glacier in subzero waters for almost twelve minutes, slightly behind our optimal pace, but safe in terms of air supply and warmth.

With Dr. Terence in tow and Mathias leading the way, I started to take in my surroundings. It was hard to miss the giant crabs crawling along the bottom of the glacier. There were hundreds of them, and they seemed to be getting bigger and bigger.

"Hey Des, you check out these crabs?"

A small army of them lined up on the glacier above us.

"Roger that. Seems a little odd, but just keep moving. It's just a distraction. We need to get back to the surface," Desmond said calmly.

"Okie dokie," I said while scanning the ceiling one last time. Only crabs. Just lots of them. I trusted Desmond with my life and returned my focus forward.

The mask Dodd had given me was made of tempered glass and was at least two inches thick to withstand the cold. I could see Desmond, Mathias, and the mass of crabs all perfectly well, as they were no further than twenty yards away. But further away, I wasn't as eagle-eyed as normal.

At first, I assumed the cloudy images in front of Mathias were pockets of algae, bacteria, or arctic jellyfish, if there was such a thing. Mathias would navigate us through them. No problemo.

Then, I felt it. I was slowing down. I swam a little harder and we picked up the pace, but again, I felt a drag, like something was pulling on Dr. Terence.

An industrial-sized plastic trash bag had landed on Dr. Terence and was slowing him down like a parachute.

Then I looked up and realized that the school of jellyfish was really an army of plastic bags. A bag suddenly swooped down and covered my face. I quickly pulled it away, only to find another and another diving at me.

"Des, Mathias, the bags are attacking!" I yanked on the tether and was able to shake a few of them loose, but they were falling like snow from the sky.

"Why would Dodd attack us when we are bringing him Dr. Terence?"

Dodd's voice appeared in my ear. "There's been a change of plans, Ms. Spencer."

I was in a tangle of discarded plastic that had a mind of its own—a mind that was intent on suffocating me. How was Dodd communicating with me?

"I planted a comm in your wetsuit hood. Seems that little sea glass prism you and your friends created set off a beacon to the SOS. Sam and your teammates are here earlier than I expected." Dodd's tone changed from mocking to dead serious.

"I had wanted you to deliver Dr. Terence safely on board before my ambush, but cie la vie." Dodd paused. "Nothing worthwhile in life comes easy, Ms. Spencer. But death, well, death comes and goes without any effort at all. Enjoy your view of the fight from your grave on the bottom of the sea. The battle has begun!"

CHAPTER 43

No sooner had Dodd declared war, than I found myself sinking to the bottom of the Arctic Sea covered in an array of discarded plastic bags. It wasn't exactly how I envisioned my role in the final battle to decide the fate of Mother Earth.

I'd become untethered from Desmond, Mathias, and Dr. Terence. I could see them in the distance, way above me, fighting through the wave of plastic attackers.

We were far outnumbered, but Mathias had enlisted help. The army of crabs had come to fight alongside us, floating down like paratroopers from the iceberg. They were the size of dogs and had bolt cutter-sized claws that snapped with such intensity that I could hear them from far below. My crustaceans defenders cut and tore the bags into pieces as they fell, but it wasn't enough.

The mass of plastic shopping bags was like a blanket of lead pinning me to the ocean floor. I checked my oxygen gauge. Less than a minute left.

Still, I couldn't help but think about all the sea creatures that had succumbed to this insidious pollution. I was one of them now, and I understood more clearly than ever their feeling of loss and hopelessness. Desmond didn't teach me that revenge and empathy were typically associated together, but I would avenge those creatures' loss by defeating Dodd. But first I needed to save myself. *Think Akela, think.*

A golden retriever-sized crab floated past my goggles and landed on my arm. Immediately, its claws started cutting away at my plastic shackles. Helpful, but not nearly enough. My breathing was becoming labored. Could I breathe in this cold water?

I mentally called out to Desmond. *"Taking off my mask. Out of air. Stuck to the ocean floor. Help me."*

With my arms pinned, I couldn't use them to release my mask and breathing apparatus. I had to wiggle my head down by my shoulder and nudge it off with all my might. In one final thrust of my shoulder, I was able to knock the mask off. Holy brain freeze.

I shut my eyes and clenched my teeth against the shocking cold. Slowly, I released my jaw and took in the slightest amount of oxygen from the water. An arrow of cold pierced my lungs and focused all my mind and body on accepting the pain along with the oxygen. It hurt like crazy, but I could breathe in this extreme water. Just tiny micro breaths, but I was buying myself time to figure out a way to release myself and to get to the surface.

My eyes were still closed when the plastic landed on my face. It hit dead center, covering my mouth, and blocking my path to air.

I bent my head forward and tried a few times to shrug my shoulders upward to remove the bag with no luck. I started to feel lightheaded, but I wasn't ready to give up.

Then I heard humming near my frozen face. The noise got louder and louder until there was movement in the water around my neck and head. I didn't know if I was hearing things due to oxygen deprivation or not. I was fading.

I felt it again, and much stronger this time. At first, it was a swirl of water, but that quickly turned into suction. The bag stuck on my face was suddenly whisked off and I could breathe again! It still hurt like heck, but I was getting oxygen.

Whatever machine or animal was in front of me was saving me. The plastic bags that plastered me to the bottom of the ocean were being vacuumed off. Little by little, the weight holding me down began to lift until I was eventually free.

I messaged Desmond. *"I'm unstuck and I can breathe."*

"Roger that. The SOS Vacuum Bots released me as well. Mathias and I have Dr. Terence and we are heading to the surface."

SOS Bots meant that my teammates were here. That was good news, but also bad news, considering Dodd's ambush plans.

"Des, I still can't see. Make some noise and I'll echo locate your position."

Desmond sang in Whale, and the vibrations bounced off the iceberg and the seafloor.

Slowly and cautiously and in complete darkness, I swam upward. Desmond's beautiful melody echoed in my ears and through my body. *"Breath in, calm, breath out, ease."*

My head broke the surface. The usually frigid arctic wind hit my face like a warm tropical breeze. I opened one eye. The glare was dizzying, but its intensity was a relief as I knew that my eyes still worked. They hurt, but they were functioning.

I bobbed in the water, patiently waiting for my eyes to adjust to the lightness while training my ears on my surroundings.

Mathias and Desmond were at the base of the iceberg with Dr. Terence bobbing behind them. Standing next to them on the iceberg was Mik and Warren. Yes! They were alright.

Behind them was a snowmobile that looked like it was built for battle. It was massive compared to my SOS teammates', but it was still dwarfed by the towering peak of the iceberg behind it. The vehicle had treads on it the size of a tank and a large, enclosed bed. I followed the tracks of the vehicle as far back as my powerful eyes could see. They led me to Mik's JetCopterBoat.

Desmond got out of the water first and lent me a hand getting out.

"The Dolphin Girl rises again!" Warren shouted.

"Happy to see me?" I asked, the warmth returning to my face.

"Yes, very," Warren said sweetly before Mik elbowed him in the ribs. She had that ever-present sparkle in her eyes.

"You okay, kiddo?" Mik gave me a hug and handed me an ear comm.

"Yeah. I'm good. Where's the rest of the crew? Any sign of Dodd?"

"Leo's at the chopper with Sam. No, nothing yet."

We pulled Dr. Terence from the water and placed him in a specially designed incubation chamber in the back of the vehicle. Mik attached a variety of electrodes and wires to the doctor, locked the chamber door and hit a button. The flashing lights of the device reflected off Dr. Terence's Antarctic Sea glass.

Mik sealed the incubation chamber. "It's something Sam had designed specifically for this purpose."

"He's alive, isn't he?" Warren asked.

"We'll find out soon enough," Mik answered. "We need to get him back to the SOS."

Next, we used harnesses to place Mathias in a saltwater-filled tank in the snowmobile.

"Leave me behind," Mathias communicated to me. He had a faraway, yet calm expression on his face.

"No chance, my friend," I answered. "Mik, where's the SOS?" I buckled my belt.

"As close as Sam could get it in limited time." Mik tapped on the steering wheel. "The JCB and this bad boy was our fastest option."

A voice I hadn't heard for days came into my ear comm. It was Leo.

"AK, you alright?"

"Thanks to you, buddy. I owe you one for taking the trash out down there."

Mik started up the snowmobile. The engine sounded like an airplane, and we started driving.

"Des, AK, your ops drysuits are in the bathroom. Go change," Mik said. We took turns changing as fast as possible. I looked out the window, we were moving, but not very fast.

"Mik, you gotta go faster," Sam said urgently. "We're both sitting ducks out here."

Mik glanced over her shoulder to look at me, Desmond, Warren, the frozen Dr. Terence, and Mathias swimming in a tank of water. "Sam, I've got a few extra thousand pounds of weight on board. I can't go any faster."

A loud boom thundered in our ears, and the snowmobile jarred to the right.

"What was that?!" Warren yelled.

Leo came over the snowmobile's internal comm. "It's a submarine, and it's breaking through the ice!"

Sam yelled urgently, "AK, man the cannon in the back!"

I got up and ran to the rear of the vehicle past Mathias and Dr. Terence. Mathias and I locked eyes for a moment.

"Release me," Mathias communicated to me.

I looked hard at him and slid open the back-panel door leading to the mounted laser cannon. The back door opened, and a rush of cold air and snow flew in, blinding me momentarily from a sight that took my breath away.

As the snow cleared from my vision, I could see the top of Dodd's submarine knifing through the snow and rising like a shark on the prowl. Our snowmobile was the prey.

"Fire that laser, Akela!" Mik yelled. Desmond was at my side now. He nodded to me.

I gripped the weapon, aimed, and pulled the trigger. A ray of light shot out from the barrel and hit directly at the top of the sub. Nothing happened. I fired again. Same thing. The laser hit the sub, but didn't make a scratch.

"Dodd's got a particle shield up! The laser won't work unless I can hack the signal and get it down," Leo shouted.

"Do it," Sam ordered.

"On it."

"Speaking of hacking." Dodd's voice came over our intercom. "I thought slowly melting the Earth's glaciers through global warming was fun, but this is simply divine!"

Dodd's submarine gnawed away at the glacier. Behind us was now a growing mouth of hungry Arctic Ocean that would soon swallow our snowmobile whole.

Mathias's voice came into my head again. *"Release me."*

"No, you won't survive either on land or by getting run over by Dodd!"

A hatch opened on Dodd's sub and Octavius appeared on a platform. In front of him was a massive harpoon.

"Hey, guys, they've got a harpoon gun trained on us!"

"The ice is thicker another few hundred yards up," Sam said. "If you get there, I don't think Dodd's sub will be able to cut through the ice."

"I don't have enough speed to do it!" Mik said.

I ran to Mathias's tank. It was easily the heaviest cargo on the snowmobile.

I looked out the back. We weren't going to make it.

"Desmond, help me."

We grabbed both latches that held the water in Mathias's tank.

"Will I see you again?" I asked.

Mathias looked at me, but didn't reply.

We pulled the latch and a rush of water flooded out, along with Mathias. I watched Mathias ride the wave of water toward the submarine and open sea. Octavius took a shot at him, but barely missed as Mathias disappeared into the cold blue.

The snowmobile shot forward with a burst of speed.

"We made it. We're on firmer ground now. The sub can't follow us!" Mik yelled.

I breathed a sigh of relief and started to high five Desmond.

"Incoming!" Leo yelled as the harpoon pierced the side of our vehicle. I was knocked off my feet and crashed into Desmond as the snowmobile tilted almost to the point of flipping, and then landed with a thud back on the ice.

"Everybody okay?" Sam asked.

"Roger that," Mik confirmed.

Desmond slowly stood tall and picked me up. Warren and Mik joined us looking out the back.

Dodd's submarine had been stopped by the thicker ice, but we were tethered to it by the harpoon. There was no sight of Mathias.

"Dr. Terence's vitals are active," Sam said.

I looked at the chamber holding the frozen doctor. He appeared to be breathing!

"Sam, the doctor is alive," I said.

The snowmobile first began to slightly move and then violently shake.

"What is that?" Desmond asked.

I ran to the back and saw a small army of wiry reptilian creatures making their way across the harpoon tether in our direction.

"I don't know, but that's not all." I pointed at Dodd's sub.

The door to the submarine opened and a swarm of bat-like beasts flew out.

"More of Dodd's minions," Mik said with disdain.

Desmond jumped behind the cannon and shot one of the flying bats as it dive-bombed at us. It was a direct hit. The bat exploded into a ball of fire and headed right for us.

"Incoming!" Desmond yelled.

A puddle of fluid splattered down at our feet and sizzled into the snow. I could smell it. The bats were made of burning oil.

"We can't let those bats touch us," Warren said.

The ice beneath us began to shake and rumble. There was something below our feet trying to get to us as well. We were being attacked on all sides.

Dodd's voice came through our snowmobile again. "Almost all the sea glass holders in one place, how convenient. Especially you, my old friend Sam."

A large crack came from the direction of the JCB. I turned my head to see Sam's copter and then the rotor tilted backwards.

"And you thought the kraken was my only over-sized pet." Dodd laughed in our ears.

Sam shot back. "Team, fight like the fate of the planet is in your hands… because it is!"

Chapter 44

Dodd had us under attack from air, land, and sea. A swarm of liquid oil bats, wire lizards and something big, something *very* big, was hammering away at the ice down below us.

We had to prioritize, divide, and counterattack.

"AK, Desmond, I need you back in the water. You let Mathias go. Find him and stop whatever's attacking us from below," Sam ordered over the roar of the JCB blades starting up. "Leo and I will try to draw the bats away. Warren and Mik, crush those critters and protect Dr. Terence!"

In the distance, the JCB lifted off.

"Who's going after Dodd?" I asked.

There was no way we could let him escape. There was no way I was going to let him escape.

"You have my orders, AK," Sam said.

I went to jump out the door and saw Dodd's wire critters were already by our snowmobile. The endless army of reptiles had barbed hooks for claws and teeth. When they got close enough, they started to catapult themselves at us. I slammed the back door shut. The sound of their hooks screeching on the metal of our vehicle was awful to hear. They were slowly tearing the doors apart.

"Sam, we're trapped inside. Des and I can't get to the water."

We stood huddled together around Dr. Terence as our vehicle shook back and forth from the swarm of creatures. They were adding so much weight, I could feel the ice cracking beneath us.

"Figure a way out!" Sam yelled back.

"I got this." Warren ran to the front door. "I'm going to lead them away from here. Those little dudes are fast, but I'm faster."

"Warren, wait!" I said, but he'd already opened the door and took off in a flash.

"Come get me critters!" Warren said, taking off toward the base of the glacial peak. To his credit, the wire creatures leapt off the snowmobile after him.

"It's working, Warren," Leo said from above in the JCB.

"*Be careful!*" I communicated to him as I watched him ascend the glacier.

The air and land battle were going full bore. It was time to take back the sea.

Desmond and I sprinted to the water. Above, I could see the JCB swooping and dodging the bats. Leo was hanging from the chopper door with a giant extinguisher that shot foam and rendered the flying fire hazards harmless. The bats splattered on the ice.

I stopped at the water's edge as the hammering below continued. I turned to see Mik firing the cannon from the back of the vehicle. The ice beneath the snowmobile holding Dr. Terence would give way soon.

Back on Dodd's submarine, Octavius had retreated inside. Dodd was in there along with his virus bomb. I had to stop them.

"Akela, we must follow orders for now! We'll get Dodd, but first things first. We need to protect Dr. Terence and find Mathias. Go."

We quickly dove back in and swam beneath the glacier. The water was so cold, but I was more relaxed now and able to keep myself warm with consistent breathing cycles.

It didn't take long to see what was doing the damage from down below. It wasn't another kraken. Hammering against the ice was a giant mechanical crab with two huge metal claws, a wide, metallic body, short, powerful, spring-loaded legs, and a glass bubble control cockpit. The mechanical creature was the size of a small building and was being operated by Dodd.

"Well, well, well," I couldn't help but say.

I swam full speed toward Dodd in the cockpit. My new suit had an air cannon in the waist holster. I pulled it out in preparation for blasting Dodd.

"Wait, Akela!" Desmond yelled, but I was already fully committed, like a great white shark locked onto a prey, there was no turning back now. I was going to crack that glass cockpit open like an egg and then make myself a Dodd scramble.

I was a few feet from landing the blow when Dodd turned and saw me. Those eyes. I didn't think I could feel a further chill in this Arctic water, but I did.

Dodd grinned a big, turd-eating smile just as Octavius blindsided me with a full body tackle. Not again.

The blow knocked the wind out of me. I tried to catch my breath as one of Octavius's tentacles covered my mouth.

"You could've just easily joined our side, Akela," Octavius said as he wrestled with me below the iceberg.

"Never," I said, launching a sharp elbow into his belly.

Desmond called out to me. *"Remember your training, Akela!"*

"I've got this," I said as I slipped another tentacle attack and used the momentum of the missed blow to grab and launch Octavius up into the underside of the iceberg. The blow appeared to knock him out.

"There you go, Akela," Desmond said and began swimming away from the fight.

"Where are you going?"

"To find Mathias." Desmond swam off.

Octavius had vanished, too. Where'd he go?

Out of the corner of my eye, a mechanical claw came flying toward me, narrowly missing. I dodged another quick flurry of claw thrusts and swings from Dodd and his machine. I swam quickly, darting back and forth. I wasn't getting to him and he wasn't getting to me, but at least I was distracting Dodd from breaking the ice and getting to Dr. Terence.

The cockpit glass, which was once clear, was now opaque. I couldn't see Dodd's face anymore. Looking for a weak spot, I navigated around to the back of the mechanical monster. With a quick burst from its pneumatic propulsion, the crab shot backwards, attempting to crush me against the ice. I pushed off the ice at a slight enough angle to avoid being smashed like a bug on a windshield.

The blow though was forceful enough to break through the iceberg. Bright light from the low hanging winter sun shone through like a spotlight into the crab's cockpit. I could see through the clouded glass. Dodd wasn't at the controls of the monster, it was Octavius!

"Hello, Akela," Octavius said. *"You didn't really think you could beat me, did you?"*

In my distraction of watching Desmond, Dodd and Octavius had switched. Which meant… oh no. Dr. Terence.

I swam as fast as I could for the surface, but found myself being pulled backwards by Octavius and his mechanical crab claw. The claw snagged onto a piece of my wetsuit.

Pulling a knife from my utility built, I cut the piece off my suit, seconds before the second claw came smashing into the first.

I made a beeline for the edge of the iceberg. As I swam, I saw a mass of sea life coming in my direction.

"Akela!" I heard the familiar language of Narwhal, as Marjorie and Malachi came racing toward me.

"The battle is just beginning!" Malachi hollered, shaking his horn back and forth like a saber.

Behind them was Desmond and an even larger assortment of sea creatures including orcas, dolphins, and seals. There were hundreds of them, maybe more. Mathias, oh thank goodness he was there as well.

"You didn't really think I'd leave you?" Desmond stopped and smiled in front me as the cavalry of creatures surrounded Octavius and the giant crab.

Mathias swam up and nuzzled his nose into me. *"Akela, this has been foretold in the depths of the oceans for as long as I can remember. Go now, get Dodd."*

Desmond echoed Mathias. *"Go get Dodd. We've got down here covered. That's an order!"*

I jetted upward, turning around one last time to see Malachi harpooning the glass cockpit and shattering the glass. Water flooded in as the army of allies wrestled Occy out of the mechanical monster.

I swam as hard as I could possibly swim. I hit the surface and launched myself completely out of the water, did a full flip and landed onto the iceberg like the amphibious spiritual gangster I was becoming. *You're a badass, Akela Spencer.*

The JCB was back on the ground and Leo was jogging toward me. I couldn't spot any more flying creatures in the air.

Mik pushed herself off the ground. She was covered in snow and oil. Her uniform had burn marks on both sleeves. For the first time since I met her, she looked tired.

"Dodd took Dr. Terence," she said.

Sam's voice came into the comm. He was breathing heavily. "He attacked us with an even larger swarm. The sky went dark and forced us to land the JCB."

"I took cover under the snowmobile. I had to. I couldn't see a thing." Mik rubbed some snow on a cut.

Sam came back on. "Dodd and the doctor are on the sub, I fear heading to a portal."

"Where are you?" both Mik and I replied in unison.

"In pursuit. I can't let Dodd get away again. Over and out." Sam's comm went quiet. Mik and I gave each other an 'oh no' look.

"Now listen up." Mik stood up bolt straight, instantly not looking tired anymore. "We won't lose Sam, Dr. Terence or let that missile go off. Leo, I want you back in the JCB. Find Warren."

"You want me to fly the JCB?" Leo asked hesitantly.

"I know you can do it. Now go." Mik pointed and Leo sprinted back to the chopper.

Mik turned to me. "Akela—"

"I know. Back in the water, right? But I get the sense from Mathias that somehow, I'm supposed to take Dodd out. How can I do that from outside the sub?"

Mik placed both hands on my shoulders and stared straight into my eyes. "Desmond and Mathias have the ocean covered. Your primary mission is locating Dr. Terence and stopping that virus from being launched."

"What about Sam?" I asked.

"We can survive without Sam. He'd want you to focus on the virus as well. None of us will survive if that missile is fired."

"What about you?" I holstered my air cannon and checked the rest of my gear.

"I'm going with you of course." Mik slapped my back and took off in a sprint. I caught up to her within a few seconds as we followed the tracks made by Dr. Terence's incubation chamber.

Scaling the submarine, we made our way to the harpoon that Occy had fired at our snowmobile. Our cannon had disabled the turret; it left an opening inside Dodd's lair.

The flashing on and off emergency lighting created a strobe light effect that was disorienting. There was also static in the air that was like a constant whirring sound that reminded me of Matea blending up power shakes for Kara before her heats, except a hundred times louder. Wow, I hadn't thought of the two of them in so long; it felt like a lifetime ago. I looked back again to Mik, the superhero of a woman who had landed in my front yard and brought me to the SOS. I shook my head in disbelief as to how far and how unreal my journey had been from Bonita Springs.

A large bang startled me from my untimely jaunt down memory lane. We froze in our tracks.

Mik gestured up ahead and to the left. The sound came again from that direction. I let her lead now and I watched the rear.

Our comm systems were on mute as to not draw attention from Dodd's monitoring network. We'd practiced a system of intricate hand signals for situations like this, and the training had come in handy. I thought to tell Mik that, but paused before I spoke. She wouldn't appreciate me speaking aloud to congratulate our learning hand signals.

The banging continued intermittently, and we followed it to the best of our ability. As we moved deeper into the submarine in the direction of the noise, the whirring got louder as well.

Rounding a corner, we arrived at a large, circular chamber with high ceilings. In the center of the chamber was a device that resembled a cement mixer, except it was spinning at an almost blinding speed.

My ultra-sensitive hearing was on overload. I activated the noise cancellation on my comm.

Mik motioned for me to go right while she continued to the left, making our way around the spinning cylinder. About halfway around my side, I saw him. Dr. Terence! He was unfrozen, alive, and thankfully not naked. He had a lab coat on and was standing behind a glass wall in what looked like the control room for the giant spinning device. I wanted to yell for Mik, but knew that wouldn't get me anywhere, so I started to run around the sphere to alert her.

The room was so large, and the device was so massive, that it may have been a full mile circumference around the room. I felt like I was running on the speed track at the SOS, that is until the guy in the black suit came sprawling backwards and fell right in front of me. I hurdled over him and turned the corner to see Mik in midair delivering a flying side kick to another of Dodd's goons. There was an army of them. Many of them were on their backs or knocked out, but more kept coming. Mik was surrounded.

I hadn't engaged in any land-based hand to hand combat other than the training I'd done on the SOS, but all the repetition and instinct to protect my teammate—no, my family —kicked right in. So that's what I did. I kicked right in, knocking my way into the center of the circle with a spinning round kick that sent one goon flying into another goon.

Mik and I were now back-to-back. I looked over my shoulder and we made eye contact. She winked, and that gave me the confidence I needed.

Dodd's goons came at us one after the other. I swept the first one's leg and used his face as a springboard to kick the next in the gut. I dodged a punch from another and used his arm to flip him onto his fellow goons. Mik had taught me well. I had three down.

Mike was spinning like a Swiss army knife on a disco ball. Dodd's men were flying left and right. I counted twenty bad guys, all knocked out, but more kept coming

Remembering that I had my air cannon holstered to my utility belt, I drew and fired. The blast sent all of the men in black flying into the wall and rendered them unconscious.

Mik wore a look of disappointment.

"Why'd you stop the fun?"

I gestured for her to follow me as I took off in the direction of the control room.

As we were running, the giant cylinder had begun to slow and along with it, the maddening noise. I switched off my noise cancellation.

"Nice butt-kicking, kiddo," Mik said as she jogged up next to me.

"I have a good butt-kicking teacher," I replied and pointed. "Dr. Terence, he's alive and looks to be controlling the virus bomb."

The doctor was still there at the controls in the glass room. I reached the door first but couldn't open it. I banged on the window, but it was extremely thick and soundproof. I continued to bang away at the door while Mik calmly walked up next to me, tapped me on the shoulder and pointed to the intercom adjacent to the door.

"Dr. Terence. My name is Mik, from the *Spirit of the Sea*. Please open the doors so we can get you out of here."

The doctor didn't look up from his controls, but he did speak. "Oh, is that so? I still have some work left to do here and then I'll be happy to let you in."

Dr. Terence pressed some buttons and an outer layer of panels that surrounded the cylinder opened to reveal a missile.

Mik shot me a look of concern.

"Dr. Terence, do you know what you're doing?"

"Well, since Jarvis Dodd rescued me, he explained he had built this cloud-seeding contraption and that he needed some help with the final calculations to get the seed optimally mixed before we launch it into the sky, and it rains down from the clouds. Quite simple, actually."

"Yikes," I blurted out.

Mik sighed and hit the intercom again. "Dr. Terence, Dodd has manufactured a virus, one deadly enough to create a pandemic. He's using you, this centrifuge, along with your cloud seeding algorithm, to spread the virus everywhere."

Dr. Terence looked at us before returning to his work. He shook his head. "Nonsense."

I reached my arm back to start banging on the door again, but I caught myself. I took a deep breath. We needed a different approach.

Calmly, I pressed the intercom button. "Dr. Terence, where are Dodd and Sam Shipman?"

The scientist, unfrozen from a glacier of ice just hours before, slowly looked up, completely unaware of what he was in the process of doing.

"I know Dodd, and I assume the man Sam you are referring to must be that awful man chasing us." Dr. Terence shook his head in disgust. "Dodd told me that Sam is trying to destroy the planet. Well, this cloud-seeding program that Dodd has here should help put Mother Earth right back on track. Now, excuse me while I program the final coordinates."

Behind me the centrifuge had opened wide, and the virus missile rotated on a pedestal which emitted an intermittent beeping sound like a truck backing up. Dr. Terence hit a button and the ceiling of the submarine started to slowly open directly above the missile.

"Dodd must have brainwashed or hypnotized him," Mik said. "Dr. Terence and Sam were once great friends."

She moved to hit the intercom, but I gestured for her to wait.

"Well, apparently Dodd and Sam were once friends, too." I stared at Mik.

Mik held my look for an extra beat. "We have to find a way for Dr. Terence to understand what he's doing."

"That or we can figure out a way to break in."

Over my shoulder, the missile started to rise on the pedestal. The tip of the weapon was now exposed to the arctic air. Time was running out.

"Wait, our sea glass." I couldn't believe that I had forgotten about the one thing that bonded all of us together. I ran back over to the glass window and pulled my sea glass out from inside my ops suit. I hit the intercom.

"Dr. Terence, you realize that you are part of a larger picture here." I pressed my sea glass of North America against the glass window. "Part of a powerful bond. You were chosen, Dr. Terence. I was chosen. We are chosen."

Dr. Terence looked up from his panel. The sea glass had caught his attention.

"It's not a coincidence that we both have continents," I went on. "You love this planet, and you lost somebody, too. I know it. Who did you lose, Dr. Terence? What brought you and your sea glass together?"

The doctor moved closer to me, but his eyes were on the sea glass. He reached into his shirt and withdrew Antarctica.

It was working. I kept going. "I lost my parents at an early age. I have no memory, but I know they died protecting me and our Earth. I've always had this sea glass, and I've always been able to breathe underwater and speak with sea life."

That last sentence brought the unfrozen scientist's eyes up to mine. "Come again, young lady? Did you say you can breathe underwater and communicate with creatures of the ocean?"

I nodded. "I'm not the only one. My friend, another man who works with Sam, Desmond, and I, along with Mathias, the world's oldest Greenland shark, we rescued you from the bottom of the iceberg. Yes, Dodd put us up to the mission, but not because he wanted to help you or the planet. He wants you to launch a virus into the atmosphere. He also wants to stop us from creating the Isle of Green."

A light came to Dr. Terence's eyes. "The Isle of Green is a myth. That's a myth. Something my friend, Sam…"

Mik gasped and my heart jumped. He was remembering.

The doctor continued, "Yes, something my friend Sam had talked about many years before."

He walked up so that he stood right against the glass and within an instant, his sea glass leapt from his chest toward mine. Antarctica and North America danced in the light only separated by the piece of glass on the door.

"I lost my wife. Here in Antarctica," the doctor said quietly as his eyes welled up with tears. I put my hand up to the glass and he pressed his against mine while our sea glass pieces did the same.

"I need to stop this awful virus missile from launching now, don't I?" Dr. Terence asked as he hit a button to open the door. Mik and I quickly walked in and watched as he pushed and pulled at the various buttons and levers, all the while muttering to himself.

"The Isle of Green is real… Well, I'll be." Dr. Terence wiped the tears from his eyes and the sweat from his brow as he rapidly tried to reprogram the launch code.

"Hey, Doc, the missile pedestal is actually going up, not down," Mik said, pointing to the rising weapon.

"Yes, well, I'm doing my best here, but it seems a counter program is overriding my commands."

Dodd's hyena-like laugh came over the submarine's loudspeaker system.

"You didn't think I really needed Dr. Terence to launch this missile, did you? I only needed his algorithm to optimize the centrifuge and to create even greater damage, but I wouldn't just leave him the keys to launch. That'd be crazy!" Dodd's maniacal laugh echoed throughout the chamber.

"Where are you?!" I screamed.

"I'm right here, my dear. Come find me," Dodd's voice said in my ear.

I jumped and turned to see an apparition of Dodd before it disappeared. My skin crawled.

"He appeared again, didn't he?" Mik asked, again not seeing, or hearing what I did.

"Dodd's still on the submarine," I said over the increasing beeping sound from the missile rising further out of the sub. "He's got Sam. I knew Dodd wouldn't have left Dr. Terence and his sea glass behind if he didn't have Sam with him.

"Let's go get him," Mik said and grabbed my arm.

"Um, ladies, just a note that the missile sequence has it launching in three minutes unless we can stop it somehow," Dr. Terence said with an air of urgency and his hands in the air. "I can't do a thing."

With each passing second, we were getting closer to Dodd, but also to the launch of the virus bomb. Then an idea hit me.

"Mik, do you think that the missile would still launch if the submarine was underwater?" I asked.

"Good question. Nuclear submarines can fire from the sea, but not if that chamber room were to flood. No, if we can fill this chamber with water, the missile wouldn't have the capacity to launch."

"I believe the pretty lady is correct," said Dr. Terence.

"Mik, you and Dr. Terence need to get out of here," I said.

"What are you going to do?"

"I'm going to sink this sub and get Sam back."

She paused and stared at me for a moment doing a mental calculation.

"It's our best option. Do it, please," I said.

Mik nodded, then winked at me. "Go get 'em, kid."

CHAPTER 45

I ran as fast as I could through the corridors of the submarine. Dodd would be in his Portal Room. It was his only escape route out of the sub without encountering us. It was also a place that both he and Sam could both pass through together. If he were to take Sam with him, not only wouldn't we be able to assemble the Isle of Green, but we'd lose our leader.

First, I needed to get to the submarine's glass floor that accessed the ocean beneath. Sprinting down hallways and corridors, I could sense a presence, a great energy of sea life that was gathering and I needed to get there to direct their fight. Through the pitch black, I followed my instincts while keeping my fear of the darkness at bay. There was nothing in the dark that I hadn't seen worse in the light of day.

When I entered the great room, my premonition was true. There, assembled beneath the glass floor were my teammates Desmond and

Mathias. In addition, my old narwhal friends, Malachi and Marjorie and an army of arctic seals, whales, octopus, and creatures, had grown to the thousands. I felt my skin ripple with goosebumps.

"Friends! We don't have much time," I said.

"You need us to sink the submarine, Akela," Mathias said calmly. Of course, he knew.

"Yes, and fast. I've got to find Sam and get him out of here before the sub floods." I looked at the caged animals around me. *"Rescue as many of our brothers as you can."*

Desmond began to sing to the whales. Mathias, like me, could speak all forms of sea languages. He circled around the seals, then to the sharks, and down the line to each assembled group of creatures, telling them the plan.

The army started swimming in circles, slowly, then faster and faster. Within a few moments, I could feel the submarine start to dislodge from the ice. They were creating a whirlpool and it was working. Hopefully, in a few minutes, the submarine would be pulled beneath the frozen surface and the missile launch thwarted. The question was whether Sam and I were going to go down with the ship, too.

Running was challenging now as the submarine was moving erratically, swaying, and tilting from the whirlpool created by the animals below. I banged from wall to wall as I moved as fast as possible to find Sam.

As I neared the Portal Room, I could hear Dodd's voice singing. His ancient words started to appear on the walls, almost chasing me as I ran. Cursive, aggressive letters of a language used to open a door to another dimension.

I slammed into a wall as the submarine movement grew more intense.

Nearing the Portal Room, I could hear Dodd's voice booming. But there was another voice singing as well. It was Sam.

I entered the room and saw them both there. The leaders of opposing causes. Enlisted warriors of two mythological spirits or possibly even the gods themselves. Standing face to face about twenty feet from each other, Dodd and Sam both chanted their mantras that would open their respective portals.

On Sam's side, his words appeared on the wall just as they had on the SOS in graceful yet bold lettering. On Dodd's side, his opposing mantra appeared as it had before. Dark, menacing, and edgy.

Calendar dates, the sun, and the moon were also moving across the room in similar patterns I'd seen before. The two patterns of numbers, letters and symbols now danced and darted around each other, but never intersected. It was hypnotic, but this time I wasn't disoriented. I could see the dates corresponding with the movements of the stars and planets. It all slowed down for me, and like many a language I discovered I already knew, I realized what it all meant.

The two men had stopped singing. Neither of them noticed me in the room.

Separate portals had opened in the walls. I could feel a warm breeze blowing through the openings to another dimension. The sub continued to shake and tilt, yet somehow both men were able to stay motionless. Sam finally saw me.

"Akela, this is between me and Dodd. I want you off this submarine now!" He said without taking his eyes off his enemy.

Dodd laughed. "So chivalrous of you, Sam. Some things never change." Dodd spun to address me directly. "Akela Spencer, you may have saved Dr. Terence, and maybe you can stop my missile, but do you really think you are winning the war?" Maybe a small victory here, but what is it that you're really looking for?"

A large explosion rocked the submarine. The vessel would be taking on water quickly.

"No, Ms. Spencer. What is it that connects you to your precious sea glass?" Dodd smiled, that evil, wide smile. "Don't you want to see your parents again?"

"What?"

"Oh, Sam never told you, did he? Right, because if he had, you wouldn't have helped him find Mathias or even be here now, trying to save him. You'd be in the portal trying to find your parents. Isn't that right?"

Dodd looked over at Sam, but Sam said nothing. Dodd returned his steely gaze to me. "You wonder where Sam is off to all the time, don't you, Akela Spencer? He wasn't looking for sea glass while you did his dirty work for him. No, he's only there looking for his son. Isn't that right, Sam?"

Sam looked over at Dodd and shook his head.

Dodd clapped his hands together and flashed an evil grin. "Do you ever think that maybe they are all together somewhere in time, somewhere lost in history?"

Another blast erupted throughout the submarine and the room started to shake and spin. I steadied my feet and my will.

"What's he talking about, Sam? My parents are alive?" My head was spinning and not just because the submarine was getting pulled into a whirlpool. I couldn't comprehend what Dodd was saying. My parents are alive, but somehow trapped somewhere in the past?

"Akela, don't listen to Dodd. You need to leave." Sam pointed at the door. "This is my fight."

Again, the submarine jolted, and I fell to my knees, bouncing back up quickly. I heard a noise coming from the corridor. Not just a noise, but a smell too. Salt water. Oh no.

Dodd started running toward his portal. "Adios amigos. Ms. Spencer, the truth is in here, if you care to join me. Otherwise, I'll say hello to your folks for you!" Dodd jumped through the wall.

I started after him. I'd no doubt I'd make it through. My parents were alive, and I was going to find them. I could sense the water coming fast behind me, but I was going to make it. I was going into the portal. That is, until I felt a hand clip my foot and send me sliding onto the floor. It was Sam.

Before I could get up, an avalanche of water poured into the room, picked me up, and slammed me against the wall that was once a portal. It was gone. The portal to my parents was closed.

I swam up toward the surface. Sam was already there, floating as the rising water pushed us closer to the ceiling. I took a quick breath.

"Why'd you stop me?!" I yelled, holding back tears.

Sam shook his head. "I need to get through that portal just as badly as you do, maybe worse, but we need both of our sea glass to assemble the Isle. Even if we stopped the virus bomb, we haven't stopped Dodd until we capture him here." He looked at me hard, reached out and grabbed my hand. The water was now pushing our heads up toward the roof. "The Isle of Green can be a sanctuary for our cause. This is bigger than you, me, or our lost families, Akela."

"You lied to me!" I cried, pushing his hand away.

"I'm sorry. I owe you an explanation, but first we need to get out of here. Especially me, the only one of us who can't breathe underwater!" Sam said with a sense of urgency as we were only a foot away from the top of the room. "You've got to get us out, Akela."

"Okay, save your breath. "I grabbed his hand and mustered up all the courage I had left.

We both took deep breaths, but Sam was the only one who really needed it. I only needed to remember how to get out of this maze of corridors. If I didn't, we'd both eventually run out of air and become entombed in Dodd's submarine.

Chapter 46

With Sam holding onto my hand, I pushed off the wall with both legs. The water wasn't as cold as it was in the open ocean, but it was still freezing. The reality was that I only had a minute or two before Sam would lose his oxygen or freeze to death.

It was pitch black now, but I had no time for fear. We banged from wall to wall as I dolphin kicked with one hand out front and the other holding Sam.

Corner after corner, I dodged and weaved through the dark hallways, not once looking back. I could feel Sam holding on and that was enough. I took a lot of blows to the face, but nothing was going to stop me from fighting to get us out and back to the surface.

My mental time count had us at well over a minute. We were getting close. I was tiring, but continued to push harder than I'd ever pushed in my life.

I swam around a corner and entered the missile chamber. The launch room was fully submerged. Mathias, Desmond, and their sea friends had stopped the missile from launching!

I kicked hard off the floor and made for the opening, pulling Sam with me as I went. We were so close to the air.

As we exited the underwater sub, we were greeted by the army of ocean animals that helped us to successfully sink the submarine.

Oh no. We were at the bottom of the sea. I'd no idea we had sunk so far so fast! Mathias was there, and I blazed past him.

Sam had to be running out of air, and I couldn't let him die. For so many reasons, but also a new one: he knew where my parents were.

All at once, I felt a rush of momentum followed by an enormous burst of speed. The army of ocean animals had gathered behind me and were driving me toward the surface like a wave machine.

Mathias's voice came to me. *"Doors open for those who never give up."*

Sam and I burst through the surface so fast that we launched into the air and landed hard on the glacial surface.

We did it, I thought to myself, until I saw Warren fly past me with a grave look on his face.

Sam was unconscious. His hand had frozen to my wrist.

Desmond rushed out of the water and was soon by Sam's side. "He's alive, but just barely."

"We need to get Sam out of here, now!" Mik commanded. Dr. Terence was shivering by her side.

"One step ahead of you," Leo's voice came through the comm as the JCB lowered from above.

I looked out over the Arctic Sea. Thousands of sea creatures swam in the water. Many were helping Dodd's animal captives to the safety of the iceberg. I saw Octavius tied up and being towed by a pair of orcas. And there was Mathias, his distinctive head bobbing out in front of the army of allies that had helped us stop Dodd.

Desmond looked at me and smiled. "You did it, Akela. You stopped Dodd today."

"No, *we* stopped Dodd, today. All of us," I said, pointing to our friends in the water. I was still holding Sam's wrist as Mik lowered the JCB to pick us up.

Chapter 47

I walked through the jungle quietly so as not to disturb the locals. Some were friendly, others were lethal, but none bothered me as I snaked and glided past trees and bushes. The humid air felt good on my skin, especially after being so bitterly cold in Antarctica.

Voices floated in the not so far distance, and I knew that when I rounded the corner and into the clearing that I would finally see them. After all those years of not knowing, all the loneliness, the void in my heart would be filled.

The Amazon sun shined down on my face, obscuring my vision until my eyes adjusted and then I saw them, finally. They looked just like the photographs I'd seen, except they were real. My mother and father were standing in front of me. With a few quick steps, we were hugging. The humid air on my face mixed with the saltwater tears that streamed down my cheeks.

Then I awoke. It was just a dream. My cheeks were wet. I'd been crying, yet I wasn't sad. It felt good knowing they were alive and that I may see them again.

I stretched my hands over my head and flopped back down on my pillow. Who would have known that this boat could ever feel so much like home, but that's how the SOS felt to me.

By the time I finally rolled out of bed and checked my ops watch, it was well past 11 a.m. We had been back two days now, and all of us—after spending time in the infirmary—were instructed to go to our rooms and rest up. Those were Sam's orders after the ship's doctors cleared him. Our leader was fine, thankfully.

Still, Sam had lied to me about my parents. They were alive, stuck somewhere in time, somewhere that only Dodd knew. Sam's son was there too, apparently. I was mad, but also felt compassion toward Sam. Sam had lost someone, just like the rest of us sea glass holders.

Intellectually, I got it, I understood his tactics. But as much as I tried, I couldn't lose my anger. He used me to further our mission against Dodd, and that plan worked. We'd won the battle. We had all the sea glass, and we had stopped the virus bomb. Octavius was in the SOS prison, and even though Dodd had escaped, the world was safer today because of us. I didn't know if it was abnormal to feel proud and angry at the same time, but I did.

My ops watch beeped and there he was, Sam, instructing the team to reconvene in the Aqua Hold.

I felt my sea glass between my fingers. We had all the pieces now. It was time to assemble the sea glass map to the Isle of Green.

As I reached my hand to open my door, I already knew who was on the other side. I could hear them, smell them, but more importantly, I knew my friends would always be there for me.

"Hi guys," I said before the door was fully open.

There were Warren and Leo. I hadn't seen either of them since we returned to the SOS. And it had been even longer since we'd had any time together that allowed us time to breath, let alone talk. I gave each of them a big hug.

"Are you guys ready for this?" I held up my necklace out in front of my face.

The boys each did the same. We let go and watched as our pieces levitated in the air in front of us. Warren and I caught each other's eyes.

He smiled at me and then loudly clapped his hands together. "Bet you guys can't beat me to the Aqua Hold," Warren said, starting off down the hall.

Leo and I started a leisurely walk after him. I put my arm around his shoulder. "You saved me more than once out there, you know."

Warren came jogging back around the corner after realizing that nobody was in pursuit.

"You saved me, too, Leo," Warren said as he sidled up next to us. "You and the JCB got to me right before those little critters almost chased me off a cliff,"

"But we chased them off instead!" Leo said with a laugh.

"You fly like a pro, buddy." Warren fist bumped Leo. He then reached for my hand, and I gave it to him. "I heard you, Akela, when I ran off. You communicated to me, and I heard you. It's coming back." He squeezed my hand.

"Promise me that we'll always be there for each other," I said, looking at each boy.

Leo nodded and Warren pressed his hand harder against mine. That was promise enough.

Entering the expansive ocean biodome still took my breath away. A large, wooden, circular table and chairs had been placed on the dock. The pathway to it was lined with lit torches.

The team was already there. Desmond was dressed elegantly in a beautiful orange suit. Professor Wild wore a rainbow lab coat with images of tropical birds adorning each sleeve. Mik looked comfortable and lethal in a yellow jumpsuit with her hair pulled back. The other sea glass holders were all there as well.

Dr. Terence was wearing a lab coat and was fussing with his hair. Mik patted it down for him. He looked amazing considering he was a human ice cube no more than forty-eight hours ago. His Antarctica sea glass glistened in the lights.

"Hello, my young rescuers!" He waved eagerly.

Mathias swam up near the edge of the water and escorted us as we walked. His sea glass necklace was almost glowing as it cut through the water. I could see the pod swimming with him. Jon, Ana, Grandpa and Rhino—the whole gang. We called out to each other, and my heart soared.

Sam stood at a large table, waiting for us. He was wearing his usual shorts, Hawaiian shirt, flip flops and an LA Lakers hat. He was casual as always, which was a relief since all us kids were woefully underdressed.

He looked a little tired, which was understandable. We all were tired, but in the best possible way—the kind of tiredness you felt after saving the world.

"Sea glass bearers, please come sit. Mik, you, too." Sam gestured toward the chairs.

"Before we assemble the Isle of Green, I have some explaining to do." Sam nodded at me. "Especially to you, Akela."

We all took our seats. The round table had a carving of Pangaea in the middle, the earliest image of our continents where all the land formations melded together as one.

Sam cleared his throat. "As at least one of you may have figured out…" Sam paused and looked at Warren, who was nodding to himself in a self-congratulatory manner. "Yes, you, Warren. I'm much older than I appear."

Leo interrupted, "Wait, Warren was right?"

"Whether I'm immortal or not, thankfully, I haven't had that tested yet," Sam said. He paused to nod to me. "But otherwise, I will no longer age."

Warren was nodding his head up and down with a big smile on his face.

"Told ya," he said.

Sam went on, "I know you've all realized by now that many stories we've been told to be mythical are actually true. Which is how—"

Leo interrupted Sam. He held his head in his hands before looking at Sam. "Hold up, hold up. That can only mean one thing. You found the Fountain of Youth, right?"

"Why would you say that?" Sam asked with a surprised look on his face.

"Well, understanding how portals work now and what Mathias said about seeing you and Dodd over the years, that's the only explanation I can think of. Well, and that I hacked the servers and saw a folder named 'Fountain'." Leo grinned sheepishly. "Sorry."

"If portals, krakens, and prophecies exist, why shouldn't a Fountain?" I said, staring at Sam.

Sam scanned from Leo to Warren and then back to me.

Sam sighed heavily. "Jeez, you guys take away all my drama. Yes, I found Ponce De Leon's fabled Fountain of Youth. And I didn't find it alone."

"Jarvis Dodd was your partner," I said.

"Yes, we were colleagues, along with your parents, Akela. Friends, too, well before you were born. Dodd changed after we found the portal and he found Chixtal. He became enamored with the idea of resetting the planet," Sam said.

"He also fell in love with power," Mik added.

"That, too, Mik." Sam slowly moved his gaze over all of us. He held up a finger. "One thing is for certain, though. Htmalo, Chixtal, and their prophecies are real and very powerful. Once Dodd was seduced to Chixtal's destructive dark side, we became adversaries and have been fighting this battle ever since," he said.

"For how long?" Leo asked.

"Time is very elusive," Sam replied.

"Dodd knows where our families are, doesn't he?" I asked.

"May we table that for a moment please, Akela?" Sam asked with a kind smile. "You and I can discuss that privately."

I nodded. After all this time, I could wait a little longer. Today, we were going to complete the sea glass map.

Sam took a deep breath and adjusted his hat. "Now, let's move onto the formation of the Isle of Green. I will need everybody to remove their sea glass and place it on the table. Right on Pangaea," Sam said with great reverence.

I got up and walked to the side of the water, where Mathias was patiently waiting, along with the members of my dolphin pod. I reached down and gently removed his sea glass necklace. While doing so, I gave him a gentle rub on the nose.

"*I know where you are going,*" Mathias communicated to me without talking. "*Follow your heart, but be warned, even I can't see what happens in the portals. If you are not careful, you may get lost, and then even your heart can't return you back.*"

I smiled at Mathias and said his words quietly back to myself. I wouldn't forget. His eyes reflected peace and tranquility.

I placed Mathias's necklace on the table on Australia. Then I removed my necklace and placed it directly on the North America carving. Sam followed me and placed his brilliant piece on South America.

Desmond stood up, towering over all of us and gracefully bowed his head to remove his piece. He carefully laid it down on the African part of Pangaea. Leo removed Asia, much less gracefully than Desmond, and placed it on the table. Warren followed next with Europe.

Last to stand up was Dr. Terence. His piece of sea glass dangled from his neck and almost matched his white hair, white beard, white glasses, and white lab coat.

"Well, I never thought I'd see another day, let alone this day here with all you brave sea glass bearers and eco-warriors. I'm honored to be part of this, and grateful to all of you for making it happen," Dr. Terence said in an emotional yet strong voice.

He bent his head forward and placed the last piece of sea glass, Antarctica, on Pangaea.

"I'm honored to be here to bear witness to this great day," Professor Wild said with his head bowed and Hope standing tall on his shoulder.

"We couldn't have done it without you and Hope, Professor," I said.

"And your caterpillars, Track. Thank you," Sam added.

We all stood staring as the continent-shaped glass began to move. The dance of the various colors and shapes was mesmerizing. As with before, the adjacent continent's glass pieces moved toward each other, turning, and twisting until they were touching at the appropriate meeting points.

The pieces had all found their rightful positions and stopped moving on the table. We all looked to Sam and then back to the sea glass, waiting for something to happen. We continued to wait while nothing happened.

Finally, I spoke up. "Is a holograph supposed to appear?"

"If it is, it's invisible," Warren said before Leo elbowed him in the ribs.

Sam placed his hands around the sea glass and moved them from one angle to the next, trying to elicit some reaction from the glass, but nothing happened.

Mik edged up close to Sam and gave him a 'may I' look. Sam nodded.

She took a deep breath and pounded her fist on the table. The glass all flew up in the air and then landed back on the table, again assembling into the position they held before. But nothing more. No map, no nothing.

"Nice punch," Desmond said with a smile.

Sam took his hat off and ran his hand through his thinning hair. I guess the Fountain of Youth didn't restore, it only suspended.

"Well, I'm stumped," he said. "The prophecy didn't say anything more than to assemble the glass and the Isle would appear. There they all are on the table—all of the major components of our precious planet Earth."

A loud splash of water got us to turn our heads toward the ocean pool. Mathias had backed away from the side of the platform and swam toward the rambunctious Rhino before coming back to the platform.

"Is everything really there? Everything that is necessary for life on Earth?" Mathias communicated to me, and I relayed his message to the team.

I looked from Mathias to the sea glass and then back to the water, just in time to see Bingo come flying out of the biodome pool and land with a gigantic splash that not only soaked us, but covered the table with water.

I reached to catch the sea glass from sliding off the table, but stopped my hand at the sight before me.

The water swept up the glass off the table and launched itself into a waterspout that hovered and spun over the table. Slowly, the swirling ball of water took the form of a globe. An audible gasp came from all of us. The sea glass, as they did on the table, started to move, but this time, instead of Pangaea, they took their spots exactly where they would appear as continents today.

"Of course!" Desmond boomed. "What is Mother Earth without water! Thank you, Mathias!"

"*And thank you Rhino,*" I communicated.

The water globe of sea glass hovered over the table, slowly rotating. It was the size of a basketball and each sea glass piece glowed and shone as it spun.

"What was once broken is now whole," Desmond said and took my hand. We all, one by one, reached out for each other's hand. "All of us, at some point, our families were shattered. But now here we have found each other, and with that, a new family, a new wholeness."

We all stood and stared, entranced by the image in front of us. As the globe continued to spin, a prism of light appeared from the Southern pole. It contained each color of the sea glass continents and shone down onto the table like a spotlight.

"There!" Leo shouted and pointed as the projection of light on the table started to take the shape of a map. At first, it was as large as the view of the Atlantic Ocean with North America and Europe on either side. Slowly, the light shifted, and the projection map started to zoom in.

"It's showing where the Isle of Green is located," Dr Terence said in a hushed voice.

The map projection eventually stopped shrinking and stopped with Florida, Puerto Rico, Bermuda, and all the areas that the surrounding islands left in view.

Nobody took their eyes off it.

"Uh, is the Isle of Green actually an existing island?" Warren said without joking for a change.

Sam walked closer to the table. He peered down on the map. "No, I don't think so."

"*Neither do I,*" Mathias communicated to me.

Just then, another beam of light shot out from the spinning globe and a triangle appeared onto the top of the other map.

Leo gasped with delight. "The Bermuda Triangle! Look, see how each corner of the triangle lands on Florida, Puerto Rico and Bermuda."

Sam laughed a joyous and surprised laugh. "The Isle of Green is in the Bermuda Triangle. Clever, Htmalo. Very clever."

Mik stretched her arms wide. "That's a large area, Sam, but much smaller than searching the entire world. With the help of Mathias and the pod, we should be able to find it. When do you want us to start?"

"Not tonight my friends. No, tonight we shall celebrate, tomorrow we shall rest and then we can begin the next mission. Who's ready to party?!" Sam shouted with a laugh just before getting splashed again by Rhino.

CHAPTER 48

Sam had pulled out all the stops for the celebration that evening. The cafeteria was transformed into a wonderland of color, sound, and flavors. Every band on board the SOS took turns playing their music to the delight of the dancing crew members.

Everybody put on their funkiest outfits to make sure that the vibes for the evening were festive and fun. The whole crew was in full-on Mardi Gras mode. That is, everybody except for me.

I sat at the table and picked at my food. It was delicious, but I wasn't hungry. I peered up from my plate to watch the celebration. Leo awkwardly spun a smiling Ahimsa, while Mik gracefully danced with a surprisingly nimble Dr. Terence. Warren was all smiles as he held a stick while Professor Wild followed Ericka in the limbo. Even Sam was still present, working the room saying thank you to the crew. And my buddy Desmond was right where I would expect him to be, next to me.

He looked down at my plate and then up to my eyes.

"Unless that's your second serving, you aren't feeling like yourself, are you?" Desmond asked, putting his hand on mine.

We connected telepathically.

"I know where you're going, Akela," Des communicated. *"I don't agree, but I understand. Your parents are out there, and you need to find them."*

My head found Desmond's massive shoulder and I rested it there.

"I do," I said.

Reaching into my shirt pocket, I pulled out the photos of me with Kaipu and Alana and the one of my parents with me as a baby and layered them to make it look as though they were one picture.

"Yes, you do have to go, Akela." Desmond squeezed my hand. *"But you also must remember that you have a family, regardless of whether you find them or not, do you understand?"*

I tried hard not to let the tears escape my eyes, but it did no good.

"Like pieces of a puzzle," I said and looked up to Desmond's smiling eyes. A tear fell from them.

I placed the photos back in my pocket.

Desmond cleared his throat and stood up. He bent his massive body over and spoke verbally again, "You know, young lady, I'm not letting you leave until I have one more dance."

We danced together, hopefully not for the last time.

As the party went on, I breezed through the cafeteria, saying hi and accepting hugs and high fives, but I found myself being drawn to the door. In a moment where all eyes were directed at Sam, who was giving a speech on the success of the mission as well as all the challenges ahead, I slipped away without saying goodbye.

I was happy, but I wasn't satisfied. I started to walk toward the door.

"AK, wait," Warren's voice said from behind me. When I turned to him, he came all the way up to me and kissed me on the cheek.

"What was that for?" I asked, not the least bit upset it happened. More wondering why he didn't aim for my lips.

"I get the sense that you are going somewhere, and I just wanted to make sure you didn't leave without a kiss."

This time, I leaned in and kissed Warren on the lips. It wasn't a long kiss, but it felt like time stood still. My skin tingled and my body warmed. He put his hand up to my cheek and I reached up and held it. I'd connected with Warren telepathically, and I could tell that he wasn't going to stop first. I pulled back. I had to go, but at least now if I didn't make it back, I knew what a proper kiss felt like.

"Be safe, AK," Warren said. He held my hand still. I let go.

"I'll see you soon, Wolf Boy." I smiled.

Walking away as if in a daydream, I followed my feet, knowing my destination, yet without a map or plan.

In the kitchen, I picked up the same knife that Sam had used to open the secret panel to the weapons room. I tossed it high in the air and in a single motion caught and threw the knife directly into the dead center of my intended target. Slowly, the wall began to move to the side, allowing my entrance to the Portal Room.

The quiet of the room contrasted so intensely to that of the celebration, it almost overwhelmed me. Desmond had taught me to appreciate the nothing—that everything must come from nothing and return to nothing. To appreciate anything beyond nothing, you had to accept that nothing was something.

At first it seemed like a riddle to me, but now, here, alone in the Portal Room, it all made sense. I appreciated all of it.

I opened my mouth and began to sing the words of Htmalo. The nothingness of the Portal Room transformed into an echo chamber of my singular voice. A sound that once made me uneasy around others was now something confident and strong. I knew the words by heart, and I knew my intention was purer than it had ever been before.

As I sang, the words of the hymn began to appear on the walls. The writing was different, though, as the portal translated each different person's song into their own specific handwriting. I continued to sing and watch as my words danced across the walls, and soon the moon, sun, stars, and calendar dates appeared as well. It was beautiful. All the elements moved together in a pattern and rhythm that I understood and that I controlled. Ever so slowly, a portal began to open in front of me.

"Akela," Sam's voice said from behind me. I was expecting him.

"Why didn't you tell me that my parents were alive?" I asked again, but already knew the answer. I could feel the warm breeze from the portal caress my skin.

Sam walked in front of me, standing between me and the portal.

"For the same reason I never told you about losing my son. Because he is just that—lost in another time dimension. Whether it's my inability to navigate the nuance of the portals, or if it's Chixtal and Dodd's actions that keep my boy and your parents out of reach, the fact remains that I can't bring them back," Sam said with a sigh.

"Like you, Akela, my son had been in the portal many times before. He was sick, very sick, though. So, I went searching for the Fountain again. You and your parents joined to help. We have all done this many times together." Sam glanced over his shoulder at the portal opening and shook his head. "But this time was different."

"Did the Fountain help?"

"We never got there. Dodd ambushed us. We all became separated. Dodd took my boy and stole off. Your parents disappeared as well." Sam stared longingly into the cave entrance. "Somehow you made it back through alone."

"The portal. It's why I felt the déjà vu and why I feared the dark. I'd been in there before, all alone," I said.

"I knew that you'd understood the portal from an early age, but I had no idea to what extent, though," Sam's eyes were sad and soft, but still with a spark of mystery. He smiled. "Are you still afraid of the dark?"

I smiled back. I wasn't afraid anymore. I wasn't afraid of anything.

"Let me help you," I said.

"Akela, I've tried to locate them and bring them back. Time and time again I've failed. I won't stop, but I'm not strong enough to fight Dodd again… yet."

I walked to the side to get an unobstructed view of the portal entrance. "I'm going in, regardless, Sam. I have to find my parents or at the very least try. I couldn't live with myself otherwise."

Sam nodded slowly. "I understand better than anybody." His posture changed and he straightened his shoulders back.

"So, where shall your search begin?" Sam said with a broad gesture to the moving wall. "I typically identify significant environmental events and start there, as my assumption is that Dodd and Chixtal are near these occurrences."

"Maybe our families will be nearby as well?"

Sam nodded.

"I have an idea where to start," I smiled.

"Everything starts with an idea, Akela." Sam walked over and gave me a hug.

I smiled at Sam and then moved closer to the portal entrance. Taking a deep breath, I stepped confidently into the beyond.

THE END

9 781835 560730